THE GAME

DANNY DAGAN

First published in 2025 by Bloodhound Books.

www.bloodhoundbooks.com

Print ISBN: 978-1-917449-6-63

Dedicated to Dave Graham for his unwavering support and eternal patience.

ONE

An injection of truth

Noah Gant's mouth was dry, a soapy taste on his tongue, his nose filled with an astringent odour of disinfectant, like a mix of vinegar and bleach. His head felt heavy, as if submerged in thick, swampy mud. When he finally opened his eyes, it took him a moment to focus. The walls and ceiling of the room were off-white. The bedsheets felt rigid, heavily starched. A drip loomed above him, connected to a cannula that was stuck into his left arm, held in place by surgical plaster.

'Good, you're awake.'

He turned his head towards the voice. On a chair to his right sat a woman with high cheekbones and probing black eyes. Her cropped hair was bleached. She was wearing a doctor's coat.

'Where…?' His voice was croaky. He coughed and tried again. 'What happened?'

'My name is Marian,' the woman said. 'I'm a psychiatrist. You've had a bit of a turn, but you're safely placed with us now.' Her accent was almost Irish but not quite, like her vowels had floated to the mid-Atlantic. 'Your throat must be dry. Let me get you some water, and then, if you're up to it, we'll have a little chat.'

'I don't understand.'

'I know. I know. It can be quite disorienting.'

She came to stand by him, picked up a water carafe from a bedside tray and filled up a plastic cup. The trickle of water as it met the plastic sounded to his ears unnaturally loud. She added a straw and held it under Noah's chin for him to drink. He shuddered with a foreboding sense that something terrible had happened. He could feel it, knew it, but his mind was muddled, devoid of answers, of any memory of how he came to be in this clinical room with its oppressive bright light.

Once Noah had sipped a little, Marian left the cup in his hand and returned to her seat. She crossed one leg over the other and reached for a metal clipboard that lay on top of a medicine cabinet. With an air of detached professionalism, she rested the clipboard over her knee, produced a pen from her breast pocket and drummed it on a stack of paper forms.

The water was a relief for Noah's cotton-woolled mouth but also raised in him a retching reflex. He swallowed bile and cleared his throat. 'Is my mother here? Have you contacted her?'

'Not the standard response I'd expect from a patient your age. Then again, people react differently to the shock of psychosis. Don't feel bad.'

The fog that had engulfed his thoughts was beginning to lift. He stared at her, confused. 'Psychosis? What did I–?'

'We'll get to that, I promise.' She slid the pen behind her ear. 'These conversations are always tough. None of us imagine we'd wake up in a secure unit one day with no memory of what happened before. Believe me, it's more common than you think. I see people who wouldn't dream in a million years they'd find themselves here. One minute they're going about their normal day, the next – bang!' She clapped her hands for emphasis, startling him. 'Something snaps inside them. No warning. My car does that sometimes. You wouldn't know, looking at her shiny red bonnet, that things were corroding inside.'

Noah avoided her gaze that felt like it was boring into him, probing, judging. He licked his lips. They felt dry and cracked.

'I know it's scary,' Marian said, 'but for your own good, let's put fear to one side and concentrate. I'm going to ask you some questions, and I'd like you to answer as honestly as you can, okay? The first one should be easy. Well, I hope it is. Do you know your name?'

'I'm Noah,' he said. 'Doctor Noah Gant.' He shook his head. 'Not that kind of doctor. I'm a PhD, English Literature. My thesis was about T. S. Eliot.'

'Impressive,' Marian said with the kind of fake enthusiasm so familiar to him whenever he confessed to his field of study. 'All right, Dr Gant, do you mind if I call you Noah? How old are you?'

'Twenty-eight.' He turned his head to look at her again. She was focused on his face, no doubt assessing him, almost as if she was trying to read his mind. His unease grew. 'Please, can you tell me what happened?'

'I will, I promise.' She glanced at her clipboard. 'Next question: are you generally happy in your life? Any recent upsets?'

'I'm lucky,' he said. 'Everyone tells me I should be grateful.'

'Why does everyone tell you that?'

'We have money, lots of it. My mother is successful. You might have heard of her? Cecilia Gant. Supposedly, I can do whatever I like with my life.'

'But you don't feel lucky.'

'You wouldn't understand.'

'Let me venture a guess,' she said. 'Most rich people are happy – delighted, even – with the kind of fake intimacy money can bring them. Nectar and butterflies. Butterflies and nectar.' She angled her head and seemed to examine his face for signs. 'But you aren't one of them, are you, Noah? No. Something tells me you desperately want the other thing, the real thing. Without it, you feel lonely, but you can never tell if they want you for you or because of your bank balance.' She nodded as if agreeing with herself. 'And you aren't allowed to complain because rich people are expected to be grateful. Am I close?'

'Cue, a soundtrack of microscopic violins.' He stared at the cup in his hand. 'You're very perceptive.'

'Not strictly my area of expertise,' she said, 'but have you ever considered dating someone like you, someone with their own money?'

'Try talking to an heiress or movie star – well, at least the ones I've met. I don't really care about fast cars and parties and massive houses with golden taps. Maybe it's me, the way I am. I just… I don't fit in with the jet set crowd.' He paused, unsure if he was being too honest with this stranger. 'I don't mean to sound ungrateful. I haven't had to struggle, but all I want is a normal life.'

'From years of clinical experience, I can assure you there's no such thing as a normal life.' She retrieved the pen from behind her ear and pointed its tip at the clipboard. 'All right, I think you're fully awake now. Maybe it's time we talked about your episode. Let's see how much you can recall, and then I'll fill in the gaps. Deal?' She gave him a clinical smile and didn't wait for an answer. 'Tell me, Noah, what's the last thing you remember before waking up here?'

Noah searched his mind for answers. 'I… I had an invitation to go to some pretentious fashion place that had just opened in Knightsbridge. I get a lot of those because my mother, well, she's in retail, and they think I'm a way in. Doesn't really work like that, and I don't usually go, but this one intrigued me.' He took another sip through the straw. 'Anyway, I get there, and it's one of those weird new concepts, like, you make an appointment, and they ask you questions about your childhood and give you psychological questionnaires, and based on that, they fit you with a wardrobe. I was the only customer there.'

'Carry on,' Marian said. She was scribbling notes as he spoke, angling the clipboard so he couldn't see them.

'So, I get there and do the interview with the consultant, Eliza, and fill in questionnaires on a tablet computer. Twenty minutes later, she gives me this box, like a massive present tied with a gold ribbon and a huge pair of scissors for the ribbon. Like I said, pretentious. She tells me to go try on my new clothes in the changing room.'

Marian put down her pen and leaned forward, her chin resting over steepled fingers, her eyes fixed on him.

'And then,' he said, 'it's really weird. I'm in the changing room, door's closed, and I cut the ribbon and open the box, and I remember a strange smell, like lemon or… or sulphur, and I try to open the door because I start feeling queasy, but I can't because it's locked, and I panic.' He hesitated. 'Then, everything goes dark, and I open my eyes, and I'm here. Where am I? Which hospital did you say this is?'

'Imagined smells are a common symptom when an episode starts, conspiracies, others trying to get you, gas meant to subdue you. That's what you're describing.' She frowned and rubbed her chin. 'You don't remember coming out of the changing room?'

He shook his head.

'All right, Noah. This is going to be difficult to hear, but…' She paused as if considering whether she should tell him the rest, then straightened her back and spoke in an even tone. 'You kicked down the changing-room door and started shouting and talking to yourself. Then you attacked her, the fashion consultant, Eliza Drummond.'

'I don't–'

'The receptionist heard screaming and ran into the room. He saw you on top of Ms Drummond. You had the scissors in your hands, and you were stabbing her with them.'

'No,' Noah said, shaking his head. 'That didn't happen.'

'They have cameras, and I'll show you the video when you're feeling better. It's gruesome, but at some point you'll have to confront it. It's part of your treatment plan, especially if you have no memory of the attack.'

'Is she… How is she?'

'You were in a frenzy. The police say you stabbed her in the throat and chest at least a dozen times.' She looked down at her boots, then up again to meet his eyes. 'I'm sorry, Noah. She didn't make it. Her two-year-old daughter, Lily, is with social services now. Father's absent, unfortunately.'

Noah's eyes stung. The room started swimming before him. The plastic cup fell from his hand to the floor, spilling what remained of the water, the straw bouncing as far as the wall. His stomach twisted. A foul, sour taste rose to his mouth. He turned his head, expecting to vomit, but only managed desperate dry retches, his eyes fixed on the floor tiles and Marian's black Doc Martens. He coughed, coughed again, laid his head back on the pillow and stared at the ceiling, his breathing a series of frantic gasps.

'I know it's a lot to take in,' Marian said, 'but I still need to ask a few more questions to ascertain your history and mental state. This is our first interview, but we'll be meeting regularly. My final report will go to the police and CPS.'

Tears wet his cheeks and rolled down to his neck and onto the pillow. A lump grew in his throat, like a giant, suffocating furball. 'Am I being arrested? I should be arrested. I don't understand what's happening.'

'Let's not worry about that now, all right? For our meeting today, I'd like to focus on some easy basics. Could you tell me about your relationship with your parents? You get on with your dad?'

He felt the burning acidity of sick in his mouth, could smell it, like mustard and rotten eggs. 'My dad's a good listener. Doesn't answer back.' He coughed and cleared his throat. 'He's dead. Sorry. Don't know why I said that.'

'It's fine to feel guilty, but remember, when you stabbed that woman, you were ill. It will take time, but you'll learn to recognise how your illness isn't you. You weren't yourself. Now, tell me about your mother. Are you close?'

'She does her best. Even with her busy schedules, she always has time for me. I'm her only child, so really, it's just the two of us. I… That poor woman, Eliza.' He punctuated his words with breathy sobs. 'I remember her face, pretty, looked like a model. Was thinking I should ask her out. Wouldn't have had the courage, of course. Not that it matters now. Nothing like this ever happened to me. I'm a logical guy, never been violent to anyone, wouldn't even know how to throw a punch.'

'It's natural to feel confused, especially about traumatic events that you've suppressed. So, you're close to your mother, then?'

'She'd do anything for me.'

'Anything?'

He contained his sobs and nodded, then wiped his tears with a fisted hand. His thoughts were spinning. A shrill, high-pitched tone like tinnitus pulsed in his ears.

'And what about you, Noah? Would you do anything for your mother?'

'Yes,' he whispered without thinking.

'People often answer this type of question in the abstract, so let me be more specific. Imagine you and your mother are climbing a mountain. Let's call it Everest.'

'What?'

'Focus, Noah. You've reached the summit, and you're heading back, already imagining the warmth and safety at base camp. Then, disaster strikes, a terrible avalanche. You both survive, but the force of the rushing snow swept away your oxygen tank. The air is thin, and you need the oxygen to survive, but there's only one tank left, your mother's, enough for one of you to get back to safety at a lower altitude.'

'I thought some people climb Everest without oxygen,' he said in a dead tone, feeling like a ghost, watching himself from afar.

'You're very literal,' Marian said. 'It's a thought experiment. Just go with it.'

He stared at her blankly.

'So, your mother begs you to leave her there. She won't take no for an answer. *Take my tank*, she says, *live*. You are standing on the edge of a sheer rock face, trying to decide what to do.'

'I'd jump,' Noah said, jolted and angry, as if dragged back into his body by the absurdity of her question. 'I'd sacrifice myself, like she'd do for me. Is that what you want to hear? I don't care about your screwed-up scenario. I love my mother, all right? Why are you looking at your watch? Am I boring you?'

'Just a professional habit. That's the fastest response I've ever had, from anyone. Didn't actually have to time it. This test was all about the speed of your reaction.'

Noah glared at her. This doctor was just a functionary, part of the system, while he was all alone with the shock of his violent, deadly actions. She would go home after this and have her dinner, feed her dog and tell her partner she'd had a good day at work, treating a case of a deranged man who killed his victim with a pair of scissors. *I love my job*, she'd say. *It's so, so interesting.*

He concentrated, trying to remember the attack, imagining himself stabbing the poor woman, the blood that must have gushed from her wounds. An image came to him of his mother being told of his crime. *No. That can't happen.* He started contemplating the most efficient way to put an end to this wrong turn he couldn't remember taking. He looked at the bedsheets, assessing if he could use them as a noose. Was the thick hook holding the grimy light pendant on the ceiling strong enough to take his weight? Could he reach it if he stood on the bed? He was tall enough, he decided. It was better for his mother to visit a grave rather than a prison. Of that, at least, he was certain.

Marian seemed to notice the change in his mood. She spoke to him softly now, in a warm, caring tone. 'One more question, and then we'll contact your mother. When you were coming out of sedation, you mumbled a person's name, Emily. Could you tell me about that?'

'I did?' he said, then lied. 'Haven't thought about her in a long time.' He cupped his cheek with his hand. His face felt hot, like he was running a fever. 'Emily's just someone I had a crush on at school.'

'All right,' Marian said. 'You've done really well.'

'What's going to happen to me?' he said, not caring. The burden and horror of it all were more than he could bear. As soon as she'd left, he would put his plan in motion, tie a noose, make his guilty thoughts stop.

'For now, I need you to rest while we make some more enquiries and contact your mum. The legendary Cecilia Gant shouldn't be hard to reach if it's about her son. The nurse will give you an injection to send you back to sleep, okay?'

'I don't want to sleep.'

Marian shrugged and inexplicably smiled. She bumped her fist on her knee, looking impatient, like she was done with him.

'Can I have some more water?'

'In a minute you won't feel thirsty. You won't feel anything.'

'My throat's like sandpaper. My mouth tastes of sick.'

Marian pressed the call button next to the bed. A woman in a blue nurse's uniform entered, a syringe in her hand. She was wearing a surgical mask and protective goggles.

'I really need another drink,' Noah pleaded.

'Best not,' the nurse said. 'This injection works better nil by mouth.' Without a moment's delay, she grabbed his right arm, traced a vein and injected him with the entire contents of the syringe, a translucent liquid. Within seconds, Noah felt himself fading away.

'Poor poppet,' the nurse said to Marian. 'You got what you needed?'

'Worked a charm,' Marian said. 'You all right? You sound a bit off.'

The nurse shook her head. 'I understand the logic, but I wish we didn't have to.' She removed her mask and goggles.

As Noah met the nurse's eyes, a violent shock of insight struck him like a high-voltage current. He started to convulse. The nurse held him down, pressing his shoulders onto the bed to keep him still. He could place her voice now. He had recognised her beautiful, dimpled face. The nurse was Eliza, the fashion consultant from the store, the one he thought he'd killed. He tried to say something. His lips moved, yet they produced no sound. Then he was gone, again.

TWO

The nun's tale

The bartender wiped his hands on his kilt, nodded at Peter Hammerson and spread out his arms in an expansive gesture to show off the rows upon rows of bottles behind him. 'What's your pleasure, sir? Whisky? If you're with the lynch mob, we have special deals on Lowland single malts. The quality stuff, which by my considered opinion is Highlands and Speyside – that's full price.'

'Neither,' Peter said. 'I'll have a double Lagavulin.'

'Well played, sir,' the bartender said. 'Not showing our hand, are we?'

'I just want a drink.'

'Fair enough, sir. Fair enough. Lovely evening for a Lagavulin. Cube of ice?'

Peter shook his head, then gestured towards the bowels of the wood-panelled pub. At a corner table, a nun in grey garb and a white head covering sat solemnly, her hands clasped. 'And one for the young lady over there. Tell her it's from me.'

The bartender clicked his tongue. 'Are you quite sure, sir? I mean, setting a gentleman's dram before a woman of the cloth… I don't want to start anything, if ya get my drift.'

'Quite right,' Peter said. 'She'll have a vodka and orange. Looks innocent enough.'

The bartender hesitated. 'Aye, still…'

'The two drinks,' Peter said, 'and some crisps, salt and vinegar. How much do I owe you?'

The bartender shrugged and gave him a curt, professional nod. 'Ice for the nun?'

Once the bartender had set the drink before the nun, spoke to her and pointed at Peter, she crossed herself and gave Peter a solemn nod of the veil. Even from a distance, he could see her disapproving pout.

Peter took his whisky glass and crisps and walked over to her table. His black dress shoes squeaked over the sticky floor, and he wished he had chosen somewhere more upmarket than this dive of a pub that smelled of stale beer and was only traditional in the sense that it had neglected to employ competent cleaners. Still, it had the advantage of being quiet – exactly what he needed for this chat.

He laid his whisky on a scuffed beer mat, sat opposite the nun, tore open the crisp packet and thrust it between them. The vinegary smell filled the air.

'Hello, Emily,' he said.

The nun produced a laminated rectangle from her pocket and raised it for him to read. The words *Vow of silence* were printed on it in Comic Sans font.

Peter took the laminated notice from her, turned it over as if to confirm it contained no further instructions, placed it on the table, smoothed it with his palm and looked at her, his eyebrow raised.

She held his gaze for a moment, leaned forward and took a sip of her drink through the bendy pink straw. Mid-sip, she stopped, sat back and shook her head, her face tight with disapproval.

'I'm glad you came,' Peter said. 'We need to talk, and I wasn't sure the nuns would give you my message.'

She tapped her index finger three times on the vow of silence note.

Peter crossed his arms, pulled back his shoulders and stared at her, letting the silence percolate between them. When he finally spoke, he did so with the kind of imposed calm he'd use in a business meeting when a multi-million deal seemed doomed, and its salvation hung on his skill to steward it away from choppy waters. 'I know you don't want to talk to me, but vow of silence? A bit of an extreme measure, don't you think? And since you're here, I have to assume—'

She jabbed at the sign again, this time more vigorously, her lips curved down like a petulant child's.

'I guess,' Peter said, 'the vow didn't apply to the homeless person you spoke to outside the train station for a full five minutes.'

Her jaw tensed, and her face – framed like a cut-out by the white coif – bloomed in an instant to a seething red. When she spoke, her voice was harsh, the words sour and indignant. 'You had me followed?'

'Just a precaution.'

'That's a new low even for you, Dad. What the fu–!' She stopped herself and immediately made the sign of the cross.

Peter held back a smile. Old habits died hard, even for a nun, and this nun, his daughter, had fostered more bad habits than most before she jumped, head first, into the cosy pool of sanctimony.

'It wasn't to check on your prayer times, all right? My security team have better things to do than tail you for giggles, but,' he lowered his voice, 'Brent thought it was essential, for your safety, and if you'd let me explain–'

'Brent's here?' she said, her face a shade lighter. 'Can I say hello?'

Peter congratulated himself on the wisdom of bringing his head of security along. Brent had been in Emily's life since she was born, looking after her when Peter and his ex-wife couldn't, driving her to school, to friends' houses, to university, to rehabs.

'He's waiting in the car down the road,' he said. 'There's no parking here, and he thinks you'll be safe enough with me.'

She looked at him doubtfully, picked up the salt shaker from the table, sprinkled two shakes on the back of her hand and licked off the granules. 'I know you don't get it,' she said, 'but I like my new life. At Vespers last night, I had a breakthrough. I felt something like… like the hand of providence. It was–'

'Someone touched you? I'll kill him.'

'Dad!'

'Look, Emily, I'm happy to tolerate your God phase, indulge it, even. Better than your cocaine phase, the new age phase, the two weeks when you thought you were a lesbian.'

She angled her head and gave him a cutting glare.

He knew that look. His throat tightened. 'That last one was fine, okay? I have nothing against lesbians. What I meant was, I've done my own searching when I was your age, and–'

'Enough, Dad. Enough. You know what? Never mind. I shouldn't have come.' She stood and looked down at him, her expression softer. 'I love you, Dad, and I forgive you.'

He took a deep breath to calm himself. Parenting was never guaranteed to foster gratitude, no matter how hard you worked at it. 'Please don't go. I really need to talk to you.'

'Can't stay. With luck, I'll get back in time for dinner leftovers. Was a mistake to even come here.' She crossed herself. 'Our Lord, have mercy on my father, Peter Hammerson, and guide him away from greed and gluttony and vainglory. I know it's a lot to ask.' She turned away, straightening a plain canvas satchel over her shoulder, preparing to leave.

To her back, Peter said, 'Noah Gant's been kidnapped.'

She spun around. 'What?'

'Sit down, Emily. Much as I enjoy your holier than thous, I came here because I'm still your father, whatever you think of me, and I'm worried, very worried.'

She squeezed into her chair without pushing it back, her tunic bunching itself to one side. 'Noah?'

'For obvious reasons I mentioned him first, so you'd sit down and listen, but there's three others from your year at school: Ashleigh Boroughs, Zayn Sayal and Jonny Salt.' He took a too-large sip of his whisky and held back a cough. 'They've all disappeared in the space of three days. Clean gone: no letters, no clues, no phones – nothing, vanished. Do you see a pattern in these names?'

'Fat cat parents? Not a huge surprise for graduates of our overrated school.'

'More than that. All of their parents have a net worth of over a billion.'

'Morbidly obese cats,' she said, then looked contrite and tugged on her ear.

Peter took another deep breath for patience. 'The only other person in your year who fits that category is you. The other parents are waiting for a ransom demand. There's been nothing yet. It wouldn't surprise me if the kidnappers want a full hand before they make their play. You're the Ace. I'm the richest.'

'Really?' she said with a deadpan glare. 'I never knew you were the richest.' Her hand shook as she removed the straw from her vodka and orange, took a swig, hesitated, then downed the remainder of the drink in four long gulps. 'Greed and gluttony and vainglory,' she said. 'Who's gonna kidnap a nun?'

'I'm liaising with the other parents on the assumption that you're on the list.'

'Be that as it may, I've forsaken that life.'

Her reaction grated on him, the mask of put-on indifference she had mastered so well, holding firm against logic, against his every attempt to get through to her. 'And Noah?' he said.

For a long moment, Emily was silent. She picked up the pepper shaker, peppered her hand and licked it, swallowed and coughed. 'Police say anything?'

'We've kept them out of it.'

'Why?'

'They'll mess it up is why. And honestly, we have budgets they can only dream of. We'll hire the best experts, best negotiators, private investigators. Whatever they can do, we'll do it better.' He swirled the remaining whisky in his glass, resisting the urge to drink it dry. 'Plus, if this gets out, the tabloids will have a field day.'

'The tabloids,' she said with a shake of her head. 'Of course, the tabloids.'

Peter placed his hands flat on the table before him. Its surface was sticky, but he focused on his daughter. 'We're going to keep it in the family for now. I'm bringing in Alex Czerniak to help us. He's a private investigator, the best of the best. He'll be setting up an incident room at Ewald House, and I've invited the other parents to join me there. Complex scenarios are my expertise, and they all know it.'

'You talk about it like it's one of your oil deals or those wind farms you're so proud of.'

'I'm serious about my deals, and I usually win.'

'Usually? Well, that's reassuring.'

'Look, sweetheart, I know you don't like this, but whatever else happens, I need to keep you safe.'

'I'm a nun. Don't call me sweetheart.'

Despite Emily's defiant expression, Peter couldn't hold back a chuckle, which erupted into full-bellied laughter.

'Hysterical,' Emily said, glaring at him. Then, her straight face cracked, and she, too, was overcome by a fit of giggles to match her father's. She wiped tears from her eyes.

Peter looked at his daughter and remembered how easy it used to be, that feeling of undiluted parental love. He missed the days when she was his little girl, before adolescence and then adulthood had dug a moat of estrangement between them. The love was still there, but it had grown spikes, shielding itself from moments like this, cherished moments.

'I've had security set up at our Inverness house, or you can come with me to Ewald. Your choice. Mind you, there are unwashed activists camped in front of our house here, protesting about wealth or oil or whatever upset them this week. Quite a few, I'm told. The bartender called them a lynch mob.'

'I've forsaken wealth and oil for lent,' she said. 'Never felt the urge to have them back.'

'You've done a lot of forsaking.'

'Look, Dad, I appreciate the offer of protection, but I don't fancy being stuck under mansion arrest.'

'Did you not hear a single thing I said?'

'I'd rather go with God's plan.'

'Emily, stop. Christ!'

'That's the one, our Lord Jesus.' She pushed back her chair and stood again, on her face the same screwed-up expression she used to wear as a stubborn toddler going through her *no* phase. She sidestepped the table, reached into the crisp packet, fished out a single crisp, placed it on her tongue as if it were a holy cracker, chewed, then swallowed. 'Leave me a message if anything happens. We don't watch the news. Goodbye, Dad.' She picked up the vow of silence card, turned her back on him and headed for the door, walking briskly, as though she couldn't wait to get away.

For a moment, Peter hesitated. Then he leapt to his feet to follow. If only he could convince his daughter to walk to the car with him, Brent would talk some sense into her. He'd drive her to their Inverness house, only five minutes away, or the airport, where a helicopter was waiting to ferry them to Ewald House and the safety of the Northumbrian countryside. To his relief, Emily stopped on the pavement outside, looking for something in her satchel.

'Stubborn,' he muttered. He wished his children were more grateful, more appreciative of the comforts they were born to. And Emily was in danger. *Why wouldn't she listen?* With his wealth, he could control nearly everything – everything, that is, except for Emily and her brother.

Three paces short of the door, the kilted bartender blocked his path and held up his hands to stop him. 'Doesn't look like the lady wishes to speak to you, sir.'

'Get out of my way.'

'Can't do that, sir. Just had my safeguarding training.'

'Emily!' Peter called out over the bartender's broad shoulders, his hand raised.

His daughter turned her head. As their eyes met through the window, a white van came to a sudden stop beside her with a screech of its tyres. The side door slid open, and two large-set, masked men jumped out, grabbed her roughly by the arms and bundled her into the vehicle. It was all over in a heartbeat. The last thing Peter saw of his daughter was the flutter of her robes and the terror in her eyes. By the time he had shoved the bartender aside and swung the pub's front door open, the van and Emily were gone, leaving an eerily quiet street.

An emaciated tabby cat, its ribs showing under bald patches, jumped on top of a bin and glared at him with savage eyes that seemed to judge him, to accuse – and rightly so. He should have stopped her. He should never have let her leave.

On the ground, on the spot where Emily had stood only moments before, lay her laminated vow of silence card, soiled by a boot print. Beside it was a Scottish five-pound note bearing only two words, handwritten in black marker ink: *Lorem Ipsum.*

THREE

Parent evening

EWALD HOUSE, NORTHUMBERLAND, 12 AUGUST

The grounds of Ewald House, set in the vast, lush greenery of the Hammerson estate in Northumberland, felt to private investigator Alex Czerniak like an airfield that morning, with several helicopter landings ferrying in passengers and equipment. On his own flight from London, Alex had played chaperone to a white Labrador named Willow, belonging to Cecilia Gant, mother of kidnappee Noah Gant. Cecilia had come straight from a business meeting in Cardiff and wished to have her pooch with her at this difficult time. It was lucky they all made it to Ewald before noon. A storm bearing gale-force winds had gathered. The treetops swayed wildly. Menacing clouds threatened thunderstorms and rain.

Ewald was everything Alex had expected of a billionaire's country retreat: a formidable faux-ancient mansion fronted by heavy grey stone. The beautiful brownish-red moss that crept up the walls was plausibly real. Inside, living quarters were a fantasy of Dickensian wood effect and period oil paintings, some depicting thin-nosed aristocrats with their gundogs. The spell was occasionally broken by modern art pieces, such as the curvy copper-and-steel human figure at the foot of the grand staircase or the giant canvas of angry red paint spatter that dominated the entrance hall.

When Alex finally managed to find Peter Hammerson's office, having lost his way twice in the maze-like ground floor of the grandiose house, he knocked on the open door and walked in without waiting for an invitation. Peter sat at his desk wearing a black turtleneck sweater and a dour expression. After Alex formally introduced himself, though he and Peter had already shared two brief video meetings and a frantic phone call following Emily's abduction, he softened his face and calibrated his tone from professional to personal. 'How are you holding up, Peter?'

Peter drew in a lungful of breath, held it in and exhaled, his eyes on the keyboard. 'Better not to ask.'

'They're all here,' Alex said. 'Second floor conference room. It's like a parent evening in West London. Only one parent bothered to show up for each kid.'

From behind his desk, piled high with bulging files and two computer monitors, Peter looked up at him, a chewed-up pencil in his hand. 'They're all divorced or separated, that's why. Except for Cecilia Gant. Her husband died a few years ago, terrible business. Well, I guess we'll have to face them. What's the mood like in there?'

'Fraught, I'd say. Theo Salt and Davis Boroughs nearly came to fists.'

'Wouldn't want to be Theo in that match-up,' Peter said. 'Wouldn't want to be Davis in the lawsuit after. They never liked each other, those two.' He gave his pencil a final chew, laid it on the mouse mat and walked around the desk to join Alex. With a pained smile, he said, 'Rich people become insufferable when things are out of their hands.'

'Yes, sir. I have had first-hand experience.'

Peter sucked in some air, then patted Alex on the back. 'Remember, Alex, we may be rolling in it, but when it comes to this, we're just people, just parents. I keep thinking back to the last time I saw Emily. I mean, we knew they could be after her – *I knew* – and still they took her. If only I'd kept my security team with me. If only I... How did they even know where to find her?' He bit his lip and shook his head. 'Sorry. My mind's racing. I can't seem to slow it down. It just... It runs away from me.'

The remorse and guilty tone, combined with Peter's anguished expression, made Alex feel for him. He had done his homework on Peter's background. The man wasn't born to wealth. He came from nearly nothing and had worked hard to build his energy company, pivoting to renewables at just the right time. And the riches he earned had not shielded him from the kind of hardships that could befall anyone, rich or poor. His younger son, Brendan, now twenty-four, was hit by a drunk driver on a pedestrian crossing in Newcastle when he was a teenager on a night out on the Toon. His injured spinal cord had left him permanently reliant on a wheelchair. Rising to the challenge, Peter became his son's greatest champion, taking interviews alongside him to talk about how Brendan's accident did not define him. Peter's marriage, however, did not survive the strain. The divorce left Rita Hammerson with a golden parachute generous enough – if the tabloids were to be believed – to allow her a dazzling, self-destructive lifestyle in her new home in LA. Rita had severed all contact with Peter and the kids, though Alex suspected there was more pain in her story than reported. And now Emily was taken. Money could only shield you so far. In Emily's case, it had made her a target.

Alex motioned to the open door. 'After you, sir.'

In the capacious boardroom, the fancy focaccia sandwiches were left to sag, untouched on their silver trays, filling the air with an aroma of smoked salmon, houmous and boiled eggs. The brutal storm outside was visible in greys and blacks through the picture window, mirroring the volatile darkness of the mood within. Beneath the well-trained game faces of the four guests, anxiety and lack of sleep revealed themselves in tiny twitches and shaky small talk. The coffee machine worked extra hard, groaning as it ground premium Columbian coffee beans and spat out steaming milk.

Peter Hammerson sat at the head of the table with Alex by his side and motioned for his guests to take their places. They were an odd mix of personalities, a pastiche unlikely to come together if it weren't for their offspring having attended the same expensively prestigious school. The children of five billionaires in one year – it was probably a first.

The plump lawyer, Theo Salt, planted himself two seats away to Peter's right, next to the formidable Nadia Sayal, owner of a food empire that had managed to break into the American market against every analyst's predictions. To Peter's left was Noah's mother, department store magnate Cecilia Gant, soft-eyed and kind and notoriously ruthless in business. Her hand was absent-mindedly stroking her dog's head. Beside her was the dandy, Davis Boroughs, father of Ashleigh and owner of a business, the nature of which would usually shun him from polite company. A breathless Brent, Peter's head of security, joined them at the last minute and took a seat by the wall, his hands in his lap, looking down with drooping eyes like a beaten hound.

'Thank you all for coming,' Peter said, sounding formal, like the esteemed CEO he was. 'I thought this might be better done in person, so we can all work together in real time and take decisions as a group. They have our kids, but we should be hopeful. There is no better equipped, better resourced group of people to bring them back safely.'

Theo Salt, founder of the mighty law firm Salt-Lather-

Reese, pulled on his red braces and let them snap back to his paunch. He cleared his throat. 'Let's get to it, Peter. We don't need speeches. This isn't Davos.'

Cecilia Gant gave Peter's shoulder a tender squeeze. 'Terrible that Emily was also taken. It must have been a shock.'

'From right under his nose, I hear,' Theo Salt said. 'If I'd been given that opportunity, the advance warning, I'd surround my Jonny with walls of concrete and steel, not wait for him to be snatched from me like some neglectful parent. You met at a pub? Seriously? A pub?'

Peter met Cecilia's kind gesture with a nod and made a point of ignoring the lawyer's harsh words, though a dark shadow crossed his face and, for a fleeting moment, he seemed to shrink into himself. He straightened his back and hardened his expression. 'We all know each other,' he said in a forced even tone, 'and you've met Alex Czerniak. He'll oversee our operation here. Alex comes highly recommended, not only as a private investigator but as someone who can get things done. For transparency, I should mention that his wife is a senior Met Police officer, but he's bound to silence by his contract.' He took a hasty breath. 'And over there is Brent de Waal, my head of security.'

Theo Salt raised an eyebrow. 'The one responsible for protecting your daughter?'

Nadia Sayal, strong-featured in a resplendent red and gold tunic over pleated trousers, fixed her eyes firmly on the lawyer and tapped her fist on the table, her bangles clinking in the act. 'We thank you, Peter, for your hospitality. Now, Alex, could you talk us through what you propose? I mean, we've heard nothing from these kidnappers, but I expect they'll make their demands soon, right?'

Alex clicked on a remote control, and the large screen on the wall brightened to life, showing the pictures, names and ages of the five abductees:

Emily Hammerson, 28
Noah Gant, 28
Zayn Sayal, 27
Ashleigh Boroughs, 27
Jonny Salt, 28

Alex clicked to change the image on the screen to a close-up of the five-pound note left behind at the scene of Emily's abduction. 'All of your adult children,' he said, 'were kidnapped under different circumstances, but in all cases, the kidnappers left a calling card. A five-pound note with the words *Lorem Ipsum* on it. As I'm sure you've already googled, it's derived from the Latin *dolorem ipsum* meaning *pain itself*. It is also used as placeholder text in documents and websites, which, well, doesn't help us much. This might be a warning or a threat. We're not sure yet. Let's keep it in mind. In my experience, every detail matters. The next thing–'

Davis Boroughs, who had not yet spoken, raised his hand like a traffic cop to stop Alex's flow. Davis was dressed like a stage actor in a brown herringbone suit, red pocket square and tan moccasins over bright-blue socks. Alex could feel the air in the conference room chill as Davis claimed his right to speak. Davis was often snubbed for the manner in which he made his fortune, selling cheap but highly satisfying adult toys to the masses through a series of well-designed websites. Behind his back, he was often referred to with a chuckle as Dildo Davis. No one would ever invite Dildo Davis to Davos.

'Begging your pardon,' Davis said, 'but we know exactly what they want. They didn't kidnap the daughter of a beekeeper or nurse, did they?'

'A beekeeper?' Theo Salt said.

Davis ignored him. 'It's just a matter of establishing the amount of ransom. We have to play this right, negotiate right, get them back safe.' He rubbed his forehead with the tips of his fingers and squeezed his eyes shut. When he opened them, he said, 'This needs to end, and it needs to end quickly. My Ashleigh, she's… She has…' His voice caught in his throat. He swallowed and fixed his gaze on his ring's substantial violet diamond, which rose like a mushroom from his left middle finger.

'If you just bear with–' Alex started to say but was, again, interrupted.

Davis pushed back his chair with a screech and stood, seeming to have regained some of his cocky composure. His sheer height towered over the conference table in a way that would have seemed threatening, but for his unzipped fly that showed a sliver of bright-pink underwear. 'I don't need a support group,' he said.

'Sit down,' Nadia Sayal said. 'We're all worried sick. You've come all this way. At least hear the man out.'

Davis remained standing, as stiff as a tin soldier, but did not leave.

'We can consider amounts when we get their demands,' Peter said, 'but we're not just going to sit here and chew on our nails. We'll try to find and rescue them, give ourselves other options, hire a mercenary platoon if we have to. That's why I brought Alex here. He knows the right people.'

Davis scratched his five o'clock shadow, shook his head and grunted, but returned to his seat.

'Before we go any further,' Peter said, 'I propose that we don't involve the police or the press. Better to hold these negotiations quietly, so we can maintain control, not let the authorities take rash decisions. Once the press gets wind of this, there will be a frenzy we won't be able to control and with it a whole world of risk.'

Cecilia Gant looked at Peter. 'You already said that when you sent us your invitations, but is this policy meant to protect our children or our businesses?'

A pained, artificial smile appeared on Davis Boroughs's face. He clasped his hands over the table, leaned forward and gave Peter an expectant look.

'I'd say it's yes to both,' Theo Salt answered for him. 'It's a solid strategy. Otherwise, we might find ourselves unexpectedly restrained, as if dangling from one of your slings, Davis.'

'And thank you for being a loyal customer,' Davis said.

'This is no time for childish arguments,' Nadia Sayal said. 'In case you've forgotten, our children, my Zayn, they're—'

'Quite right,' Theo interrupted. 'Forgive my… *friend* Davis here.'

Alex reflected on Theo's acidic reactions. The parents were coping with the crisis in their own individual ways. For Theo, it was through a mixture of contempt and lashed-out anger. He reminded himself not to judge the man too harshly. His son had been kidnapped. Beneath the abrasive lawyer's façade would be a boiling soup of emotions, not least fear and a crushing worry for his Jonny.

'All right. All right,' Peter said. 'Are we all agreed? No police. No press. Do this on the quiet. Get our kids home quickly. Pretend the whole thing never happened.' He looked at each of them in turn. Davis nodded, then Nadia. Theo took a long moment but relented. Cecilia Gant looked down at her dog and patted its head but did not voice an objection.

'What happens next, then?' Davis Boroughs said. 'Or did we drop everything to discuss a butchered Latin phrase and our comms policy?'

A bolt of lightning flashed to hit the paddock, followed by a rumble of thunder that reverberated through the window's glass. Willow the Labrador growled at the window, then whined softly.

'Shh. Shh. It's okay,' Cecilia hushed her dog, then leaned down to hug it. Alex noticed a tear running down her cheek, leaving a streak of mascara in its wake. There was so much pent-up worry in the boardroom, so many stunted emotions.

'As soon as they get in touch,' Alex said, 'our best chance is to respond as a united group, with one voice. Having you all here means we can gather quickly when we need to. In the meantime, I'll speak with my contacts and put things in motion. Whatever else happens, my priority is to try and locate your kids, see if we can put an end to this on our terms, not theirs.'

'And remember,' Peter said. 'Discretion, discretion, discretion. It's absolutely paramount.'

There then came a knock, and the door opened. Peter's son manoeuvred his wheelchair into the room and to the head of the table opposite his father. On his lap was a tablet computer.

'And who might you be?' Davis said.

'My son, Brendan,' Peter said.

'Ah, the spare!' Davis said.

Brendan narrowed his eyes and glared at Davis for a long moment. He pulled forcefully, almost violently, on the lever of his wheelchair's handbrake. 'You have to see this,' he said. 'Dad, click the TV to Screencast. A few minutes ago, the kidnappers released a video. It's already been shared all over social media.'

Davis Boroughs tutted. 'Discretion, discretion, discretion, eh?'

FOUR

Robin's Brigade

Alex stood and leaned his back against the wall, his hands folded. His instinct told him to stand apart from the circle of angst formed by the parents. Whatever came next couldn't be good. He needed to keep his thinking focused, detached from emotion, alert to any clues and nuances in the kidnappers' message.

Brendan tapped on the tablet and shared his screen. It displayed a video's opening frame. The image under the triangular *Play* icon was of a one-armed doll dressed in a green felt Robin Hood costume. On the screen's top-left corner was a logo constructed of two words in dramatic black lettering: *Robin's Brigade*. Brendan pressed play.

The doll's image faded out to be replaced by a woman staring forward with intense hazel eyes. She wore a Robin Hood hat, a waistcoat and a skinny green tie. Alex assessed her age to be in the mid-twenties. When she spoke, she sounded educated, posh. 'Citizens of the world, the downtrodden, the exploited, the oppressed,' she said with pathos. 'We are Robin's Brigade. We stand with you. We have stolen from the rich, and we will give to the poor.'

'Oh, bollocks,' Davis Boroughs said. 'Socialists.'

The screen changed from the announcer to five framed video images of the abductees, each in what looked like a hospital bed, connected to a drip. Alex could almost feel the collective intake of breath in the room.

A whimsical trumpet played in the background while the announcer said, 'These are our bargaining chips, and this video is intended for their unjustly rich parents.'

Peter rushed to the side of the screen and stared at the image of his daughter, lying still in a nun's uniform, her eyes closed. When he returned to his seat, he clutched his chest and looked pale. The other parents, too, had their gazes fixed on their children until the picture changed to show a partial view of what looked like four stacked wooden boxes.

The music subsided, and the announcer's voice returned, yet the wooden boxes remained in the frame. Alex shuddered when he realised what they were. 'Dear billionaire parents, we're going to play a fun game together. We call it *Heir Loss*. That's heir with an "H". The rules are simple. The game has two levels, two rounds. In each round, your offspring will earn points. At the end of the game, the participant who earns the most points will be returned to you safe and alive. The other four, well, they'll also be returned,' she paused for effect, 'in one of these coffins.'

Cecilia Gant's hand rushed to her mouth. Theo Salt crossed his arms, locking them tightly against his chest as if to shield himself from the horror on the screen. The parents all looked like they were drowning, struggling for air.

The images of the five abductees reappeared, and the voice on the video changed to a lower tone, serious and businesslike. 'Now, in order that we follow the thread of natural justice, it's not your children who'll be playing for points – it is you. For those who don't know yet, these are the sons and daughters of some of the wealthiest people in our land. Their combined net worth is in the many billions, an amount that could pay to feed millions of hungry mouths, raise millions more from destitution, provide essential medicines to those who will die without treatment. In the abstract, these are just numbers, but think of one child – one child – they could save with a sum that wouldn't put a dent in a single tin of their beluga caviar. Think on that while you consider what they do with their cash.'

Captioned pictures flew onto the screen, of Theo Salt's private jet, of Cecilia Gant's immense holiday villa in Grenada, of the collection of Bugattis, Ferraris and Rolls-Royces parked in Davis Boroughs's hanger-sized garage, of Nadia Sayal's thoroughbred racing stallion, worth millions. The images then layered over each other at a dizzying speed: bottles of vintage Dom Pérignon, diamond-studded stiletto shoes, gold bullion, a satellite image of Ewald House. Then the video darkened, and a single image expanded to take over the entire screen. It was of what appeared to be a homeless young girl, about five years of age, staring down at them through wistful eyes under dark matted hair. She was bare-footed, wearing a filthy gingham dress, standing in an alcove on a cobbled street. She was sucking her thumb and clutching the familiar one-armed doll dressed in the Robin Hood costume.

The announcer reappeared. 'We've set the stage. Now, let's play the game. Each of you *obscenely* rich parents will receive an email shortly. Don't bother trying to respond. It's from a one-time email account. You'll know it's from us because it will contain two words that only you will know, words we left behind for exactly this purpose. In this email will be details of an account into which you will transfer an amount of money in cryptocurrency within twenty-four hours. We'll call it 1pm tomorrow. We hope it will be a large sum, but that's up to you. The only condition is that you send *something*. If you send nothing, your child will immediately be disqualified, and you know what that means…'

There was a pause into which Davis Boroughs interjected, 'Up to us?'

'Listen closely,' the woman on the screen continued. 'We're not here in the name of greed. We're here for justice, for redistribution. The funds you send us will be promptly transferred into the accounts of organisations that support the poorest, the persecuted, the hungry and the sick – either directly or in trusts that will pay them an annual sum. Does that sound fair to you, gentle viewer? Of course it does. And we promise complete transparency. Everyone in the world will know how much each parent paid and where the money went. We take nothing for ourselves. Not a single penny.'

The announcer stared at the camera for a long moment as though she could see the startled faces of the parents looking back at her. 'And herein lies the key to this round,' she said. 'Each of your children will receive a number of points based on the amount of money you send. The highest amount will win your child the most points. The lower amounts, less. And remember: more points mean a better chance of winning. Not enough points: a coffin. We will be in touch again, 1pm tomorrow, with the results of the first round. And whatever you do, I can guarantee you this: within six days, your children will be sent back to you, one way… or the other.'

The screen returned briefly to the image of the homeless girl, and then went dark.

The parents stared at the screen in stunned silence until they were interrupted by another knock on the door. It was Darren, the estate manager.

'Sorry to bother you, sir,' Darren said to Peter. 'There's an ITV News van parked outside the outer gate. Thought you'd like to know.'

'How on earth did they get here so quickly?' Nadia Sayal said.

Brendan spun his chair and wheeled himself to the door.

Before leaving the room, he looked back at the assembled. In a dry tone, he said, 'I guess you're no longer working together on this, yeah?' He looked at his father. 'Remember, Dad, your responsibility is to Emily. You don't have to play nice. I can guarantee you this lot won't.'

FIVE

Game theory

Theo Salt locked the door of his allocated bedroom and double-checked the handle. He kicked off his shoes, sat hunched forward on the edge of the bed and held his head in his hands. A single length of breath escaped him like a stunted sigh. He wished his ex-wife Ruth was with him still, so he could hold and comfort her, thereby comforting himself. If only he could tell her – and himself – that everything will be all right, that Jonny will come home unharmed, back to his wife and son. The notion was fanciful, he knew. Ruth had fled his love to live an itinerant off-grid lifestyle, *away from it all*. Last he heard, she was in some bearded guru's ashram in Tamil Nadu where she could live a simple existence, bathing in the river and surviving on rice and curried vegetables, secure in the knowledge her bank manager would always welcome her back like a much-loved, lost relative.

Sometimes, Theo dreamed of doing the same: getting on a plane, shedding his responsibilities, the suffocating tie, the too-tight belt around his too-full belly, the unnecessary red braces. Then, he would remind himself that he was the lucky one. Joyful moments with his grandson Evan – Jonny's five-year-old

– were worth more to him than any fantasy escape to mantras and daal.

Theo stared at his dry knuckles, at the brown age spots on the back of his hands. In this dark and fraught moment, he felt so desperately alone, trying with all his might to keep his flimsy composure intact, or else he would shatter to nothing. *But no, I have to keep my cool. For Jonny's sake, I have to think straight.*

He checked his watch, reached into his leather attaché case, pulled out a thin silver laptop and opened it. He signed in to his law firm's secure platform and navigated to the conferencing app. After a couple of clicks, the company's London boardroom appeared on screen: glass and chrome, and the two other managing partners at Salt-Lather-Reese.

'Afternoon, gents,' he said, reining in his tone before it cracked. 'You've read my email?'

'We've been gaming scenarios since we got it,' Jim Lather said. Jim was a sharp-suited American lawyer with quick wit, a deep Southern drawl and an encyclopaedic knowledge of tricky international cases adjudicated on both sides of the Atlantic. 'But first, we're all real sorry for what happened, and the firm is one hundred per cent behind you in getting Jonny back from those bastards.'

'Sentiment noted,' Theo said, 'but what have you got for me?'

'It's a tough one,' Jim said. 'We have some thoughts on how to play this. There are no guarantees, of course.'

'I'm not a client, Jim. Don't flannel me.'

'Sure, Sure,' Jim said. 'So, here's what we have: five parents, each trying to figure out the sum they'll pay to be the highest bidder. I didn't mean bidder as in...' He winced, then shrugged. 'Anyway, we asked ourselves: how does each of the other parents decide what to pay?'

'Yeah, yeah, okay,' Theo said, scratching the bedspread out

of the camera's sight like an aggravated cat. *For goodness' sake, man*, he thought. *For goodness' sake, get to it.*

'Just being thorough, that's all,' Jim said, for once reading the virtual room.

'The issue on this end…' Theo said. 'Well, I saw the look on Cecilia Gant's face. There's no telling how high she'll go for her Noah. The moon, probably.'

'Theo, it's Avery,' Avery Reese said, even though Theo could clearly see his muscled, bull-like frame that took up a third of the screen. 'We've brainstormed options, and we have a plan to suggest to you. In our opinion, the best move is to influence the other parents. We need to anchor their thinking to a specific ransom amount. There's obviously no rate card for kidnappings, but an anchor of seventy thousand pounds per hostage should do it. We lock their thinking to it. They pay a little over. You go about double. You end up on top.'

'Seventy sounds low,' Theo said.

'Low, but deliberate,' Avery said. 'They're all in turmoil, second-guessing amounts. Their heads are exploding with numbers. If you dangle certainty before them, something to latch on to, they'll feel relief. In a crisis, relief trumps logic. It's simple psychology.'

Theo took a silent moment to think. Avery and Jim had clearly thought of some kind of plan. For the first time in his life, the lawyerly vocabulary felt trite and inappropriate, yet it was the only edge he possessed, the only card he had to play. International law firms like his own thrived on complex negotiations, on having the best-trained minds dedicated to weighing up options and strategies. If it brought Jonny back to him, back to his wife and son, he had to press this advantage to its fullest.

'Theo?' Jim said.

Theo tapped his fingers on the wooden bed-frame. 'The

other parents aren't stupid. How in God's name will we get them to do what we want? With hypnosis?'

'Not quite, but close,' Jim said.

'Well, out with it,' Theo said with a huff.

'Our designated hypnotist,' Jim said, 'will be Beth Grisham.'

'The US media mogul?' Theo said.

Jim nodded. 'She's rich, takes no bullshit and is above suspicion.'

'I'm sorry,' Theo said. 'I don't follow.'

'Here's how it'll work,' Jim said. 'Beth will call each of the parents to express her sympathies. She'll let slip that her news team has found a way to get hold of the actual sums paid by the others. Something to do with hacking bank transfers or cryptocurrency purchases. She'll ask them to call her before they make their payments. When they call, she'll say the others all landed under seventy thousand pounds. She'll swear them to secrecy. She only told them because she loves them above all of her other dwarves.'

'And why,' Theo said, 'would the ruthless mogul who takes no bullshit back me?'

'You're gonna love this,' Avery said.

Jim shrugged with one shoulder and gave the camera a crooked grin. 'She and I have a history. Let's just say she owes me one. Either that or a paternity test for her twins.'

Theo blinked. 'You… and her?'

'She needed an oil change, that's all,' Jim said.

'He's a right prince, our Jim,' Avery said.

Theo shut his eyes, shut them so tight he saw red circles pulsing to the beat of his heart. When he opened them, he said, 'This strategy makes sense, but what if we're wrong? My gut tells me to pay above and beyond, reduce the risk, do everything I can to save Jonny. This isn't some acquisition contract we're negotiating. My son's life… I…' He shook his head, unable to complete the thought.

'We know, Theo. We know,' Jim said. 'It's a tough spot, but you've got the advantage here. If it were my Hilary, I'd remind myself how emotional clients make rash decisions based on their gut and indigestion. If the other parents are tied to the anchor we push, you'll end up on top. Otherwise, you're just playing a lottery with random numbers. Do that, and all bets are off. We're offering you a solid solution, Theo, at least for this round.'

'It's a good plan,' Avery said and shrugged. 'If I'm honest, it's the only one we have.'

Theo took a moment, finding it difficult to focus. He scratched his chin, chewed on his lip, then gave his partners a single nod. 'All right. All right. Let's go ahead. Thanks, gents. I appreciate it.'

Jim straightened his tie. 'Leave it with me. You rest now, Theo. You look terrible.'

Avery hesitated, then raised a tentative fist in the air. 'Stay strong, Theo.'

'We're all very–' Jim started to say, but was cut short when Theo hit the disconnect button.

Theo washed his face in the en-suite bathroom and looked into his mirrored bloodshot eyes. He hadn't slept much since Jonny was lifted from a restaurant opening, two days earlier. The tiredness, coupled with the endless cups of coffee, made his hands shake and his frayed nerves hum. He returned to the bed, arranged the excessive number of pillows and cushions into a nest and rested himself in their midst. He clicked on the TV's remote.

A BBC reporter was interviewing shoppers on a high street in Sunderland. The caption on the screen read *Billionaire kidnappings*. A microphone was thrust in front of a woman carrying a sackcloth shopping bag. She had shoulder-length pink hair with three sea-glass beads hanging from a braid to the side of her face.

'Of course, taking anyone's daughter or son is wrong,' the woman said, 'but put that to one side for a minute. Don't you think these kidnappers have a point? I mean, how is it right that people go hungry, go to food banks, don't have money to heat their homes? People are dying from famine all over the world. They're dying here in England. How do you justify having mansions and private jets and… Nobody should have billions. Nobody.'

'And if,' the reporter said, 'as the kidnappers threatened, they'll kill four of their five victims, how would you feel then?'

'I'm against any killing. I'm not heartless. Of course I'm against killing them. But think of the thousands of people all this money will save. Are they worth less than the lives of those who've had it so good?'

Theo clicked angrily to another news channel. Home Secretary Nessa Thorns was sitting stiffly in the studio under the title of some political programme, wearing a politician's straight face.

'You will be aware, Home Secretary,' the silver-haired interviewer said, 'as anyone who has followed social media over the last couple of hours would be, that the hashtag *WeAreRobin* is trending.'

'The government condemns the kidnapping in the strongest terms,' the Home Secretary said. 'We all believe in social justice, but this is not the way to bring it about. And remember, these billionaires have built businesses that employ many thousands of people. They contribute to the economy, create jobs and prosperity. They're not bad people.'

'Naturally,' the interviewer said, 'but what do you say to those who, while they disagree with the kidnappers' methods, are protesting the stark disparity between the haves and have-nots?'

'Gutless, crackpot idiots,' Theo hissed at the screen. He clicked the television off, slammed the remote onto the bedside table and stared at the ceiling, his chest tight with anger.

His phone buzzed. It was a video call. His grandson's face appeared on screen, red-cheeked, his mouth round with what Theo recognised as his worried pout.

'Grandad, Grandad,' Evan said without a greeting, 'I was at school, and Freddie showed me the video of that woman talking about Daddy, and Freddie says *no chance. He's never ever coming home. He's so dead.* And Mummy says it's lies, and you'll get Daddy back because you're the best law-i-yer, and…' His lips quivered, and he opened his mouth, then closed it. He scratched his nose and swayed from side to side.

Leila appeared behind the boy. She wrapped her arms around him and held him close, speaking to the camera in a forced jolly tone, 'Of course Grandad will bring Daddy home.'

Theo resisted his lawyerly instinct to inject logic into the conversation. He could not guarantee a thing, but the desperate plea in his daughter-in-law's eyes overwhelmed him. 'We'll bring him home, Evan,' he said with as much confidence as he could muster. 'We'll bring Daddy home.'

'Promise?' the boy said.

'I promise,' he said, against his better judgement.

'When?' Evan said.

Theo hesitated.

'Let's not bother Grandad,' Leila said. 'He's got a lot of work to do for Daddy. Okay, sweetheart?'

'When?' Evan repeated.

'Evan, I…'

The boy's lower lip trembled, and his voice shook. 'When?'

'Call me when you know anything,' Leila said and hung up.

Theo lay back on the bed, closed his eyes and thought about the many unfulfilled promises he had made in his life: to his ex-wife, to his son, to the people who should have mattered the most. His phone beeped with a message from that useless PI, Alex: *Dinner and updates at 7pm, Family Dining Room downstairs. The Home Office asks that we meet with their rep for an important update. He is due later this evening.*

He switched off his phone, thinking that he should get some sleep. He might be able to, now he had calmed a little. Jim and Avery's plan was a good one. To quieten his dread further, he allowed his mind to play a little confidence trick on itself, welcoming a newly forged sense of hope. He imagined the look on Davis Boroughs's face when the results were announced for the first round of payments, how the man would seethe and curse and act out the frustration born of his own gullibility. *I won't gloat,* Theo decided. *I'll just sit there calmly with a little smirk on my face. Yes, that would show him. That would humble the smutty, preening peacock.*

SIX

Mr Smith

Alex Czerniak considered what he should wear for dinner and settled on a white dress shirt, blue jeans and formal black shoes, the image of one who is respectful yet not beholden. It was essential to keep himself above the brewing tensions in the house. The parents were at odds with each other, the veneer of a cordial *we're all in this together* having worn dangerously thin. They were worldly, intelligent people, supposedly meant to understand that whatever happened between them had no bearing on their children's chances. Still, Alex understood the rising frustration that could drive them to lash out. If his own girls were held to ransom– *No!* He interrupted the thought before it ran away from him. For a parent, some things were too awful to consider.

He was about to leave his bedroom when his phone rang. It was Darren, the estate manager, calling to inform him of the visitor's arrival, in from the storm, damp and impatient. Alex asked that the guest be dispatched to the formal lounge, where he would receive him. He felt like a member of the landed gentry when Darren did not hesitate to confirm that, 'Very good, Mr Czerniak. I'll have him taken there,' adding, 'Shall I arrange for another place to be set for dinner?' and then, 'Will there be anything else, sir?'

Alex had met quite a few affluent people in his line of work as a top-tier PI. He observed that even when their lives were marred by heartbreak and personal difficulty, there was a certain ease with which the trivial took care of itself without them having to give it a second thought. Peter Hammerson would never have to do the laundry, cook a meal, change a light bulb. *I could get used to this*, Alex thought. Then, he reminded himself that once you got accustomed to a hassle-free lifestyle, it no longer felt like a privilege. After a while, even the wondrous became mundane, luxury became a habit, clicked heels and whim-fulfilment were taken for granted. *Even so*, he thought. *Even so.*

Alex left his bedroom and walked along the upstairs corridor, his steps swallowed by the plush burgundy carpet. Beautiful gaslight-style wall lanterns projected a soft ambience of shade and light. He stopped in front of one of the bedrooms, the one allocated to Cecilia Gant. Muffled voices were coming from within. Cecilia sounded agitated, her tone raised. A male voice – Peter Hammerson's, he realised – was responding in kind. Even though Alex could not make out the words, he sensed the two were having a heated exchange. *What on earth could they be arguing about?* Then a thought occurred to him. *Could it be that one had some leverage, some information that could force the other into paying less?* It was unthinkable. What kind of parent would sacrifice a child in response to blackmail? No information, no matter how shocking, could compel such a result. And both Cecilia and Peter seemed like good, decent people. It was far-fetched that either would stoop so low. Then again, they didn't become billionaires by being timid. He carried on walking and filed the question in his mind. Something to figure out later.

When he reached the formal lounge, the visitor was already

there, standing stiffly in a cheap suit, his small eyes tracing the shelves and antique furniture, a stale whiff of cigarettes about him.

The man held out his hand. 'Tom Smith, Home Office Liaison. It's nice to meet you, Alex. I've heard a lot about you.'

Alex took the proffered hand and shook it, doubting the man from the Home Office would have heard much about him, let alone a lot. 'Looks rough out there,' Alex said. 'Gale-force winds. Did you drive all the way up from London?'

The man gave him the thinnest of smiles. 'Not quite. I'm seconded to our Edinburgh office. Even so, I'm telling you, it was a scary ride: trees on roads, flying debris, detours. Wasn't sure I'd make it.'

'Well, you're here now,' Alex said, keen to do away with the small talk. He motioned to two high-backed leather chairs, inviting the visitor to sit. As the man undid his jacket button, Alex felt a tremor of unease. His gut told him there was something ominous about this man with his generic name, Tom Smith, in his generic Marks & Spencer suit, whose shoulders were covered with a dusting of dandruff.

They sat, their legs crossed, eyeing each other.

Smith raised his chin and pushed out his chest. 'Will Peter Hammerson be joining us?'

'He's delegated all external communications to me,' Alex said, keeping his tone formal. 'Which Home Office department did you say you work for?'

'I report to the Home Secretary directly,' Smith said. 'I troubleshoot situations that require her close ear. The Home Secretary and I go back a ways. Sheer luck I'm currently in this neck of the woods. All her other minions don't imagine there's anything north of the M25. Northumberland could well be on another planet.'

'And what are your instructions regarding… our situation?'

'I'd rather discuss these directly with their intended

recipients.' Smith said this with so much pomposity that Alex felt like punching him in the mouth.

'You're welcome to join them for dinner,' Alex said, 'but I have to warn you: these are powerful people. They prefer the owner, not the lapdog.'

'No need to worry on that count,' Smith said. 'This lapdog has bite. Also, after I've had my chat with them, I'll need a moment in private with Nadia Sayal.'

'What for?'

'A personal matter. I'm sure you'll be keen to help us. We're all on the same side, after all.'

Are we? Alex thought but did not say. Instead, he approximated a nod of agreement.

'I do have one question, if you don't mind,' Smith said. 'You're a private detective, and I assume you've done some background work on the unfortunates that were kidnapped: light profiles, mugshots, that sort of thing. Out of interest, what did you find when you looked into Zayn, Nadia Sayal's son?'

'Nothing remarkable,' Alex said, thinking there was no harm in sharing well-known trivia. 'Zayn Sayal's grades at school weren't spectacular, so he didn't carry on to university. He's not bad-looking and loves attention, so at first, there was talk of maybe a career in the movies. His mother pulled some strings to get him an audition in Hollywood. He flew to LA for it but never showed up at the studio. Apparently, he got to LAX and immediately boarded another flight to Tokyo, where he went on a three-night bender, larging it in exclusive clubs and parties. As far as I know, that's the lifestyle he's lived since school: New York, Berlin, Moscow, Beijing, the Algarve. In winter, he prefers Bali and the Emirates.'

'Nothing exceptional, then,' Smith said.

'Zayn is a good-looking party boy with an unlimited line of credit. The story writes itself.'

'My thoughts exactly,' Smith said and straightened his damp hair with fat, nicotine-stained fingers.

Alex eyed him suspiciously. 'What aren't you telling me?'

Smith shrugged. 'Nah. Just interested to know if there was more to him. Clearly not. You said it yourself: a rich, good-looking bum is still a bum. A bit surprising though, considering his impressive mother.' He rubbed his hands together. 'The man at the door – what is he, the butler? He said they're all gathering for dinner. I hope he won't get in trouble for leaking tonight's menu. Crab cakes and truffled venison sound lovely. Shall we go and join the poor bastards?'

The Family Dining Room was modest by Ewald's standards, but large enough to host a party of twelve. It was distastefully furnished, combining a Tudor-style table with modern chairs alongside a Victorian fireplace and an Art Nouveau chandelier. Peter Hammerson revealed himself as caring little for interior design, or perhaps it was his ex-wife's doing. Around the table sat the five parents and Peter's son, the starter already before them, crab cakes on a bed of flash-fried marsh samphire. An extra place had been set for the new arrival. Darren had clearly relayed the message. Alex sat down between Nadia and Cecilia. The guest remained standing, eyeing the parents as if taking an inventory.

'This is–' Alex started to say but was interrupted.

'Tom Smith, Home Office Liaison. Thank you for inviting me to join you. If it's not too much trouble, I was hoping to stay the night. I don't fancy my chances driving back to Edinburgh tonight. I didn't want to presume and ask the butler.'

'We don't have butlers,' Peter Hammerson said, then

nodded to an aproned woman who was standing in the corner. She bowed her head in acknowledgement and left the room.

'I'll introduce you,' Alex said.

'No need,' Smith said. 'I know who you all are. Please don't let me interrupt your meal.' He joined them at the table. 'If you don't mind, I'd like to talk to you about something important, maybe after dinner? I'm starving.'

'Important?' Theo Salt said and put down his fork. 'What is it?'

'Better on a full stomach,' Smith said.

'No,' Theo said. 'If it's important, we'll talk about it now.'

Smith picked up the soft white roll from his bread plate, broke it in half with his thumbs and used the main-course knife to smear it with a thick layer of butter. They were all staring at him, waiting. He shoved the roll into his mouth and bit off half of it in one. He closed his eyes, chewing vigorously, his Adam's apple rising and falling as he swallowed. Still chewing, he said, 'Pardon my manners. I had to rush to get here, and it took me ages. Had nothing to eat since breakfast. My blood sugar was in my big toe.' He raised his wine glass at them, drank from it and sighed with contentment.

Alex was unsure if it was anger etched on the faces of the impatient parents or perhaps disbelief. Somehow, they held back, though their eyes told him they were ready to pounce.

'Well, then?' Theo said.

With his middle finger, Smith dislodged a piece of bread that was stuck between his gum and upper lip. 'The Home Secretary,' he said, 'wishes to convey her deepest concern about the situation you find yourselves in. His Majesty's Government is committed to doing everything in its power to return your children to you safely. I am here, as it were, in my capacity as a back-channel intervention.'

'You mean like a suppository?' Theo Salt said.

'I understand,' Smith said, 'the strength of feeling around this table, and—'

'Do you indeed?' Theo said. 'Tell me, Mr Smith, do you have children?'

'I don't see how that's relevant,' Smith said.

'Of course you don't,' Theo said. 'Please, deliver your message.'

'All right,' Smith said. 'Before I do, I have just one question. Have any of you already sent payment to the kidnappers? A show of hands would be fine.'

No hands were raised.

'Let me put it another way,' Smith said. 'How many haven't?'

'That's two questions,' Davis said, 'and it's none of your business.'

Smith took his time, seeming not in the least rattled by the growing tension in the room. He wiped his mouth with a napkin and discarded it over the bread plate. 'Very well. I have been instructed to tell you the following. The Cabinet met today. As I've already said, they are very sympathetic. However, they're also concerned for the safety of every British citizen should this campaign be allowed to stand. If political, cause-driven activism pays, who's to say the next target won't be, for example, the Prime Minister's daughter with a demand for a change of policy, or even the Home Secretary's dog.'

'Her dog?' Nadia Sayal said.

Smith ignored Nadia's interjection. 'After careful consideration,' he said, 'with the full agreement of the Prime Minister, it was decided to designate the kidnappers as terrorists. I'll explain the implications in a moment, but—'

'You can't do that,' Theo said. 'How could they possibly be classed as terrorists?'

Smith brought out his phone and read from it. 'Dictionary definition,' he said. '*A terrorist is an individual who employs unlawful violence for the purpose of promoting political goals or causes.*' He returned the phone to his jacket pocket. 'Kidnappers usually want money for themselves. This lot is different. They are involved in a campaign for a defined political aim.'

'It's nothing to do with politics,' Theo said.

'Let's not split hairs,' Tom Smith said, 'and as a learned lawyer, I'm sure you'll refer yourself to Part Two of the Terrorism Act 2000, as the Cabinet did in its deliberations. The Home Secretary can outlaw an organisation by issuing an order. It usually has to go before Parliament, but our *outstandingly* efficient government has managed to amend the law recently. Now, in cases like this one, they can issue an emergency ban. It's called a Terrorism Designation Order. Catchy name.'

'Theo,' Nadia said, 'could you explain to us non-lawyers what this means?'

'The snakes,' Theo said, the vein on his forehead pulsing. 'It is illegal to fund terrorism. If we pay the kidnappers any money, we'll be committing a serious offence for which we could be arrested and prosecuted.'

Nadia turned to Smith. 'You're asking us not to pay?'

'Not so much asking. Any payment to these terrorists will be treated as a criminal act, subject to immediate detention and the freezing of any or all of your assets and bank accounts.'

'Tell your boss,' Theo said, clutching a bread knife and pointing it at Smith, 'that we wish to speak with her immediately.'

'I'm terribly sorry,' Smith said. 'The Home Secretary and Prime Minister are both attending an important summit at Chequers for the next couple of days. Their staff are under strict instructions not to disturb them. In any case, the Terrorism Designation Order has already been issued.'

'Maybe, Mr Smith,' Cecilia Gant said, 'you and your boss

haven't been paying attention. The kidnappers were very clear. If we pay nothing, our kids will die – all of them. Ghosting us is not an option.'

'I sympathise. Honestly, I do,' Smith said, 'but as I've explained, there are bigger issues at play here. And, Mrs Gant, I wouldn't worry. How likely is it that these terrorists would kill their only leverage? One doesn't kill a diamond-shitting chicken, do they?'

'A what?' Cecilia Gant said.

'The Home Secretary is grateful for your cooperation,' Smith said. He drank some more of his wine and smacked his lips in appreciation. 'Why don't we let the idea settle while we have our dinner?'

The parents' seething silence lingered in the room until, at last, Peter Hammerson spoke. 'Thank you for delivering your message, Mr Smith. Luckily for you, we don't shoot messengers here, however tempting it might be at this particular moment. That doesn't mean we have to dine with them. My staff will show you to your room. I'll have a slice of yesterday's cold quiche sent up.'

Smith put down his glass and stood, shedding breadcrumbs to the floor. 'Very well. Cold quiche is disappointing, but it will have to do. I appreciate your time.' He turned to Nadia. 'Mrs Sayal, if you don't mind, could you stop by my room after you've had your dinner? I have something private to discuss with you. I'm certain you'll want to hear it.'

Nadia Sayal did not answer but gave him a reluctant, almost imperceptible, nod.

With breezy steps, Tom Smith left the room.

Alex thought back to the kidnappers' video and the words of the woman in it, *the only condition is that you send* something. *If you send nothing, your child will immediately be disqualified, and you know what that means…* Even if the parents defied the government and paid before the first deadline, their assets would be frozen, and they would not be able to do so in the next, dooming their kidnapped children.

'They just expect us to leave our kids to die?' Nadia Sayal said.

Theo nodded, his face grim. 'They've tied our hands,' he said. 'As far as they're concerned, the sooner this ends, the better. I bet you they're nowhere near Chequers. Forgive me. I'm going to go now. I've lost my appetite.'

As one, the other parents rose from their seats and dumped their napkins on their plates. In a sombre procession, they left the dining room.

Brendan wheeled himself along the table and positioned his wheelchair next to Alex. 'I'll stay and eat with you if you like,' he said. In his eyes was a look Alex recognised. It was that of one who wished to confess something important.

SEVEN

Game and wine

Brendan refused a staff member's offer to pour the wine. Instead, he asked for the bottle of Châteauneuf-du-Pape and, with a flourish, overfilled Alex's glass and his own. The table was cleared, the starters taken away, leaving only Alex's dinner set and the one newly laid for Brendan next to him. Alex sniffed, then tasted the wine. It was spicy and sweet, no doubt of some exquisite vintage, though Alex was no connoisseur. To him, wine was wine, perhaps with the exception of the bottom-shelf vinegar-and-piss varieties he remembered from his student days, along with the hangovers that invariably followed.

'Will sirs wish to have candles lit for the main course?' asked a scrawny young man with an angelic face and a Polish accent. He wore pinstripe trousers and a velvet vest over a lively chartreuse shirt, making him stand out like an extravagant scarecrow against the whites and blacks of the other waiting staff.

'Thank you, Lucas,' Brendan said. 'It's not that kind of dinner.'

'Candles always add, I find,' Lucas said, 'regardless of

dinner purpose, but as you wish. Remember, your father warns not to drive wheelchair when you are over drink limit. For this, I am ready to help. I will wait for your message.' He left the room in a confident stride, his hands clasped behind his back.

'Spunky, isn't he?' Brendan said. 'Joined last year as my personal all-sorts. Don't let his pouty face fool you. He's brightened up the place no end. Good heart, firm hands.'

'My parents are Polish,' Alex said. 'I know all about the hidden-joy pout, but how did a Pole get to be in the wilds of Northumberland?'

'I found him online,' Brendan said, looking pleased with himself. 'If it were up to my dad, he'd get me some matronly type. So far, Lucas, bless him, has managed to sabotage every single one of my suicide attempts.' He gave Alex a cheeky grin that did not reach his eyes.

Alex shuddered but decided not to take the bait. He would have liked to help this young man, to listen to his troubles, but the countdown to the kidnappers' deadline was ticking in his mind. Brendan knew something important. Alex's gut told him so.

Brendan looked down at his electric wheelchair's controls, his smile gone. 'To be fair, I wasn't trying too hard. Not recently. Things have been better for a while, not to mention Dad wants grandchildren, and now Emily, she's...' He hesitated.

'A nun?' Alex said.

Brendan shook his head. 'Done. As good as dead, so... it looks like I'm *it*, responsible for delivering the Hammerson dynasty's future offspring spawn. Makes you think, doesn't it.' He raised his glass for an imaginary clink, and then his tone sharpened. 'Oh, don't give me that look, Alexander. Yes, it still works. Want me to show you? No? All it takes is a firm hand and a lab beaker.'

'I know it's tough,' Alex said, 'but don't lose hope. The ghastly man from the Home Office was right about one thing. The kidnappers won't give up their only bargaining chips if they don't get paid. Especially if they don't get paid.'

'You haven't got a clue, have you?' Brendan said. 'Dad didn't tell you, eh?'

'Tell me what?'

Brendan turned his head towards the opening door. With forced cheer, he said, 'Oh, look! The dead deer is here.'

The main course was laid before them, steaming plates of venison medallions, their centres pink, along with flash-fried asparagus and a small mound of cubed butternut squash. Brendan shooed the staff out of the room.

Alex tried a cube of the squash. It was crisped to perfection and tasted of butter and a hint of rosemary. He started on the truffled meat, buying time to consider how to approach this young man who was intelligent and self-assured but potentially volatile. He put down his cutlery. 'Well, then,' he said.

Brendan dissected the venison on his plate into tiny shreds but delivered none to his mouth. 'I hate having the other parents here,' he said. 'Competitive hostage negotiations are a shit spectator sport. Mind you, Emily would have loved the attention. She'd pretend she didn't care, but, believe me, she'd bask in it.'

'You two close?'

'She's my sister.'

Alex raised an eyebrow and angled his head.

Brendan skewered a tiny piece of meat with his fork, then shook it loose. He downed half the contents of his wine glass in one go, then refilled it nearly to the brim.

'Aren't you going to eat?' Alex said.

'Wine works better on an empty stomach, especially with a chaser of Prozac.'

'Tell me about your sister. What's she like?'

'Why?'

'Just background.'

'Do you have to study to become an investigator? Is there, like, some special school for PI magic, or do you learn from YouTube videos and then use terms like *wire-tap* and *femoral artery*?'

'My trade secret,' Alex said, 'is that every detail matters, including background. I asked you about your sister.'

'All right. All right,' Brendan said and laid his fork down, its tip resting on the edge of his still-full plate. 'My poor sister, let's see. Emily's hard to pin down, gets obsessed with things: drugs, relationships, ideas. Doesn't value her life much, thinks it's all useless and the world is fucked, except now she has *what's his name*, God. What else? She's very good at hiding things, and she's stubborn. Heart of gold, waxworks face, except when it comes to our parents. With them, the mask sometimes cracks – but not recently. Last I heard, she wasn't talking to Dad until, you know, the last time he saw her in Inverness.'

'Any particular reason they fell out?'

'The usual. She can't get her head around being rich. *Materialism* this, *spiritual life* that. It's ironic, really, her being kidnapped by social justice warriors. Wouldn't be surprised if she broke out the guitar and is singing 'Kumbaya' with them by now. Dad gave her a few million as a bribe to stay clean when she was doing okay for a while. I reckon she hasn't touched a penny. She treats money like it's dirt.'

'When did you last speak to her?'

'Just before she left for nun-land. Nothing since. She deleted all her social media in the name of our Lord, probably exorcised her phone for sixty seconds in the microwave. Still, it was never going to stick, you know.'

'The convent?' Alex said.

Brendan nodded. 'Nothing does with her. Okay, maybe the drugs lasted for a while, but then she discovered luxury rehabs. She loved those. Given half a chance, I reckon she'd spend her life in recovery centres, pretending to talk about her feelings and drinking green smoothies. They discharged her when she ran out of excuses to stay. I guarantee you she'll cancel her God subscription by Christmas and find something else to obsess about. She wants her life to mean something, probably give away all her money to some scammy well-digging project in Asia.' He reversed his wheelchair a few inches, then edged forward and parked himself in the exact same spot. 'Look,' he said quietly, 'you asked me if we're close, and I… I don't want to give the wrong impression. We don't talk about feelings in this family, but Emily's my only real friend.'

'The only one?' Alex said.

'That I'm not paying for,' Brendan said.

'I'd like to ask you something in confidence,' Alex said. 'Maybe you can shed some light.'

'Me and Lucas?' Brendan said.

'That's none of my business.'

'For shame,' Brendan said. 'What's your question?'

'On my way down here, I overheard your dad having an argument with Cecilia Gant. Any idea what that's about?'

Brendan's face tightened, and his eyes grew cold. He picked up his fork and wagged it at Alex. 'Why would you spy on my dad? If he found out, Mr Private-Investigator-who-works-for-us, he'd sack you on the spot.'

'Would he, really?' Alex said, keeping his voice even against Brendan's sudden change of temper. 'Like I said, every detail helps.' The young man's reaction suggested that Alex had hit a sore spot.

Brendan's fingers closed over his wheelchair's control joystick. 'I think I'll tell him,' he said. 'Yes. I'll go see him right now. Sheesh, everyone's got an angle, *everyone*.'

Alex reached for the wheelchair's handbrake and pulled it back, holding it firmly in place. The chair's engine groaned and shuddered as Brendan tried to reverse, but the wheels did not budge.

'You will let go,' Brendan hissed, spraying droplets of spittle as he did, his face blood red. 'Right now. Let go!'

'I know you're worried, Brendan,' Alex said, 'but if you care about Emily, you'll cool your temper, and you'll work with me. I'll do you the courtesy of explaining why, and you'll do me the courtesy of listening, okay?'

'No,' Brendan said and once again pulled back the chair's control, eliciting another prolonged mechanical groan. 'Let go!'

'I have a team of investigators working round the clock to pinpoint the kidnappers' location. There are a dozen ex-special-ops fighters armed with dubiously legal weapons ready to board helicopters or a jet the minute we know where to send them.'

'I don't care. I–' Brendan said, but Alex wasn't finished.

'I have a legal firm of bulldogs on speed dial, in case our fighters have to use lethal force and need cover, and I have contacts at the very top of the Met Police. What they know, we know. I'm your sister's best chance – probably her only chance – so why don't you stop acting like an entitled rich-kid cry-baby fool.' He stiffened his voice. 'Is that clear, Brendan? Am I clear?'

Brendan inhaled noisily and held his breath. Finally, on the exhale, his muscles loosened, and he gave Alex a reluctant nod. He raised his palms in surrender and placed them on the table before him. His top lip quivered. 'It's triggering,' he said. 'You should never stop a person's wheelchair like that. It's not right. It's not done. It's… demeaning.'

'I understand, and I'm sorry, truly,' Alex said, 'but just so you know, if you had use of your legs, I'd kick much more than your pride to keep you here. We don't have time for games. Every minute counts.' Alex seized the stem of the young man's wine glass with one hand and the bottle with the other, placing them out of Brendan's reach. 'Now, here's what's going to happen. You're going to stop drinking, and you're going to answer every question I ask because, as I've already explained, every detail matters. And you're going to eat. None of this is up for discussion. Do you understand?'

'Okay. Wow. Okay.' Brendan rounded his lips to make a *kapow* sound, demonstrating an explosion by joining his hands and parting them wide. 'Wouldn't want to be your wife in an argument. Jesus.'

'Eat,' Alex said, 'and if you met my wife, she'd quickly set you right on that assumption.'

Brendan picked up his fork and skewered three asparagus tips, which he chewed and swallowed. Then, he made a show of shovelling increasingly loaded forks of venison and squash into his mouth, making theatrical 'mmm' sounds as he did.

Alex waited in silence until most of Brendan's plate was clean. 'Good,' he said. 'Now to business. You looked upset when I asked you about your father's fight with Cecilia. Why was that?'

'I…' he hesitated. 'You can't tell my dad I told you.'

'Speak.'

Brendan bit his lip. 'That argument is why my sister doesn't stand a chance. Unless your commandos reach her, she's already… well, it's not definite, but my gut tells me she's as good as dead.'

'I'm listening,' Alex said.

Brendan pulled the cuffs of his knitted brown sweater over his fingers, looking like the fight had gone out of him. Then, in a quiet voice, almost a whisper, he went on to explain. When he was done, Alex patted him on the shoulder and considered what he had learned. For the first time, he doubted the wisdom of his suggestion that all the parents assemble in one place. Still, there was nothing for it now. What was done was done. He was not entirely convinced by Brendan's logic. A parent would not give up on his child, but what he revealed made matters more complicated – a hundred times so.

EIGHT

Nightmares are also dreams

When Noah Gant woke again, he found himself dressed in a fluffy white dressing gown, lying on his back in a four-poster bed: plump pillows, crisp white linen, a woven bedspread threaded ochre, green and gold. He took in the room, which oozed the ambience of a five-star faux-rustic hotel suite, complete with a sliding door to an en-suite bathroom. The furniture, all constructed from reclaimed wood, included the bed, a bedside table, a wardrobe, a writing desk and chair. There was no television, no bedside clock or phone. Sand-coloured curtains rustled softly in whispers of warm breeze from an open window. The air was humid and salty with a pleasant scent of beached seaweed. On the bedside table stood a bottle of mineral water with its label peeled off.

Noah grabbed the bottle and sat on the edge of the bed, gulping down mouthfuls, stopping once to cough when he nearly drowned himself, trying to drink too much at once. His whole body felt like it was bathing in sweat.

The view from the window was a wonder. Light sparkled over gentle waves of an azure ocean lapping onto a pristine sandy beach. Leafy trees provided shaded areas. A raffia hammock hung between two palms.

His thoughts began to clear. First, he had awoken to the nightmare in the hospital. Now, he found himself in what resembled a congenial dream. As much as he hated nightmares, Noah did not trust in dreams. His most frequent one recurred at least once a month. In it, he is having a succulent roast lamb dinner with his parents, laughing and telling jokes, logs crackling in the fireplace: a perfect family picture of contentment and warmth. Then, without warning, the dream turns on him. There's a knock on the door. Two uniformed police officers – a man and a woman with standard-issue kindly expressions – inform him that his father was crushed to death when his car hit a tree. *He died instantly. We know it's a shock. We're sorry for your loss.* When he looks back at the table, he sees only his mother, sitting alone, her face frozen, her eyes bottomless wells of grief.

Noah stood and waited for his cramped leg muscles to steady. He hugged himself, his fingers squeezing the bathrobe's soft material. His eyes traced a fly that landed on the wall, the ceiling and the wall again. He took a step, then another.

The en-suite bathroom was sparkling clean. Fluffy towels and luxurious toiletries were laid out for him. He washed his face and armpits, patted himself dry, applied a generous spread from the citrus-smelling deodorant stick and returned to the bedroom. In the wardrobe, he found a selection of clothes, casual and formal, shorts and longs, underwear and socks, shoes and sandals, a black silk bow tie. He opted for cream cargo shorts and a black T-shirt with a white logo he did not recognise, formed of the words *Lorem Ipsum*. He selected a pair of light-brown loafers, which he wore without socks. Everything fitted him perfectly, as if made to measure.

Noah walked over to the room's door and, with trepidation, turned the doorknob. It was unlocked. He took a deep breath, pushed the door open and stepped outside. He found himself on the second-floor mezzanine balcony of a house that reminded him of his mother's plantation-style holiday home in the Caribbean. Internal clapboard walls were painted mayonnaise white. The floorboards were dark-stained wood. A staircase spiralled down to the expanse of a light, airy room with rattan seating, a dining table and various pieces of elegantly carved wood furniture. The effect was colonial meets seaside. Tall open doors led to a sunny veranda.

Noah scratched his left arm and for the first time noticed the skin-coloured plaster. *The cannula*, he remembered. *The nightmare*. He pushed away the memory and descended the stairs, one deliberate step at a time, looking around for anyone who might have an explanation, any explanation. His ordered life had taken a turn that was beyond comprehension. Nothing made sense.

The house seemed empty. An archway led to a kitchen with marble worktops, a fridge and wall-hung cupboards. In the wall to his right, incongruous within its surroundings, was a heavy-duty security door made of bare steel, familiar to Noah from his mother's panic room. It was of a kind that would require high-impact explosives to break open, or at least so the brochure promised. Next to it was an entry keypad with illuminated numbers. *Why?* He looked up to the mezzanine. There were four doors next to the room he had woken up in. *More bedrooms?*

'Hello?' he called out.

No answer.

A large woven fruit basket on the dining table was piled high with mangoes, pears, guavas, grapes and apples. Noah picked a giant green apple and bit into its flesh, relishing the sharp taste on his tongue like a spray of lemon zest needle pricks. By the time he stepped outside to the veranda, he had devoured the entire apple, core and seeds, and his rumbling stomach thanked him by settling down. He gazed beyond the whitewashed balustrades at the faint line of oceanic horizon where the water ended and the cloudless blue sky began. He walked the short trail from the front of the house to the beach and sat down on the soft, warm sand, hugging his knees. He shrugged off his shoes, buried his toes in the sand, closed his eyes and let the pleasant warmth of the sun wash over him.

In that moment, with the sound of the lapping waves, the melodious tweets of an unfamiliar bird and the salty scent of the sea, Noah no longer wished for answers. More than that, he wished there were none beyond this beach and its magic. He wished to be frozen in time, with no regard for what came before or what was yet to come.

A voice startled him out of his dreamlike state. 'Hey!'

He opened his eyes and squinted at the brightness. A nun was walking towards him along the waterline, bare-footed, the sun surrounding her curls like a halo. When she got closer, he recognised her and his heart skipped a beat.

'Noah!' she shrieked and waved.

When he did not respond, she closed the distance between them and came to sit beside him.

Noah looked at her, unsure of what to say. For a moment, he questioned his sanity again. He observed his feet, the grains of sand between his toes, then swallowed and met her eyes that were as bright and flighty as ever. 'Hello, Emily,' he said. 'Why are you dressed like a nun?'

'You didn't get the memo, about the dress code?'

'Tarts and vicars and… nuns party?' he said.

'Not much of a party, as you've probably gathered.'

'Still gathering,' he said.

'Yeah, so, before all that, I am duty-bound to say that I'm not a nun yet. Just a novice in a Highland convent. Cranky Sister Maria would insist.'

'A novice,' he said, 'in a convent. Well, holy blimey flying pigs. Aren't you boiling in that uniform?'

'You should see me in full garb. Had to take off my head covering. I prayed on it. Pretty sure God understands.' She placed a hand on his shoulder. 'It's so good to see you.'

Noah stared down at his knees, shuddering to her touch, waiting until she retracted her hand and placed it on the sand next to his. 'Feels like I've died and gone to the tropics.'

'That out-of-body sensation,' Emily said, 'that's the kidnappers' sedatives wearing off.'

'Kidnappers,' he mumbled, thinking back to his blackout at the fashion store and what followed. 'Right.'

'Want to hear the rest of it?' she said.

'Actually, no. Don't tell me yet.' Emboldened by the surreal encounter, Noah did something he would never have dared in his other, real, life. He covered her hand with his own and gave her soft, sandy fingers a squeeze. 'Emily, erm… Notwithstanding that you're a nun now or… a novice, do you remember the letter I wrote to you at the end of school? I know it's a long time ago now, but still…'

She looked down, avoiding his eyes. 'Of course I remember.'

'You never mentioned it, never got in touch, after.'

'Noah, Noah, Noah,' she said, then tutted. 'Here's the thing to tell your younger self: you want to send a letter, send a letter. Don't hide it in a book and give it as a graduation present like some weird Victorian snowflake.'

'You don't like Jane Austen?'

'I love Jane, I do. But the complete works? That's what? Two thousand pages? I never got past *Pride and Prejudice*. Mr Darcy annoys me every time. My dad found your letter, four years later.'

Noah's cheeks felt hot. He imagined Peter Hammerson reading his teenage outpourings with his afternoon dram.

'Beneath the nerdy exterior,' Emily said, 'you're such a sensitive boy, aren't you?'

He shrugged. 'It is a truth universally acknowledged.'

'All right,' she said. 'I'm going to explain what happened with the letter, but look, you're being strange. Probably the chemicals in your brain and a couple of days of sedation, so before we talk about ancient history, can I tell you about this place?'

The words *ancient history* pierced him like poison darts, but he nodded, unconvinced, acutely aware of how his hand now felt leaden over hers. He dared not move it.

Emily cleared her throat. 'Remember you once told me they'd have to kidnap you to get you to a class reunion?'

He swallowed hard. 'Who?'

'Zayn, Ashleigh and Jonny. Last I saw them, they were under the mango tree behind the house.'

'Great,' he muttered. 'Just great.'

'If it's any consolation, Zayn's all grown up now, don't worry.' She crossed herself, then looked up to the heavens. 'Sorry, God. Shouldn't lie. He's still every bit the pretty-faced, six-packed, entitled fool he was at school.' She looked back at him. 'But Jonny's here and cheerful as ever, and Ashleigh's been subdued, so this reunion's not all bad.'

'That's... nice,' he said.

'From what we've pieced together, everyone's been lifted by what feels like a professional operation, well funded, well organised. There's palms and heat, so it would have been a long flight. Not sure about motive, but it's an easy guess, considering the guest list they put together for this exclusive place.'

'Who are *they?*' he said.

'Haven't seen any of the *they* yet.'

Two grey birds, possibly cormorants, flew overhead. Noah tapped the middle finger of his right hand on his knee and stared at Emily, angling his head, waiting, tethering his patience.

'Jonny's still big,' she said, 'but he wears it better. He has a son. I guess one of us had to be normal.'

'Normal,' Noah echoed. 'Are we done with the resort briefing? Sounds like we don't know anything except that we woke up in an empty Club Med.'

'Just a villa and a beach. Zayn and Jonny were going to look around, see what's what. Nobody's been awake too long, and we're all still a bit dazed. When Ashleigh came to, she did what prom queens do in a crisis situation, put on a bikini and went for a swim. To be fair, looks like she's grown up a bit. She calls herself a writer now, busy working on her novel, bless her perfect boobs. Why are you looking at me funny? I'm rambling, aren't I?'

'I don't mean to push you,' he said. Her easy manner grated on him, along with the way their conversation seemed to mould itself so naturally into their old school's vernacular and its teen-like rhythms.

She withdrew her hand from under his, made it into a fist and placed it in the folds of her habit.

'Look,' Noah said, 'I'm not stuck on some teenage fantasy, all right? It's just… If you tell me, it'll help.'

'You overthink,' she said. 'I remember now. That's what you do.' She wiped her forehead with the back of her hand, hesitated, then spoke again. 'When my dad found your letter, he told me not to answer it.'

'So, you wanted to.'

She gave him what might have been a tiny nod.

'I thought your dad liked me,' Noah said.

'It was more… well… He took me on a long drive to Bamburgh beach, sat me down for what he called "a serious chat". At first, I thought it was about my ten million pound *welcome to adulthood* present. He'd been holding off releasing it to me until I was clean for a while.'

'Okay,' Noah said, wishing she'd get to the point.

'I was wrong,' Emily said. 'It wasn't that. He wired the money that week. What he actually wanted to say was that I couldn't see you – not like that.'

'Please explain and cite sources,' Noah said, echoing their pedantic classics teacher, Miss Bluntforth, though the reference made him cringe as soon as he said it.

'He and my mother,' Emily said, 'had a turbulent relationship from the start, crazy ups and downs. When my brother had his accident, they finally split up, but even in the years before then, the two of them were like drowning ferrets in a cage. It was heartbreaking.'

He tensed. 'So, you weren't allowed to date anyone because your dad messed up his marriage? You do realise that's riding the bonkers bus, right? Is that why you joined a convent? No fights, no drowning ferrets, a gold-star Jesus husband?' The words came out angrier than he intended.

She picked up a fistful of sand and let the grains cascade through her fingers. 'This is hard,' she said.

'Tell me.'

'Not easy,' she said.

'That's what hard means.'

She blinked a few times in quick succession and scratched her wrist. 'When my mum and dad were going through one of their lows, he had an affair with a married woman. It was almost twenty-nine years ago. They only saw each other a few times, but it was enough.' She waited a long moment, then finally looked at him. 'I was sworn to secrecy.'

Noah caught his breath. The sun suddenly felt scorching on his head, too hot to bear.

'You have my father's eyes,' she said. 'They're quite distinctive. Do you understand what I'm telling you?'

He shuddered, and then his whole body shook. His instinct was to deny Emily's revelation, to argue she could not be right, yet like the final missing pieces in a vast incomplete puzzle, the truth exposed itself to him in the many unspoken signs that had been there all along: his hair, his eyes, his voice, his dimpled chin, the long skinny limbs that were nothing like those of the man who had raised him.

He tried to say something, but his voice betrayed him, sounding like a cough.

'They stayed in touch all these years,' Emily said. 'My dad and your mum. She'd send him pictures of you, school reports, tell him how you're doing. You should know that he always considered you his son. He cared about you, from afar.'

'From afar,' Noah whispered, though now he remembered how Peter Hammerson had rushed to his mother's bedside when she suffered her heart attack in September. At the time, he thought it odd to see Peter there, more than once, bearing flowers and chocolates, at the private hospital where she was recovering from an operation to implant a pacemaker. 'I'm here if you need me, for anything,' he had told Noah. 'Anything. All right, son?' *Son.*

Without thinking, Noah started shovelling sand with his hand, digging a trench in the space between them.

'You're lucky,' Emily said. 'Before I was kidnapped, my dad told me all our parents were going to gather at Ewald. That's our house in Northumberland. At least you'll have two parents rooting for you when the negotiations with these kidnappers start. I don't think my mother would bother sobering up enough to be there.'

Noah slipped on his loafers and stood. 'God suits you,' he said. 'Suits you perfectly.'

'Noah, please, sit down.'

'You could have told me. All those years. *All those years.* You could have got in touch. Instead, I have to hear it from some effing overdressed nun on an effing random beach.'

'What could I say, eh? Oh, by the way, Noah, my adulterous dad is also your adulterous dad. Congratulations, brother, we both deserve better?'

'When my father died,' Noah said, 'it would have been nice to know there was a spare out there.'

'Now you're just being spiteful.'

'Not spiteful, angry. There's a difference. Maybe pray on it.'

Without giving her an opportunity to speak, he turned and walked away, kicking sand as he went.

NINE

Class reunion

Noah dragged a rattan chair out to the veranda and sat facing the beach, his head drowning in thoughts. Emily returned to the house but stood a few paces away, her arms at her sides, staring out to nowhere. At least she had the wisdom to stay silent, though it must have been a struggle for her. The Emily he remembered was never one for quiet reflection. He supposed that being a nun may have taught her some composure or, at the very least, how to pretend one. He tried to imagine referring to her as his sister or half-sister. The idea rang strange after a life lived as an only child. He tore off the plaster from his arm where the cannula's needle had pierced him, then scratched off the sticky glue deposits it had left behind. And to think she let him dream of her *in that way*, his own sister. It made his guts churn with embarrassment and not a little anger.

The dense silence between them was broken when their three former classmates appeared from around the side of the house, all in flip-flops, ambling to join them, looking like tourists on holiday. Ashleigh was wearing a two-piece swimsuit, a towel over her shoulders. Her perfectly proportioned face was sallow and chalky. She looked thin, almost emaciated.

Zayn grinned, his teeth whiter than Noah remembered, his biceps bulging from sleeves that were folded two inches too high, showing off a scorpion tattoo on his left arm. He was wearing a black baseball cap with the words *Lorem Ipsum* emblazoned on it. 'Well, well, well,' he said. 'Here he finally is, the runt of the class. Were you hiding in the library again?'

Noah pushed himself up from his chair. 'Hi guys.'

Ashley waved, and Jonny gave him a friendly salute.

'What's up with you, chump?' Zayn said and made a show of sniffing the air. 'I smell tension with a hint of nunnery. Did Mother Superior try to convert you?'

'It's great to see you too, Zayn,' Noah said. 'I've missed our deep *intellectual* chats at school.'

Zayn laughed off the comment, approached Noah with open arms and gave him a hug and a kiss on the cheek. His sweat smelled like the tropics, vanilla and lime. 'Just like old times, eh?' he said.

'God, I hope not,' Noah said, though it was nice to have Zayn and the others with him now, to break the pattern of his incessant thoughts. Zayn's tight embrace and genuine warmth were a tonic to his nerves. He felt a little lighter, a little less wretched in his turmoil, though he could still barely bring himself to look at Emily.

'I'm thirsty,' Ashleigh said. 'I'll be inside.' As she climbed the veranda's steps and walked into the house, Noah couldn't help but notice her awkward gait, like a newborn fawn taking uncertain steps. At school, she had been athletic and full of spirit. Here, she seemed like a shadow of her younger self.

Still grinning, Zayn nodded at her back as if to say, *I'll go,* then followed her, leaving Noah with Emily and Jonny outside.

'I've been trying to figure out where we are,' Jonny said. 'Southeast Asia, maybe? Or the Caribbean? Mangoes and palms, I mean, they have them in so many places. One thing's for sure: it's a long way from home.'

'Have you seen anyone, any guards?' Noah said. 'If we've been kidnapped, it's odd no one's watching us.'

'Zayn and I took a walk around to reconnoitre,' Jonny said.

'Reconnoitre?' Emily said and giggled.

'My dear Miss Hammerson,' Jonny said, 'don't pretend you didn't attend the same uppity school as I did and, considering your current affiliation, you'll know God loves all his words equally, be they big or small.'

Emily gave him a warm smile. 'A good point, well made. As a nun, I always like to hear about God's love.'

'I thought you were a novice,' Jonny said. 'Only six weeks in the convent?'

'When it suits her,' Noah said. 'What did you find on your walk?'

'They don't have to watch us,' Jonny said. 'You can't see it from here, but there's a twelve-foot fence with razor wire on top. Big signs saying *Electric fence. Danger of death.* Thick jungle beyond it. The only way out is a locked gate with CCTV on the beach, left-hand side, a few minutes that way. I'm sure you saw the security door in the front room. Maybe someone's in there? Bottom line, we can't go anywhere. Our zoo enclosure is about the size of a football field, slightly longer on the beach end. I don't like it. It's too elaborate. None of it feels like an afterthought.'

'What about the sea?' Noah said. 'Can't we swim around the fence?'

Jonny shook his head. 'The fence goes out quite far into the sea with cameras on top. Like I said, elaborate.'

'Let's not dwell on the negatives,' Emily said, trying for a cheery voice but sounding more like a provincial vicar delivering a Sunday service. 'If you'd asked me to imagine being held hostage, I'd think crummy basement smelling of cat piss. Look around you. Isn't it gorgeous? There's a fridge stacked with food. We can build sandcastles. Why not think of it as a holiday? God has a plan for us. I can feel it.'

'Oh, Emily…' Jonny said. He covered his cheek with his hand and winced like he was suffering from a nasty toothache. 'You know I love you like a sister-wife, but someone drugged us, took us by force and brought us to this place. For all we know, they might just kill us. I have a five-year-old at home, and his dad's disappeared into thin air. I don't mean to be rude, but please, *please*, not again with the forced positivity and God's plan.'

'You've lost weight,' Emily said and punched him playfully on the shoulder. 'Looks good on you.'

'I didn't,' Jonny said gruffly, 'but honestly, I don't care about that. I haven't cared about my weight in years, all right?'

'Jonny, I…' Emily's face seemed to cycle through different emotions until the edges of her mouth rose into a plastic smile. 'I'll go inside. Maybe I can find some crayons to keep Zayn busy.' She left without looking back at them.

'She means well,' Noah found himself saying. 'You know what she's like.'

'On a normal day, it's charming,' Jonny said. 'I've always liked Emily and her sketchy ways, but here, today, I'm sorry, I just don't have the patience for it. I know our school brainwashed us to hide behind masks, but God almighty, I can't stomach that level of cheer just now. We're in serious trouble. I have a bad feeling, here, at the pit of my enormous belly.'

Noah decided to change the subject. He had defended Emily but had no wish to talk about her more than necessary. 'What's your son's name?'

'Evan. Was supposed to take him to Disneyland this week, give Leila some space. He's been obsessing about the rides, can't decide which ones to do first, treats it like it's a life or death decision. Last I heard, it was *Pirates of the Caribbean*. By now he would have moved on to *Star Wars* or the submarine. Oh, to be a kid again.'

Noah wanted to say something, to hear more about Jonny's life, but a lump had formed in his throat. They stood under the veranda's awning, an empty silence between them. Noah felt a sudden displacement and an unexpected yearning. Emily had God, Zayn lived in his own world of carefree joy and Jonny had his family, a son to miss, to go to Disneyland with. He shifted his weight to the balls of his feet and finally found his voice. 'Is Ashleigh okay? She seemed a bit off-colour.'

'Who knows,' Jonny said. He squeezed Noah's shoulder. 'Sorry to be such a downer, mate. Might be the hangover from the drugs. I got an injection in the neck. Someone was waiting for me in the back seat of my car. The stuff of horror films, right?' He patted his stomach. 'Food will help. A full belly, and maybe I can do the fat happy clown act everyone expects of me.' He raised his hands, clicked his fingers and did a little jig, his hips swaying, a cringed smile on his face. 'Shall we go join the beauty pageant inside?'

In the sitting room, Ashleigh handed out water bottles from a twelve-pack that stood on an antique chest of drawers. They, too, had no labels. Jonny went into the kitchen and returned with a tray of bread rolls, cheese squares, sliced ham, strawberry conserve, chocolate spread and a large ramekin of butter. He sliced the rolls and took orders for preferred fillings, which he handed out between bites of his own fully stacked ham and cheese creation. Emily ate her sandwich quietly in the corner.

Noah refused the food and stood with his back to his classmates, gulping down water while inspecting a marble bust that was set on a plinth. It was of a man with stern features and a prominent nose. The inscription was so worn it was unreadable. 'I wonder who that is,' he said to no one in particular. He was keen to delay the conversations that were bound to follow, about another life all those years ago, a life he'd rather forget: the prim Mademoiselle Ducasse, French, the pervy Mr Brewers, maths, Headmaster Crampton-Hughes and his blinkered authoritarian regime. He kept his eyes firmly on the lifeless marble head.

'That statue would be my great-great-grandfather, Wilhelm,' a voice thundered at him from the veranda's door, a rich baritone with a thick Germanic accent.

The man's sudden appearance nearly made Noah choke on his water.

'Our old European aristocracy,' the man said, 'had a fondness for this kind of commemorative nonsense. As for me, well, I do not see the appeal in the slightest.'

TEN

Wilhelm

The man at the threshold stood tall, supported by a walking stick. He wore a cream cotton jacket over a Hawaiian shirt, light seersucker trousers and canvas shoes. His steak-red face was adorned with a grand handlebar moustache, and his hair was styled into a perfect side parting. By his side was a pit bull terrier, panting in the heat. 'Like the man this head belonged to, I am also Wilhelm, and this is my hound, Loxley. Ach, yes, however.' He fingered his cheek. 'You can call me William, if you please. That is how they referred to me at Cambridge, Trinity College, where I acquired my education in the classics.'

Limping forward with the support of his walking stick, Wilhelm stepped in and came to stand by Noah's side in front of the statue. He brought with him the sweet whiff of expensive cigars. The dog followed obediently, then spread itself on the cool floor at his master's feet.

'Hmm,' Wilhelm said to Noah. 'My ancestors, even the royal ones, mostly ended up like this one, in a forsaken property, shielded from seeing their empires crumble. And crumble they did, as they rightly should have.'

Zayn cleared his throat. 'Well, Wilhelm, or William, or

whatever... do you often kidnap people, or is that just an aristocratic hobby, like something to do when you're bored?'

Wilhelm turned to face the group, and Noah turned with him. 'I urge you to be careful with your words, Zayn Sayal,' Wilhelm said. 'You do not fully comprehend your situation, I think.'

'What do you want from us?' Ashleigh said, using her towel to wipe beads of sweat from her face.

'You are guests here,' Wilhelm said, 'and guests must abide by house rules. First rule: civility. Do not hurry an old man. You are in this beautiful place, not yet harmed in the slightest. What could one ask for more than this?' He knuckled his throat and rubbed it in a circular motion. 'Now, let us look at you all, our prized acquisitions: Zayn Sayal, gallivanter, yes? Party, party, party. With the right education, even a fool can make himself look sophisticated and appealing. The Veil of Ignorance plays cruel games.'

Zayn planted his hands on his hips. 'No one asked for your opinion, Herr Kaiser,' he said.

Wilhelm raised his walking stick and struck Zayn's arm with a force that belied his frail appearance. 'Respect,' he said. 'That is also an absolute rule here. You must remember this, yes?'

The dog raised its jaw from the floor and growled, its small, dark eyes set on Zayn.

Zayn grunted in pain but stood his ground. 'With the greatest respect, sir,' he said, his voice firm but tinged with indignation, 'if you hit me again, you'll regret it.'

'I see,' Wilhelm said. He took out a small black notebook from his back pocket, opened it, and scribbled something in it. 'Where were we? Ah, yes. Ashleigh Boroughs, daughter of naughty rubber man, Davis Boroughs, and here we have fat Jonny Salt, the son who didn't want to be a lawyer like his father, choosing instead to eat and eat and invest his time in brothels. Ridiculous, yes?'

Ashleigh turned to Jonny. 'Brothels?'

'My new restaurant chain. I called it *Jonny's Brothels*. We serve broths and stews.'

'Oh,' Ashleigh said.

'It's just a brand,' Jonny said to Ashleigh as if to justify himself. 'Each dish is named after a girl. Candy's sweet potato soup, Samantha's goulash, Kimberley's veg broth.'

'Yes, yes,' Wilhelm said. 'The typical crassness of the *nouveau riche*.' He raised a finger to warn Jonny against responding, before completing his round of judgements. 'Then we have Emily Hammerson, bride of cocaine, then bride of Christ, and finally, Noah Gant. Nothing of note to say about you, yes? There are dark horses and then others are simply beige.'

'If you're quite done with your round of insults,' Zayn said, 'I'd like to use your phone now, Herr kidnapper, if I may. I would respectfully ask to get out of here. Please arrange transport.'

'Thank you. I appreciate your new politeness,' Wilhelm said. 'See how one learns? And of course, old chap, you are welcome to leave on the boat. In fact, we insist on it. We practise the campsite rule here and never leave garbage behind. But you see, we are very remote. The boat only comes on Thursdays, and then there is a minor detail to settle with your parents to do with the type of cabin you must sail back in: first class or hold. Do not worry your conventionally pretty head about it. We can discuss all that later.'

'I don't care which class you put me in,' Zayn said, 'as long as I'm out of here.'

'Hmm,' Wilhelm said. 'Thank you. This is noted.'

'The boat comes on Thursday?' Ashleigh said. 'What day is it today?'

Wilhelm ignored her question. 'You are our guests, and…' He stopped, for a moment seemingly distracted by Ashleigh's figure, exposed as it was in her bikini. He rubbed the tip of his moustache between finger and thumb, then looked around the room, his eyes taking in each of them in turn. He spoke his next words in a tender, more serious tone. 'Some friendly advice for you all: one must enjoy his days on this earth, for one never knows if they are his last, hmm?'

'Where are we?' Jonny said.

'Lorem Island,' Wilhelm said, 'far, far away.'

'Lorem?' Jonny said.

'We named it so,' Wilhelm said, 'in your honour. We refer to you five as *Lorem Ipsums*, placeholders for the money your parents will send, placeholders for five destitute people we will save with it, or five thousand, or five million, perhaps more. We are good people, you see, maybe not good to you, but otherwise excellent. We do what we must.'

'What do you mean?' Jonny said.

'Ach yes, many questions, so many. But I consider we have had ourselves enough chitter and chatter, and you are required elsewhere.' He retrieved a walkie-talkie from his jacket pocket, raised it to his mouth and spoke. 'It is time. You may enter.'

ELEVEN

A spark of recognition

Four men in camouflage fatigues that bore the *Lorem Ipsum* logo on their breast pockets burst into the room. They each carried a weapon which Noah recognised from his PlayStation days as a Mini-Uzi submachine gun. They positioned themselves in a semicircle, holding their guns to point in the general direction of the five hostages. Any superficial illusion of a pleasant beach kidnapping had evaporated, to be replaced by the menacing scents of sour sweat and gun oil.

'Some bad news, I'm afraid,' Wilhelm said. 'It is unfortunate, but now introductions are over, your vacation is to be interrupted. We must hold you in a more contained place for now. It does not please me one bit, but circumstances dictate it. I ask that you comply and avail yourselves of our basement.'

'W-why?' Jonny stuttered, looking from the armed men to Wilhelm. 'It's not like we have anywhere to run.'

'Speak not,' Wilhelm said.

'I'm not going into a basement,' Ashleigh said, taking a step forward towards Wilhelm, her arms crossed.

'Quiet,' Wilhelm said. 'Step back, Miss Boroughs.'

'No,' Ashleigh said, 'I won't.'

One of the armed men raised his gun and pointed it at Ashleigh.

After a moment of frozen stalemate, Ashleigh fell to her knees, the gun's barrel following her. 'Shoot me,' she said, looking up into the eyes of the man with the gun. 'Don't look at your boss. I'm right here. Pull the trigger.'

The man retracted his gun's charging handle. It made a mechanical click and clack as the mechanism slid back to arm it. He adjusted the gun's muzzle to point at Ashleigh's head, his finger hovering over the trigger. It was a strange sight. Ashleigh's face was white as chalk, but her eyes were hard and determined.

Noah felt a rush of fear. His breath quickened and on his tongue he tasted rusted metal. He glanced around him. Jonny was holding his hand to his chest, squeezing the fabric of his sweat-soaked shirt. Emily's face was a mix of bewilderment and disbelief while Zayn fixed his eyes on the loaded firearm, his fists clenched to his sides. It was as if the truth of their situation, the mortal danger they were in, had made itself real, visible, undeniable, and it had dawned on all of them – except for Ashleigh, whose defiance seemed to Noah uncalled for and dangerous.

'Ashleigh, no,' Jonny pleaded. 'What are you doing? Get up.'

'Miss Boroughs,' Wilhelm said, 'you are premature and a little dramatic, no? A slight change of scenery, and you ask to die? I must warn you, this is not some schoolyard game.'

'You have no idea,' Ashleigh said, her voice shaking. 'Put me out of my misery. A shot to the head. Quick and painless. Go on, do it.'

'Ashleigh, for God's sake,' Zayn said. 'Don't provoke them.'

'Spoiled brats,' Wilhelm said, for the first time seeming to lose his temper. 'I have no time for this nonsense.' He looked down at Ashleigh, his eyes harsh and cold. 'I will count to five. If you do not stand and retreat, I will grant your wish and order my man here, Cody, to shoot you in the head. He is already an accomplished marksman, but from zero distance, with this gun, it is like picking off billionaires in a bank vault. Your classmates will then be tasked with cleaning your brains from the floor. Sometimes what is required is a tough early lesson. It will make things easier for all of us after. Last chance, Miss Boroughs. Last chance. You still will not move?'

Ashleigh stared forward, as if she hadn't heard him.

Noah felt as though he was transported back to how he had felt at the hospital when he thought his life was over and all hope was lost. *And now this? Now this?* The threats, the guns, the countdown. Ashleigh seemed determined and unmovable.

'Can't you just take her there?' Zayn said. 'You have four strong men. You'd rather shoot her than force her down some stairs?'

'Be quiet!' Wilhelm said.

The armed man looked at Wilhelm, nodded and focused back on Ashleigh.

'Wilhelm, please,' Emily said, 'can I talk to you for a minute? Just the two of us? I'm sure we can work this out.'

Wilhelm ignored her and started a slow, angry count. 'On my mark. One… Two…'

Ashleigh made no attempt to move. She simply glared at the weapon and the man bearing it.

'Come on, Ashleigh,' Noah pleaded. 'Our parents will pay them whatever they're asking – of course they'll pay – and then we'll be home.' He couldn't begin to comprehend what would cause her to behave so irrationally.

Ashleigh clasped her hands as if in prayer and closed her eyes.

'Three…'

Without pausing to think, Noah rushed forward and

positioned himself between the gun's barrel and Ashleigh, shielding her with his body. 'Cody, don't,' he said, staring into the armed man's eyes and using the name Wilhelm had called him in the vague hope it might help.

'Four…'

Noah heard movement and looked behind him. Ashleigh had pushed herself up and stood, her hands raised. 'Don't hurt him.'

Wilhelm gave Noah a quizzical look. 'Mr Gant,' he said, 'perhaps I underestimated you. Please note, all of you. Do not make us kill you before we have to, because we will. It is not your living body we need for ransom, just the idea of you being held, okay?'

'You would have shot her, just like that, in cold blood?' Jonny said.

'Well, yes, Mr Salt,' Wilhelm said, 'exactly like that. Know this: I am a good person, a good man, but when it comes to you five, I have no compunctions about dealing with trouble. Do not test me. Do not become trouble.'

'A good person?' Zayn said.

Cody aimed his gun at him, and Zayn held up open palms to placate him.

Noah turned to Ashleigh. With his hand on her shoulder, he guided her back a couple of steps, away from the gun-toting men. 'You're okay now,' he whispered.

Through gritted teeth, she muttered at him, 'You had no right.'

'Silence!' Wilhelm said. 'This afternoon's entertainment is over. Honestly, it is like kindergarten here. You put one with their classmates, and one reverts to being a child.' He marched over to the security door, held his finger up to the code pad and punched in a sequence of numbers, which he shielded with his other hand. He pulled the door open to reveal steep steps descending into darkness. He motioned with his hand towards the entrance. 'Down you go, like Dante to the underworld. *Alle zusammen* – all together now.'

The armed men herded them to the door, their fingers on the triggers of their Uzis. Zayn went down first, then Jonny. Emily wrapped her arm around Ashleigh's shoulders to guide her, but Ashleigh shrugged off the embrace and walked by herself through the door, a sullen Emily following.

Noah hesitated, staying behind for a moment. He was about to take his first step past the threshold when he stopped, looked back and met Wilhelm's eyes. 'You know,' he said, 'I kept thinking you looked familiar. It just hit me. We've met before, and–'

Without giving Noah an opportunity to complete his sentence, as quick as lightning, Wilhelm signalled to the armed man closest to Noah, drawing what looked like the letter "Z" in the air with his index finger. In barely a second, the man dropped his weapon so it hung on its sling, unclasped a stun baton from his belt and stuck its coiled end to Noah's neck. It buzzed and sparked as Noah shook and fell. The man grasped his arm to stop him from tumbling down the steps after his classmates.

'Out with him,' Wilhelm said. 'Take him outside. When he is able to walk, have him brought to my quarters. Mr Gant and I need to have a little chat. God in heaven, they really are like children. I shall go ahead. I have important business to attend to.'

Still stunned, unable to speak, Noah felt himself dragged away. He was thrust onto the ground in front of the villa with so much force that he bit his tongue and tasted blood. Through his shock, he vaguely had a sense of his hands being pulled taut behind his back and restrained with a plastic cable tie.

TWELVE

Heartstrings

Noah was frog-marched away by two of the armed men who wore sweat-soaked fatigues, dark sunglasses and khaki baseball caps. His shoulders were drawn backwards by the awkward position of his arms, which were stretched and bound behind his back, making it difficult to walk upright. His escorts were tight-lipped and relentless. Their firm hands dragged him forward at an uncomfortable pace as he struggled not to trip, his calf muscles burning from the strain. On the trail from the villa to the beach, his left shoe had acquired a sharp stone that moved around to bore into the soft skin of his sole with every step, yet there was nothing he could do about the piercing pain. He was bound and helpless, at the mercy of his captors – men who didn't care, who were prepared to pull the trigger without a second's thought.

As he continued to hobble forward, the pain began to focus him, and his mind replayed the ghastly scene of Ashleigh's near-murder. His dread and anxiety were subsiding, to be replaced by waves of fury, of imaginations of what he would do to these people – these animals – given a weapon and half a chance.

When they reached the gate at the far end of the beach, one of the men pressed a button on an intercom box and waved at the CCTV camera. The gate's lock buzzed. The man pulled the gate open and shoved Noah through it, causing him to lose his balance, trip and stumble forward. He somehow managed to right himself before an almost certain fall. When he looked up, what he saw made blood rage to his head. Waiting for him there, a satisfied smirk on her face, was Marian, the woman who had made him think he was crazy, who had made him believe he had killed someone.

In contrast to her previous attire as a psychiatrist, Marian was now dressed in khaki shorts and a too-tight camouflage blouse that revealed too much. She was wearing dark aviator sunglasses and a generous application of blood-red lipstick. Droplets of sweat glowed between her nose and upper lip like a water moustache.

'You!' Noah growled and spat on the ground.

Marian removed her sunglasses with a flourish and placed them on top of her cropped hair. 'Hello, Noah,' she said. 'Sorry about our last meeting. Well, not exactly sorry. We do what we must, as the boss likes to say.'

Noah glanced at his two armed escorts and tempered his anger. 'Not a psychiatrist then,' he said to Marian.

'Actually, yes,' she said. 'I'm here as a consultant to the project. Mostly, I'm hands off, but you're a special case, a *special* boy.'

'Tell me this, Ms Consultant to the Project,' Noah said. 'Why all the mind games?'

'Mind games?' she said. 'I don't know what you mean. Anyway, mustn't linger. Let's get you to shade. You're no good to anyone burnt to a crisp.'

Marian turned to the man to Noah's left. 'You can untie him now, Curtis. I'll take it from here. You boys go back to the bunkhouse. Send Cody up to wait by the bungalow. Oh, and the boss wants his dog taken to your encampment. Apparently, he's been chewing on the furniture. Radio ahead. Send someone right away.'

'Untie him? Are you sure, miss?'

She planted her fists on her hips. 'Don't make me ask twice, and mind your manners.'

'Yes, Doctor. Sorry, Doctor,' the man said, looking like a chastened schoolboy. He fished out a Swiss Army knife from his pocket and, with a sawing motion, cut Noah's hands free. The severed cable tie fell to the ground, and Marian crouched down, picked it up and placed it in her pocket. She waved away the two guards, who left them alone.

As Noah rubbed his sore wrists, Marian put her hand on his back to guide him forward. 'Come on. You don't want to keep William waiting. I can see you're upset, but if you have any funny ideas, forget them. There's nowhere to run. Plus, knowing you, you'll want to complete that electrifying chat I heard you had with Willy earlier.'

Noah removed his shoe and shook away the stone that had pained him. 'You think you know me, do you?'

'Eliza ran a battery of personality tests in the store, and then I assessed you, so yes, I have an idea. Of our lucky group of guests, I'd rate you as the most risk-averse.'

'At least you look more authentic, dressed like a survivalist stripper. It rings true way more than a white coat.'

'Interesting,' she said. 'Didn't expect defiance from you yet, but then, in my field, I love to be surprised.' She pointed to a square shape in the sky. 'We have drones and guns, so settle down. Running won't get you far, and believe me: the cost and pain aren't worth it, not to mention a potential early death.'

He followed her up a rocky trail alongside high cliffs that protruded over the ocean. Thick jungle extended to their left, as far as the eye could see. After ten silent minutes, they approached a small whitewashed bungalow nestled within a lush garden where birds of paradise flowered in disorganised rows. An open-air terrace at the front of the property was shielded by a metal frame with trailing grapevines. Marian knocked. Wilhelm opened the door, ushered them in and signalled with a pointed finger for Noah to sit on a scuffed plastic chair.

'My dear doctor,' Wilhelm said to Marian, 'there is a pitcher of iced tea in the fridge. Could you get it for us? Cups are in the cupboard.'

'I'm fine,' Noah said, even though he felt parched.

'You will drink,' Wilhelm said and sat on a chair opposite him. 'Europeans in the tropics often forget the necessity for rehydration. Then they shrivel and die, most prematurely.'

The room they were in was a mix between a sitting room and an office. A desk was set against the wall. On top of it were a computer screen and CCTV monitors, all dark. Noah tried to be discreet as he searched the room for a phone. If he could get a message through, hopefully, the call could be traced. He could see none, but with all this technology around, there had to be lines of communication. If the computer was connected to the internet, he should be able to broadcast his location. He would have to be careful, figure out a plan.

Marian served the tea, then stood by the computer desk, her back against the wall, arms folded.

Noah relented and drank the iced tea. It was cool and sweet. He gulped down the entire content of the glass. 'You don't remember me, do you?' he said.

'Yes, yes,' Wilhelm said, after taking a sip of his iced tea, 'you have said this already in the villa. You are mistaken. My kind and yours, the aristocracy and nouveau riche, we do not mix. Oil and water is what we are to each other.'

'Interesting,' Noah said. 'Is that why you shut me up with a stun gun as soon as I mentioned it?'

'I'll humour you, Mr Gant,' Wilhelm said. He put down his

glass on the tray and leaned forward. 'What is it you think you know?'

'You can drop the act,' Noah said. 'Your limp is gone, and you didn't seem to need your walking stick when you opened the door. That's grey dye in your hair isn't it? You're not that old.'

Wilhelm smiled and motioned with an open hand for him to continue, as if intrigued by some wild theory Noah was about to share.

'Six years ago,' Noah said, 'you came to my mother's house in London.'

'That is fanciful indeed,' Wilhelm said. 'You must mistake me for someone else. Why would I come to her house? And London is such a sprawling, dirty city. I prefer the Bavarian Alps. If you twist my arm, then Paris and Vienna are tolerable cities with a little more to recommend them.'

'Maybe you didn't notice me,' Noah said, 'but I was there. Not at the meeting, but I saw you. You were invited to present to my mother and her team. They were looking at security arrangements for her company's office in Abuja. Does that refresh your memory? I never forget a face. You're Bill Drake of Black Scythe Security.'

Bill gave Noah a slow clap. In his German accent, he said, 'Heartfelt congratulations. Well done, *Schatzi*.' Then, in a gravelly London accent, he added, 'Congrats, mate. Frankly, I'm baffled by how stupid you are, but thanks for telling me. Cheers.'

'I'll tell you something else,' Noah said, his anger driving him to speak with an authority that felt new. 'My mother showed me your proposal, including your company's brochure. You're a mercenary: protection jobs, discreet missions, sordid little operations. You're a hired gun, so it's obvious you don't call the shots here. Now, be a good errand boy and tell *Wilhelm* to tell Bill to tell your boss I want a word. Is that clear enough for you?'

Bill dragged his chair forward, settling in front of Noah, his moustached face only a few inches away. The space between them was ripe with the smell of warm tobacco breath. 'Shh, boy.' He placed his fat finger over Noah's lips. 'It's my turn now.'

Noah met Bill's gaze with a defiant glare. He didn't like bullies. He pushed his chair a few inches back, away from Bill. His hands curled into fists over his thighs.

Bill turned to Marian. 'Got to give it to you, Doctor. Your evaluation was spot on. How did you describe him?'

'Timid on the outside,' Marian said, 'but he has a strong core, typical of someone who was showered with love as a child. I'd say his toughness was buried under six feet of emotion.'

'Yes. Yes,' Bill said, sounding excited. 'I think we might have just exhumed it. I can see the bare steel in him. Good job, Doctor. This version of Noah is exactly what we need, considering the circumstances.'

Noah cleared his throat but said nothing.

'You're an emotional lad,' Bill said to Noah. 'Nothing wrong with that. But here's the thing, mate, some worldly wisdom, in case you make it out of here alive. When we let our feelings control us, we force issues that don't need forcing. Sometimes, it's better for things to stay where they belong, clenched inside. I'm surprised an intelligent guy like you hasn't learned that lesson, but there you have it. Maybe it's the money. Having money makes people stupid.'

'You read that in Marian's self-help book?' Noah said.

Bill leaned forward. With a sudden, violent thrust, he slapped Noah across the face, so hard his ears rang. 'Quiet,' he whispered. 'You think you know what's going on here, but you don't. You haven't got a clue.'

'Rattle you, did I?' Noah said.

'Yeah, shook me to my arthritic bones. Here's the thing, mate. The key to *sordid little operations*, as you call them, is to prepare for *every* eventuality. There was always a chance you'd seen me in London. Like a child with no self-control, you've just confirmed it. Thank you, and congratulations. You leave me no choice but to recruit you. Welcome to the team.'

Noah shook his head.

'Show him, Doctor,' Bill said.

Marian agitated the computer's mouse, and the screen came to life. On it was a central panel which displayed a wave pattern and a pulsing circle surrounded by rectangles that bore rapidly changing numbers. At the top was a row of what looked like clickable buttons.

'Rich people,' Bill said, 'they have this uncontrollable need to buy the most expensive gadgets. I mean, I get it. You want state-of-the-art and all that, nothing but the best. With that in mind, young Noah, care to guess what you're looking at?'

'Your stock market valuation?' Noah said. 'Your evil beating heart?'

Bill slapped him on the face again.

Noah took the hit in silence, but his insides screamed. If it happened again, he decided, he would push Bill backwards, upend his chair and kick him in the head. Then he'd go for Marian. Noah was not a fighter, but if there were ever a time to start, this was it. He'd had enough. He was grateful Bill's pit bull wasn't in the cottage. A dog like that was not something you wanted to take on. As soon as the thought struck him, he decided he didn't have to wait, not for more slaps, not for more insults, not for more pain. He'd have to pick his moment carefully, time it just right. He looked around for anything he could use as a weapon. On a shelf behind Bill was an ornamental ceramic head with phrenology lines imprinted on it. It would have to do.

'Eyes on the screen, Noah,' Bill said. 'Look carefully. What do you see?'

Noah glanced at the screen but, from where he was seated, he could not read the numbers or headings. 'I'm done playing your game,' he said, his body tensing, preparing to strike.

'Tell you what,' Bill said. 'You're right. I'm being unfair. You're one of us now, so I'll give you this one for free. Last year, your mother had a pacemaker put in her. Not any old pacemaker, mind. This one was the cutting edge 5TS-3R model. Only *very* rich people can afford it. It's so advanced, her cardiologist can control it from anywhere in the world, make adjustments, keep her well. All it took my *sordid little operation* to hack it was a breach of the hospital's server to create a relay. See your mother's name? Top left-hand corner: Cecilia Gant. That's her pulse up there. Ba-boom, ba-boom. Now, with a click of a button, Marian can pull at your mother's heartstrings if she wishes. Pull at them so hard that her ticker will literally beat out of her chest.'

Noah felt dizzy. His heartbeat sped up as if it was his own pulse they were controlling. All fight had drained from him. He slumped into his chair.

'Here, have some more iced tea,' Bill said, filling up his glass. 'Honestly, there's no need to worry. Your mother is perfectly safe. Marian would never dream of harming her, okay? Our bosses are good people, upstanding. I daresay, if you met them, you'd love them. Drink up.'

Noah took the tea from Bill and held it. His hand shook so badly that he spilt some on his lap. He took a sip and placed the cup back on its tray.

'Marian, dear,' Wilhelm said, 'turn that screen off. Thank you. You can leave us now. I think young Noah will co-operate.'

On her way out, Marian stopped by Noah's side, leaned in and kissed him on the cheek. After she had closed the front door behind her, Bill grabbed Noah by the shoulders and placed his meaty forehead against his, remaining in that position for a long moment. Then, he gripped Noah's head with his hands, his fingers over Noah's ears, boring painfully into his scalp. 'Don't get any ideas in that massive intellectual head of yours. Our system gets pinged every few hours. No ping, and an automatic script runs. Result: your mother's heart explodes. Understand?'

'Yes,' Noah whispered.

'What's that, pup? I didn't hear you?'

'I understand, you bastard.'

'Excellent,' Bill said. He let go of Noah's head and spoke softly. 'It's all right, mate. No need to stress. Everything's under control. *Everything* is under control.'

Noah felt faint. His temples throbbed. He shivered with a sudden cold flush.

Bill put his arms around him and pulled him into a bear hug, burying Noah's face in his chest. 'There-there,' he said, gently rocking him. 'Uncle Bill will look after you now. Uncle Bill is your friend, and friends help each other. All I ask of you is to keep shtum about who I am and our new alliance. You will not, under any circumstances, share it with your classmates, all right? I don't need much from you. You're just, how shall I put it, a failsafe, that's all. And you will do exactly as I tell you – exactly – because you love your mother. You would jump off Everest to save her.'

Bill held Noah a moment longer, then released him and wiped the tears from his face with his fat thumbs. 'There-there. All better now. I'll explain what I need from you, and then one of the lads will take you back to the villa. We're keeping your friends in the basement, and you will join them. Do you understand, *Schatzi*? *Verstehen Sie*?'

THIRTEEN

A prayer and a hymn

Noah was escorted back to the villa by the guard whom Bill had called Cody, the same man who had pointed his gun at Ashleigh earlier. His hands were not bound this time, at least not physically, but the threat to his mother was worse than chains. He thought of his time with her, the Christmas before last, when they stayed in the Burj Al Arab hotel in Dubai. His mother had insisted they avoid any elaborate holiday celebrations and make the most of their time together, uninterrupted by the constant demands of her work. She had left her laptop and phone behind, and they spent the day at the beach, eating skewered lamb kebabs in sweet tamarind sauce and cold meze dishes, the efficient waiters serving them a succession of beautifully presented pisco sours and Hemingway daiquiris. It was Noah's brightest memory from recent times, though once the drinks had gone to their heads, their lips loosened, and they reminisced about Noah's father – the man who raised him – and wished a thousand times he could have been there with them. Noah had a vague memory of them staggering back to their hotel suite, merry and a little tearful.

Noah and the guard trod down the steep rocky trail

towards the beach until his escort broke the silence. 'Look, man, I'm sorry about what's happening to you guys. It's real rough.' He spoke in an earnest American voice and an accent that Noah thought might be from somewhere in the US South. He was a muscled man with chiselled cheekbones, like an all-American model in an advert for power tools. His right wrist bore a braided multicoloured surfer bracelet, his left an oversized diver's watch with an orange strap. A faded purple paisley-print bandana around his neck completed his action-figure trio of personalised items that rebelled against the backdrop of his uniform and gun.

'You were going to kill Ashleigh,' Noah said. 'You didn't look sorry then.'

The man's sunglasses made his face unreadable. 'That's fair,' he said. 'But you gotta understand, a job's a job.'

'They tell you to shoot someone, you shoot?' Noah said.

'Pretty much. Same as I did for Uncle Sam.' He coughed up phlegm and spat it to the ground. 'But I gotta tell ya, here pays better.'

'You're a soldier?' Noah said.

'Used to be. United States Marine Corps, honourably discharged. Then some wild times in San Diego, way wilder times in TJ.'

'TJ?' Noah said.

'Tijuana, Mexico, party town for misplaced souls. Lost my way, then found it again with this here employer. But see, I'm not a bad guy. All I want is enough in the bank for a little house off-grid in the desert: Nevada, maybe Arizona or even Big Bend, devil's land, primal as heck, do me a world of good. I like the heat, being away from people, red sunsets, cactus, beers.'

'That's a pretty picture,' Noah said.

'Still a ways to go on getting there. I want me top-of-the-range off-grid stuff. Grow roots, ya know? Not to worry about money.'

'How many murders will it take to achieve this lovely dream?'

'Told you about that already.'

'Yeah, a job's a job,' Noah said, 'pays well. I understand.' He hesitated, then plucked up the courage to make his gambit. 'Our parents would offer you enough to build a town of little houses if you help us, but look, I'm not going to disrespect you by making an offer. I can tell you're a loyal guy. Bill's lucky to have you.'

Cody stopped and turned to face him. Noah blinked at the intense glare of the sun, but kept his gaze locked on the guard's dark sunglasses, hoping to meet the man's invisible eyes. In his peripheral vision, he saw a gecko scurrying for cover under a mound of rocks. The rush of the sea sounded louder, as if risen by a swell. For a moment, Noah dared to hope. Then came the guard's answer. With a swift, vicious strike, Cody planted the stock of his Uzi into Noah's solar plexus.

Noah lurched forward, gasping, his hands clasped over his stomach.

'People think marines are stupid,' Cody said and spat again.

Noah coughed and wheezed. 'I never meant–'

'No more talking,' Cody said. 'Forward march!'

The steps behind the security door in the villa led underground to another fortified door, this one as thick as a bomb shelter's. Cody turned the arm of the bolt mechanism and heaved the door open to reveal what felt more like a bunker than a basement: a twenty-square-metre room with cement walls painted industrial white, bare concrete floors and fluorescent tube lights. A waist-height garden tap protruded from the wall, and next to it was a shelf bearing upturned plastic cups. A flat-screen TV hung on the opposite wall, showing the *Lorem Ipsum* logo. At the far end, a narrow corridor with barely any lighting led to open doorways.

Cody shoved Noah into the room and shut the heavy door behind him with a clang. The outer bolt thudded as it was locked into place. Noah's classmates were sitting on plastic chairs at a round table that was screwed to the floor. They looked subdued, welcoming him with nods and timid waves, except for Zayn, who got up to greet him.

'You all right, chump?' Zayn said. 'Glad we got you back safe. When we went downstairs, we heard a commotion, but couldn't work out what happened to you.'

'Thought I recognised the German guy,' Noah said, 'so they freaked out.'

'Who is he?' Jonny said.

'Mistaken identity,' Noah said. 'At least I got to see some of the scenery: cliffs and ocean and jungle. Not sure why they'd lock us in here. Doesn't look like we can go anywhere, and even if we did, there's drones and patrols and guards with Uzis.'

Zayn gave him a friendly clap on the shoulder. 'Welcome to the Lorem Ipsum Hotel. Come with me. I'll give you the grand tour.'

The dimly lit corridor led to three doorless box rooms, each with two thin blue plastic mattresses that lay on the floor, bare of any bedding. At the end of the corridor was a bathroom with a plastic shower curtain for a door. The entire space smelled of fresh paint and fresh sweat and stale air. When they were in the furthest box room, Zayn put a finger to his lips and motioned for Noah to sit on the mattress at the far corner of the room. Zayn came to sit beside him and whispered in his ear, 'There are four hidden mini-cameras in the communal area,' he said. 'Chinese surveillance model, TX56. They stream video and sound, but they shouldn't be able to pick up our voices from this distance. I've scanned this bedroom inch by inch. Fairly sure there's nothing here. Keep your voice down, just in case. Don't look at me like that. Playboys have to be very careful. Sex tapes are all the rage in my circles. Now, tell me, what else did you learn out there?'

'Not a thing.'

Zayn tsk-tsked at him. 'You were always a lousy liar,' he said. 'We need to work on that. Who is Wilhelm? And what's this thing about saving millions with our ransom?'

'I told you already,' Noah said, loud enough for any microphone to pick up his voice if they could hear him. 'Didn't recognise him. Don't know anything.'

'All right,' Zayn said, then whispered, 'Don't worry. I got your back. We'll get out of here, I promise.'

'So,' Noah whispered, 'you're a surveillance expert, a lie detector and a mutant turtle ninja warrior now?'

'Me?' Zayn said with a dismissive, limp-wristed wave. 'Stop it! You're making me blush.'

'Anything happen while I was gone?' Noah said.

'Ashleigh's still being quiet and awkward. I mean, the theatrics earlier, asking for a bullet to the head. I can't quite put my finger on it, but something doesn't fit.'

'Have you tried asking her?' Noah said.

Zayn shrugged.

'I'll have a go,' Noah said.

'Good luck. Other than that, we've had some God chatter from Emily, something about praying together. They allowed her to keep her uniform and a prayer book. Seems like God gets a free pass.' He shrugged again, looking sheepish. 'I might have called her a praying mantis.'

Noah grimaced. 'You didn't!'

'I'll admit, not my finest hour. She gets under my skin. Don't know what she has against me. Honestly, mate, I'm glad you're here. I don't have much in common with Jonny; Emily's being pious, and Ashleigh's lost it.' He squeezed Noah's arm. 'If you ever want a teammate for a future kidnapping, I'm your man.'

'You'll be my first call,' Noah said.

Zayn leaned his back against the wall and rubbed his hands together. 'How's life been treating you, outside of here, I mean? You got someone special?'

'Nah,' Noah said. 'My life's boring. Academia has its moments, but then I get home, install a dating app, scroll through a million Marthas and Cassandras and bloody Norahs, despair, uninstall. Weekends, I swim, go for a walk along the river, maybe see my mother. I'm not like you, Zayn. I wish…' He trailed off, surprised by his honesty. Perhaps it was the setting or Zayn's kindness, but this was the closest he'd ever been to admitting the gloom he felt, alone in his Central London flat at the end of another empty day, lying in his bed, staring into the deep, depressing darkness. He swallowed, attempting to loosen the tightness in his throat.

'Being glamorous,' Zayn said, 'is not as exciting as it looks on my Facebook feed.'

'I'd settle for five per cent of it,' Noah said. 'You must get laid a lot. I'd settle for a fifth of that as well, less than a fifth.'

'Sex is just sex,' Zayn said, 'and I think you might have missed the memo about money being like honey.'

'To prostitutes?' Noah said.

Zayn shook his head. 'Ninety per cent of the population.'

'I guess I'm more of a sucker for the ten per cent.'

'By the way,' Zayn said, 'weren't you into Emily at school? You used to be all puppy-eyed around her.'

'Let's not get nostalgic,' Noah said. 'Shall we rejoin the others?' He stood, offered Zayn his hand and pulled him up.

Back in the common room, Noah and Zayn took their seats next to each other.

'I hope the accommodation is to your satisfaction, sir,' Jonny said. 'Cheap plastic mattresses are all the rage in Biarritz this season.'

'I can see the appeal,' Noah said, then looked at Ashleigh, who appeared shrunken, her hair messy, her gaze fixed on an invisible spot on the tabletop. She was wearing her beach towel over her shoulders like a shawl to cover her bikini top. 'Ashleigh,' he said, 'talk to me. What happened up there?'

As slow as a sloth, Ashleigh raised her tired eyes to look at him. 'None of your business,' she said.

'Considering he almost died for you,' Jonny said, 'I'd say he deserves an answer?'

'I can't be responsible for other people's stupid choices,' Ashleigh said.

'If they'd shot and killed him,' Emily said, 'you'd have to live with the guilt for the rest of your life.'

'Good thing there's not much left of my so-called life,' Ashleigh said.

'Seriously?' Jonny said. 'That's your answer? I had a hunch you might be anorexic again, but–'

'All right everyone, back off,' Noah said. 'Ashleigh, listen. I know this is difficult, but a few days max and we're getting out of here.' He stopped and observed Ashleigh's gaunt cheekbones, her sunken eyes and pale-grey lips. With a tender, caring voice he'd sometimes use with his more sensitive students, he said, 'Ashleigh, what's really going on with you?'

Ashleigh brushed her hair with her fingers and scratched her neck. Finally, she spoke. 'Pancreatic cancer,' she said. 'Stage four. They caught it too late, and it's spread. Happy now?'

The room felt hot and airless, devoid of sound except for the buzz of the fluorescent bulbs above them.

'Oh,' Jonny said.

'Save your apologies,' Ashleigh said, 'and your commiserations, okay?'

'Why didn't you say something?' Zayn said.

Ashleigh rubbed her eyes with her fists. She gave Zayn and Noah a pained smile and spoke to them as if Emily and Jonny weren't there. 'It's not like I know you. Not really. Not for a long time, but okay. Funny thing is, I had the scans, the tests, the prognosis. I made a bucket list. I was going to enjoy every second. Then, I got grabbed in the hospital car park, and I found myself here, so I thought to myself: beautiful beach, coconuts, excellent. What a glorious finale, eh? I'm sorry, Noah. When they said they'd lock us up, I lost it. I have two or three weeks left if I'm lucky. There's a hospice bed with my name on it, probably for next week.' She stared at her hands. 'By the time our lovely stay here is done, so will I be. With all this stress, they'll probably just wheel me straight to the crematorium. I don't...' She paused and caught her breath.

'That sucks,' Zayn said.

'A bullet would have been a kindness,' Ashleigh said. 'Now I'm stuck in this shithole in my fucking bikini with my fucking classmates and my fucking cancer death spiral. Would be nice if they had morphine. Could you pray me some fucking morphine, Emily?'

Zayn got up and came to stand behind her. He placed his hands on her shoulders. 'Ash, listen to me. It's rotten and unfair. I can't even pretend to understand what it feels like, but I promise you – I promise – we're going to make this the most fun kidnapping ever, okay? We'll make memories together.'

'Don't fuss,' Ashleigh said. 'Please don't fuss. It's annoying.'

'You're sure there's no treatment?' Jonny said.

'I have – I mean I had – the best oncologist. They triple-checked the tests, got a second opinion. Advanced stage four. There's no stage five. Can we please stop talking about it?'

Noah went over to the tap, filled a cup with water and drank it, taking slow, deliberate sips.

Emily, who had sat in silence since the revelation, finally spoke. In a hushed voice, she said, 'I'm so sorry, Ashleigh. I was an idiot.'

'If I die here,' Ashleigh said to Emily, 'will you say a prayer for me? I know I wasn't much for God, but since you're here, it would be nice to know…'

'You'll get the full nun treatment. A prayer and a hymn. I have my prayer book.'

FOURTEEN

Best of three

The *Lorem ipsum* logo on the basement's screen flickered. They heard a static noise, and Bill's dogged face appeared in an unflattering close-up that was mostly moustache. He spoke in his German accent, being Wilhelm. 'I trust you have settled well into your accommodations, yes? The time has come to explain why we have sent you down to the holding basement. We were not certain, but it has now been confirmed. I am very sorry to report this, but I bring sad news. It appears His Majesty's government has ordered your parents not to pay your ransom. In light of this, action must be taken. It is a most unpleasant business, most unpleasant, but so it goes.'

Bill sat back, away from the camera, his entire face now visible on the screen. 'Since we require payments from your parents, a warning must be sent. It is regrettable, especially for you, but there it is. We – you and I – must send a stern message, a moving message, one that will make your parents spring into action. It is therefore my duty to inform you that, on this day, after all, one of you must die.' He paused and took a sip from a glass of iced tea.

Nobody spoke. It was as if Bill's announcement had momentarily frozen the room and turned its inhabitants into petrified statues.

Noah crushed the plastic cup in his hand and found himself reclining with his back against the wall until he sat on the floor. He felt dizzy but forced himself to watch the screen.

'After we complete this task,' Bill continued, 'those who remain will once again be allowed out. We only keep you locked away until the deed is done. This is merely to avoid any insurrection or defiance on your part. We do not wish to eliminate more of you than is necessary at this time.' He looked away for a moment, then back into the camera. 'I have pondered long and hard over this question: which one of you to choose? Which one? You see, I have no favourites in your pathetic group – so how does one decide?'

Ashleigh perked up. Her cheeks reddened. She stood and raised her hand, clearly hoping that Bill could see her through his cameras. Jonny shook his head, mumbled something unheard, and buried his head in his hands.

'Ach, well,' Bill said. 'I will bother you no further with tales of my deliberations, for I have come to a conclusion. This problem is not my problem, so to speak. It is yours and your parents' alone, not for me to play judge. I am merely the executioner.' He stared into the camera with what could have been a grimace or a crooked grin. 'It is therefore *you* who will choose. *You* will decide who is sacrificed today. Your problem, your decision.'

'What?' Emily whispered. 'No. No.'

'My men will be with you in three minutes,' Bill said. 'By then, you must have a volunteer ready. He or she will get a nice meal, a shower and some time to write a letter. Then, very shortly, when it is morning in the United Kingdom, the execution will take place, and a video will be sent, along with the contents of the letter. We do what we must.'

Noah's eyes hurt, the confined space closing in on him. He was tempted to speak, to expose Wilhelm for the Bill he really was. The fake German persona was grating on him more and more with each word, and he wondered how the others couldn't see through the lie. Perhaps it was only obvious to him, because he knew of Bill's deceit, but he couldn't tell them or even hint at it. His mother's life depended on his silence.

Zayn lowered himself to the floor and sat next to him as if sensing his turmoil.

'Oh, and one thing further,' Bill said. 'Any one of you may volunteer, except for Ashleigh Boroughs. Her father has already made payment. Good, good, well. Be ready with your decision. Three minutes.' Bill's image disappeared, and the screen displayed the *Lorem Ipsum* logo once again.

Ashleigh uttered a loud, frustrated grunt. She left the table and rested her forehead and palms against the wall, panting and shaking her head.

Emily stared at the screen, the look on her face not so much shock and despair like the rest of them, but a pure seething anger. 'I don't understand,' she said. 'I have to talk to them. I have to.' She called out to the screen. 'If you can hear me, I need to talk to Wilhelm.'

'I don't think they–' Jonny started to say but was interrupted by Zayn, who raised his hand.

'I'll go,' Zayn said. 'I'll do it.'

'Why you?' Noah said.

'Jonny has a wife and child,' Zayn said, 'so he's definitely off the list. That leaves the three of us. The nun doesn't like me, so she'll support my claim. I'm a vacuous, worthless person, right?'

'And me?' Noah said.

'It's not going to be you,' Zayn said.

'Says who?'

'Shut up, both of you,' Emily said and came to stand

before them, her anger seeming to have ebbed a little. She tousled Noah's hair and spoke to Zayn. 'Get up.'

Zayn stood and faced her. 'Yes, dear?' He spoke so calmly that Noah wondered about his mask of cool and nonchalance. Zayn had always treated everything like a game. Perhaps he didn't entirely register the gravity of what was about to happen. He was volunteering to die with the enthusiasm of a football player keen to be picked first for the team.

Emily cupped Zayn's cheeks with her hands, drew his face close to hers and kissed him on the forehead. She pulled her head back and looked into his eyes. 'By God, Zayn, it kills me to admit it, but you're a totally different dog breed to the one I–'

'Woof!' Zayn said.

Emily brushed his neck tenderly with the back of her hand. 'No one is more surprised and disappointed than I am.' Her face creased, and she hid her mouth with a trembling hand. Then, she embraced Zayn for an awkward hug. 'I'm so sorry,' she whispered. 'I'm so sorry.'

'Shit happens,' Zayn said quietly, for the first time sounding like he understood the magnitude of what he was about to do. 'I have my reasons. I can't go into it, but I'm the right choice here. It's part of who I am, of what I have to do.'

Noah rose to his feet. 'No,' he said to Zayn, 'I'm still in the running. Emily doesn't get to decide, and neither do you. You have your reasons? Well, I have mine. If you don't back off, it's going to be rock, paper, scissors, best of three.'

Jonny looked up at them both, as though he couldn't believe his eyes, their eagerness for an execution, but he said nothing.

'Noah, listen to me,' Zayn said. 'You're an awesome guy, really awesome. I'm glad we got to spend this time together. Now, fuck off and let me go. It's not up for discussion.'

Before Noah could object, they heard the door's bolt turn, and then the creaking of hinges. Cody appeared, along with one of his fellow guards. 'Who's coming with me?' he said.

'I am,' Zayn and Noah said in unison.

'If you don't choose, I will,' Cody said.

Emily turned to Cody. 'You look like a decent person,' she said. 'Maybe not good, but decent. Will you allow me to say a prayer for the person leaving us?'

'Back off, little nun,' Cody said.

'God will look favourably upon you,' Emily said in her pious Sunday voice. 'When you stand before your maker, this little act of kindness might just make a difference.'

'I doubt it,' Cody said, then shrugged. 'You know what? What's the harm. But make it double-quick.'

Emily turned to Noah. 'Will you get my prayer book, please? It's on the mattress in the second room.'

'I can see what you're doing,' Noah said, 'getting me out of the way so Zayn can go. That's not happening.'

'I don't have time for this,' Cody said. 'You both go fetch the nun's friggin' book. Then I'll choose.' He slapped his gun. 'Go on now, *get*, before I change my mind.'

Noah followed Zayn to the second bedroom. Zayn knelt next to one of the mattresses to pick up a small brown book that looked heavily thumbed. Its pages were frayed and yellowing at the edges. Noah played forward what was about to happen, the moment of selection, and how fate was going to take control. His thoughts spun like a centrifuge until they distilled in him one single-minded decision. He spun a half-turn to gain momentum and then, with all his force, kicked Zayn in the head. It was an unpractised move, poorly executed. As his foot connected with Zayn's skull, the pain of colliding bones sent Noah into a spasm that nearly floored him – but it had worked. Zayn landed on the mattress, senseless.

'Sorry,' he whispered to the unconscious Zayn, who lay flat on the mattress, his shirt riding up to reveal a thin line of hairs trailing down from his navel. He picked up the book and hurried to get back to the impatient guard, limping but with his head held high, feeling an odd sense of relief and purpose. Rather than being fearful of his upcoming death, he looked forward to it, looked forward to no longer posing a threat to his mother's life. *That'll show Bill and his stupid threats.*

As he hobbled down the corridor, he started to consider what he'd put in the letter Bill said he could write before his execution. *What do you say in a final letter?* Some fragments came to him. *If they return my body, I'd like to be buried next to Dad. I'll also say goodbye to my other father, Peter Hammerson. What else? I love you, Mum. I love you. I'm sorry I had to die.* He felt an emptiness inside him and an overwhelming sense of disappointment. *Is this all that my life amounted to? If I had to do it all again, I'd live differently, live brightly, not hide in the gloom of routines.* He allowed himself an ounce of comfort. *At least I'll save my mother.*

He imagined his classmates sad upon his death, especially Emily and Zayn. Maybe they'd even cry for him. It would make for a nice gesture.

As Noah entered the common area, he heard the basement's door bolt lock shut. Jonny and Ashleigh both looked at him with blank expressions.

'Where are they?' he said. 'Where's Emily?'

'She went with him,' Jonny said, 'volunteered herself.'

'And you did nothing? You let her?' Noah said.

Zayn stumbled into the room, his hand on his cheek. 'She's gone?' he said. 'Well played, Emily. And well played you, Noah. God almighty, it's like a death cult in here.' He curled his hands into fists and approached Noah, who waited for him, his shoulders slumped, wishing for the blow he deserved, wishing to be knocked out from the suffocating loss he felt. But Zayn did not strike him. Instead, he put his arms around him and held on tight, so tight that Noah could barely breathe, could barely sob, could barely comprehend the truth: Emily was going to die.

Five hours earlier

FIFTEEN

The Home Secretary is an honourable woman

EWALD HOUSE, NORTHUMBERLAND, 13 AUGUST

When Alex and Peter Hammerson entered the converted barn annexe at 7.45am, they found ITV presenter Tanya Sharp and her crew of three gathered around the dining table, the remnants of breakfast before them: charred toast-ends, orphaned baked beans in eggy smears, knife blades that carried evidence of Marmite, butter and yolk. Hefty black equipment boxes with metallic frames were lined up against the wall. A thick tangle of cables was rigged through the window, out to the news van that carried a satellite uplink dish on its roof. Tanya looked fresh-faced and glamorous, her perfect hair and make-up a complete contrast to her unshaven male colleagues in their crumpled clothes.

'It's so generous of you to let us stay here,' Tanya said to Peter. 'I can't imagine spending the night stuck in the van with these smelly outcasts. The wind was outrageous. We might have been blown away. Good thing it's calmed down a bit now.'

A crew member who was caressing a mug of tea grinned at her with nicotine-stained teeth. 'You love us, really. Don't you, m'lady?' He turned to Peter. 'She lives for off-site broadcasts. We're like her surrogate husbands.'

'Husbandry, more like,' Tanya said.

'I see you've been fed,' Peter said.

'To perfection,' Tanya said. 'Ready for your interview? We've set up a studio in the back office. Going live in ten minutes. Follow me.'

In the annexe's tongue-and-groove-clad office, the furniture had been moved aside, leaving two chairs facing each other among snaking cables and stage lights. Alex leaned against the wall while Tanya guided Peter to his seat and powdered his face with a brush. 'Just a tiny bit of mosaic powder,' she said, 'to stop you looking shiny. Remember, don't focus on the camera. Look at me when you speak, and my crew will do the rest. Try to relax. Imagine you're having a chat with a concerned friend, which, in a way, I am.'

A concerned friend? Alex thought. He doubted Peter would fall for that one. However sweet she appeared, Tanya was known for razor-sharp questions delivered in a warm, caring tone. She was a mercenary in sympathiser's clothing, relentless against evasion, a chaser of soundbites, dangerous. He noticed that Tanya had said nothing to Peter about Emily's abduction, no words of comfort. She was a consummate professional, saving prime lines for the live broadcast. This compounded his worry. There was no guarantee the broadcast media would be sympathetic to the parents' plight, tragic as it was. Their constituents were their viewers. All the better if they could be frenzied into a baying mob that would watch hours upon hours of non-stop coverage. Hating equalled ratings.

'Thirty seconds,' called out the producer with the greasy mullet and a belly that lurched forward from his tight, black Nirvana T-shirt.

Tanya settled in the chair opposite Peter. 'You'll do just fine,' she said. 'Look at me, not at the camera.'

The producer held up his finger and thrust it forward, mouthing, 'You're live.' The monitor that had shown a live feed of *This Morning's* studio now switched to Tanya. 'I'm in Northumberland for an exclusive interview with Peter Hammerson, whose daughter Emily was kidnapped only two days ago. We appreciate you joining us, Mr Hammerson, in what must be a terribly difficult time. How are you coping?'

Peter's image appeared on the live feed, and Alex saw him as others would: grey-faced, as if drained of life and colour. Despite this, his back was set straight, his chest pushed out, the pose of an experienced CEO. *This kind of fortitude may be a good thing*, Alex thought, *or an absolute disaster*. He was reassured by a slight tremor in Peter's voice when he spoke.

'I know,' Peter said, 'any parent watching this would understand the awful things that go through your mind when your child is taken from you and threatened with death. And then to be told that my Emily, she… She only has a twenty per cent chance of surviving. Yes, it scares me. It terrifies me out of my wits, and now things have become…' He swallowed his way out of the sentence. The camera zoomed in on his face, revealing the dark circles under his eyes that had surfaced to defy the chalky make-up.

'By twenty per cent,' Tanya said, 'you mean you have to compete with the parents of the four other victims. The kidnappers announced they would return only one of the five hostages alive, to the parent who pays the most. They call their cruel game Heir Loss. That's heir with an "H".' She took a beat, made a show of hesitating, then said, 'Your first deadline to pay the ransom is one pm this afternoon. What are you planning to–'

Peter interrupted her. 'It's not a game.'

'Of course. What I meant is–'

'If it were a game, then we've already lost. I'm devastated to say this, Tanya. I'm heartbroken, but I don't think any of our kids will come back alive. You see, there will be no payments, to anyone, by any of us. No charity will get a donation. This whole thing is just one big sorry tragedy and an absolute mess.'

The cameras cut to Tanya just in time to catch her confusion. Her chin was pushed down to her neck while her eyebrows shot upwards. 'Forgive me. Did you just say you're not paying? You won't pay the ransom to save your children?'

'I know,' Peter said, 'some people support these kidnappers, applaud them, even. They want to take from us, the rich, and donate to the poor. I understand the sentiment. Wouldn't you, Tanya?'

The camera switched to Tanya, who angled her head but did not answer.

'It makes sense, doesn't it?' Peter said. 'We have all this money while there are so many others who are less fortunate: homeless, sick, hungry. Wouldn't the world be fairer if we just gave our money to them? Honestly, I see the logic. I do. In fact, I was planning on sending them a lot of money, a hefty sum. We all were.'

'You meant to send money, but now you won't? What changed your mind, Mr Hammerson?'

That's right, Alex thought, *make her sweat for it.*

Peter leaned forward, stroking his chin. Then, he sat back again. 'I know most of you don't care about me. I'm not asking you to. But Emily, she'll always be my beautiful little girl. She's a nun now. Did you know that, Tanya? My Emily, the wild child, the rebel. When she was sixteen, she used to sneak out of our house in London, through the garden and over the fence, to go clubbing in Brixton.' He looked up, conjuring the memory, a sad smile on his face. 'We pretended we didn't know. Teenagers being teenagers. I was going to draw the line when she started smoking spliffs in her bedroom, but then, funny thing: it turned out her mother was her dealer.' He chuckled without joy and wiped a tear from his eye. 'You work so hard to raise them, love them… You imagine them all grown up and out in the world, and then… I hate to say this, but I think Emily would approve of the kidnappers' cause. Maybe not their actions, but the general idea of it.'

Tanya let the sheet with her list of questions drop from her hand to the floor. The producer was signalling for her to wrap up. 'Mr Hammerson, please,' she said, for the first time in the interview losing her mask of sympathy and patience, 'I'm sure our viewers would like an answer: the money for your children.'

'Of course we'd like to save them,' Peter said. 'Of course we'd like to pay. We've made all the arrangements. Even a small chance that Emily would survive is better than nothing, and the funds would supposedly go to good causes. Isn't that what the kidnappers said? But you see, Tanya, the government has told us we should not, under any circumstances, agree to those terms. They designated the kidnappers as terrorists. If we send even a single pound, we'd be arrested, and our assets will be frozen. If that happens, we won't be able to pay anything in the next round. Whatever we do, our children will die. All of them.'

'Who told you this?' Tanya said.

Peter looked straight into the camera. 'It came directly from the Home Secretary. She is an honourable woman. I don't doubt she means well. Her representative told us this decision was meant to prevent other groups from using the same methods in the future to force the government's hand or extract money from others. As an example, he painted a scenario where someone would kidnap the Home Secretary's beloved dog and then demand a change in government policy. I'll leave it to your viewers to draw their own conclusions on that one.' He looked down, then back into the camera. 'But let me reiterate, Tanya. We understand why the Home Secretary did what she did, but the result is a death sentence for our children, for my Emily, and no one will benefit, not even those despicable kidnappers with their allegedly benevolent scheme.'

'If there's no chance the kidnappers will get their funding,' Tanya said, 'what do you think they'll do next?'

Peter looked at her gravely and shrugged. 'I don't know. All we ask is that the media and everyone out there respect our privacy. Please leave us to pray for our children and hope against hope they'll come home safe. We don't want mass demonstrations in London this morning, not for us, not for the payments to be allowed.'

The mulleted man behind Peter signalled to Tanya that her time was up.

'I'm afraid we have to cut to the news now,' Tanya said. 'Thank you, Peter Hammerson, for joining us in what must be a terribly difficult time.'

'And, we're off air,' the producer said.

Tanya's smile straightened to an even keel. 'Just so we're clear,' she said to Peter, 'I know exactly what you were doing. If it weren't for the situation with your daughter, I would have called you out.'

'I have no idea what you mean,' Peter said.

'Respectfully,' Tanya said, 'and I say this with the utmost sympathy, don't insult my intelligence.'

'Fair enough,' Peter said. 'Do you think it might work?'

'I doubt it,' she said. 'The world's a lot more cynical than you give it credit for. People won't go out and demonstrate just because you planted the idea. And a bit of inside Westminster gossip for you, Peter. It's not the Home Secretary who's pushing this agenda. It's the Prime Minister himself. Robert Cunningham is a stubborn man, and he never backs down.'

SIXTEEN

Twice as deadly

'You wanted to see me?' Alex said to Davis Boroughs. Davis had sent him an invitation text, more of a summons, bare of any niceties: *Come meet me. Downstairs library*.

The room contained floor-to-ceiling shelves crowded with books, some neatly arranged, their spines level, others in disarray that did not look intended. This suggested to Alex that Peter Hammerson's family were actual readers. The library was not an interior designer's fiction.

Davis pulled out a book and thumbed through it absent-mindedly. 'Jane Austen,' he said. 'Hmm, one for the girls. Ashleigh would love this room. She reads a lot, too much.' He replaced the book and turned to face Alex. 'You saw Peter's interview?'

'I was there with him. We prepped for it together.'

'And?'

'Can't say I'm hopeful, but he gave it his best.'

Davis scoffed. 'His best? Ashleigh's life depends on a man who'll look like a distinguished CEO even if you dressed him in rags. We should have sent Cecilia to flutter her long lashes and cry for the camera, maybe with her dog. Yeah, dogs definitely get more sympathy than us. Then, it might have worked, but this? Nah. I don't think so.'

'Let's not lose hope.'

'Leave out the platitudes, Alex. If I already sent my payment to the swines, which I'm not saying I have, well… If Peter's little stunt doesn't work, and the government freezes my bank accounts, I promise you this: I'll make it my life's work to destroy them, that incompetent Home Secretary and her boss, our shit-for-brains Prime Minister.' He pretended to spit. 'By the time I'm done with them, they'll be bankrupt, working as cleaners, catapulted from public life to public loos.'

Alex let the furious words hang in the air until Davis seemed to regain his composure, his face returning to its natural baseline: a wealthy man in control, not to be messed with. In Alex's experience, it was a common gift of highly successful people that they could compartmentalise, park one issue and move on smoothly to the next.

'You know,' Davis said, 'you look familiar. Have we met? I mean before all this.'

'Your second wife recommended me to your third,' Alex said. 'You would have seen me in court. She paid well. They both did.'

'Ah,' Davis said. 'You're the whoreson with the telephoto lens.'

'My apologies,' Alex said.

'Tell me, Alex, considering how massively buggered we are, what have you done for us so far? You're supposed to be this illustrious PI, the crème de la crème. Please tell me we're any closer to finding and crushing these Marxist scum.'

'We're making progress,' Alex said. 'I planned to brief you all at eleven thirty.'

'Enlighten me, whoreson, who do you actually work for? Are you more forthcoming with Peter because he's the one who cuts the cheques?'

'It makes no difference who pays me. I'm doing everything I can to bring your children home, all of them.'

'And yet,' Davis said, 'isn't a dog more loyal to the hand that feeds it? Indulge me, what have you been fed?'

"Peter paid me a £300,000 retainer plus expenses, and he placed a million into escrow as a bonus if his daughter comes home safely.'

'Then you see my problem,' Davis said. 'It's like you used one of my Series Five Extreme butt plugs on me,' he hissed the next words angrily with rounded lips, 'without my consent.'

'We agreed on the terms before we knew how this would play out,' Alex said. 'Peter thought–'

'Yes, he may well have. He's a thinker, our Peter. Thinks of himself a lot.'

Alex held Davis's gaze. 'You make a fair point,' he said. 'In fact, I've had the exact same conversation with Nadia, with Theo and with Cecilia. The way things stand–'

'I'm going to match the retainer and offer you double the bonus if Ashleigh comes home safe.'

'No,' Alex said.

'No?' Davis said, his voice a pitch higher. 'You'd take photos of me doggy-styling my mistress through a lodge window, but you won't take my money to save my child?'

'Of course I'll take your money, but only as long as it's exactly the same as Peter and the other parents paid me, on the exact same terms. The last thing I want is to start another bidding war on top of the one you're already having.'

Davis eyed him suspiciously. 'Are you claiming to be decent? Is that what you're doing?'

'I promise to fight for Ashleigh,' Alex said, 'whether you pay me or not. That said, I have a Catholic mother. She buys her peace of mind with prayers, so I understand the value of insurance. You can buy yours with a bank transfer to me and into escrow for the bonus. Have your office contact mine for the contract and details, if that's what you want.'

'Done,' Davis said. 'To mark our new alliance, I'll also send your wife a gift, our best-selling Wench Box. Oh, don't play coy. I insist. Would have sent her the Cop Ensemble, but I understand she already has that one.'

Alex cleared his throat, trying to hide his elation. He didn't mind Davis gloating as though he'd won some sort of victory. With each of the five parents paying a retainer, he was already a million and a half better off. Then, there would be a million-pound bonus for each living child. He would have worked hard for all of them anyway, but these sums – they were colossal. To his clients, of course, they were a pittance.

'Now you're on my payroll,' Davis said, 'give me that briefing, starting with the frontwoman, the one in the video. Surely someone knows her. We find her, we find our children. See, did your job for you.'

'My tech team are good at what they do, especially Gabor. He's the geek you want on your side in a crisis. It took him ten minutes to find her. Her name is Cherry Brightstar.'

'What kind of name is that?'

'Technically, she's called Cherry Brightstar Version 5.8.'

'An AI character?' Davis said. 'Shit. I should have known. I just assumed these socialists would prefer to have their moment of glory in person.'

Alex nodded. 'The video was uploaded through the Tor network and VPNs in an anonymous cross-server route that circumnavigated the globe. We can't track its origin, and there's no helpful metadata. They knew exactly what we were doing. The video's a dead end.'

'Buggery,' Davis said. 'What else?'

'I'm more optimistic about phone tracking. All of your children's phones went dead where they were kidnapped, probably destroyed – except for Emily who didn't have one, but we know the exact time and place where she was taken. Gabor is using an advanced tracking model to locate any other devices that might have been present in more than one of those locations at the time your kids disappeared.'

'So you're looking for… What are you looking for?'

'If we find the same phone signature in at least two of the abduction spots, there's a good chance it's one of the kidnappers. Wherever that other device is now could lead us to them and hopefully to your daughter.'

'Will the police be doing the same thing?'

'Potentially, but they have to deal with a mountain of bureaucracy just to get data from the mobile companies. I'd say we're well ahead. The police, for their part, are looking at CCTV around the abduction points. That'll take time. CCTV always does. The vehicles the kidnappers used all seemed to disappear without a trace. It's a professional operation. Of that, we're certain.'

'So your tech geek is doing all the work, and you're here eating canapés?'

'Not quite,' Alex said. 'Tech is where it starts, but our net is much wider. I have access to… what did you call it? The Cop Ensemble? The police agreed to share their findings with me, and I've also put together an extraction team, well-trained tough guys. If we get a location, we'll be there in a heartbeat. We're using a company with military-grade surveillance capabilities. If we have a phone to pinpoint, anywhere in the world, they'll be our best chance. Oh, and we're also trying to see if we could get anything from a boot print found on the site of Emily's kidnapping. It's a long shot, but we leave no stone unturned.'

'Do you know how much ransom the other parents are paying?' Davis said.

'I'm bound by the Seal of the Confessional.'

'Anyone mention Beth Grisham to you?' Davis said.

'Beth Grisham?' Alex said, 'The owner of Grisham Media?' He shook his head and made a mental note to look her up, unsure why Davis would ask about the American media mogul.

'All right. All right,' Davis said. 'It was worth a try. Trust Peter to hire someone half-decent.'

Davis looked down at his oversized hands and took five breaths in quick succession. His entire face, which had been tight and disapproving, suddenly sagged. When he looked up again, all his bitter conceit and arrogance were gone, like a mask removed by sleight of hand. His eyes were full of sadness, pleading.

'You want to tell me why we're really here?' Alex said.

'Seems like you're keeping everyone's secrets.'

'The word *discretion* is written in gold letters on my business card,' Alex said, 'and for good reason.'

Davis waited a moment as if considering whether to share his secret. Then, in a low voice, he said, 'Ashleigh is dying. Cancer. She has weeks, maybe days. We only found out a few weeks before she… Before she was taken from me. I…' He choked and covered his eyes with his hands, unable to complete the sentence. He took a handkerchief out of his jacket pocket and blew his nose.

'I'm so sorry. I can't imagine…' Alex said, looking for an appropriate way to complete the sentence but coming up short. *What do you say to a parent whose daughter is dying?* It was a shocking revelation, even under the circumstances. Ashleigh was only twenty-seven. He looked down at his shoes.

'I didn't tell you this for sympathy,' Davis said.

'Why did you tell me?'

'I've seen how these scum operate. They're creating a sophisticated campaign to capture the public's attention, to engage them and make them feel like they're part of their sick Robin Hood fantasy. What if the next round of their "game" isn't just ransom money but also some sort of public vote? If that's the case, and a nosy journalist finds out about the cancer, how do you think the public will react? I'll tell you how. They'll think my daughter is expendable because she's already dying. They'll discard her like she's a reality TV contestant.'

Alex met his eyes and gave him a slow nod. Davis had a point. The kidnappers were ruthless. They seemed to know how to engage the baying mobs of public opinion. Their video had stayed at the top of social media feeds since it had come out.

'I'm only telling you all this,' Davis said, 'because I expect you to find her. No delays. No excuses. Stop at nothing. Ashleigh needs to come home, and she needs to come home now. If you require more money for an expense – any expense – then I'm here, any time, day or night, blank cheque, whatever you need.'

'Understood,' Alex said and got up. 'In that case, please excuse me. I need to get the latest from my team.'

Davis looked up at him, his cocksure bravado entirely gone. His shoulders sagged. He looked fragile, lost, devoid of all his masks. When he spoke, his voice was that of a broken man. 'I'm begging you, Alex. Please find her. I can't lose my daughter. I can't. Not yet. We need more time together. Every minute is precious. She is everything to me.'

SEVENTEEN

Dogged determination

LONDON, 13 AUGUST, 10AM

Home Secretary Nessa Thorns had cancelled her constituency surgery for an urgent return to Whitehall. Her lower back ached as it always did at times of high-stakes stress. She tried to find a comfortable position, shuffling in the back seat of her black ministerial Range Rover as it made its sluggish way through Central London traffic. A hot flush made her reach for her leather briefcase, where she found a bound asylum policy document of just the right thickness to fan herself with. She wondered if she had remembered to apply deodorant that morning. She must have. Had she? She discreetly smelled her armpits. *It's fine. You'll be fine.*

On the radio, a prim-voiced presenter was interviewing Robbie Sage, the trade union representative for the employees at Hammerson Oil. 'Our employees' advice to Peter Hammerson,' Robbie Sage said in a broad Yorkshire accent, 'is that he should pay – and pay generously. What are a few million to him, a few hundred million, a few billion – especially if they're going to good causes, *and* they could save his daughter. Give as much as you can, Peter, and pay no heed to the government's silly games. If you show yourself to be generous, and the government moves against you, please know that all of us at Hammerson Oil, *all of us*, will stand by your side. Go on, Peter, dig deep.'

Trafalgar Square was heaving with demonstrators, many wearing Robin Hood hats or costumes alongside a sprinkling of Friar Tucks and Maid Marians. Their placards bore variations on the same theme: *Robinistas unite!, Death to Capitalism, Government = real terrorists!, Let the pigs pay.* A riotous racket rose in a sinister wall of sound: megaphone cries, tambourines, rattles and whistles. Flares amidst the crowd launched smoke pillars in yellow, red and blue. The air was alive with the acrid smell of sulphur. The scene felt to Nessa like a raucous festival that might turn feral at any moment. Mounted police officers positioned their horses on the sidelines while their colleagues in riot gear readied for cordons.

At a traffic light stop, a scrawny woman with dirty dreadlocks and a vintage floral dress approached the vehicle. She screwed up her pockmarked face and thumped menacingly on the car's window with both fists while trying to peer in. Nessa felt a jolt of fright, causing her to almost jump out of her skin. Then she remembered the car's windows were bulletproof and fully tinted. Still, she looked away and rushed to put on her sunglasses. Mercifully, the woman became distracted, perhaps by someone calling for her, and moved away, skipping and shrieking and windmilling her arms, her dress swaying about her like a windsock.

Nessa took three deep, elaborate breaths, the way her yoga teacher had taught her, and tried to calm herself, resolving not to let the sight of the protestors affect her. But then she saw it – the abomination – and her hand rushed to her mouth. In the midst of the crowd stood an eight-foot effigy with a picture of *her* face stapled to its head. It was stuffed with straw and dressed in gold finery and a villain's dark cape. A misshapen wig on its head was clearly intended to approximate Nessa's straight, black hair, though it made the figure look like a scarecrow in drag. A banner draped over its chest read: *Sheriff of Nottingham*. An arrow with silver fletching had been used to pierce its heart. Dark-red paint dripped from the wound, or at least she hoped it was paint.

A cheer rose from the crowd as a topless, tattooed man with a broken nose and shaven head approached the strung-up figure. In his hand, which was held up high for the crowd's adulation, was a box of oversized matches. He grinned and bowed to his baying audience. Then, he lit a match.

'Don't look, ma'am,' the driver said to her. 'We'll be at Number 10 before you know it.'

Nessa did not expect her tenure as Home Secretary to be so bloody difficult. She had envisioned a job that – par for the course – came with hostile media interviews and unruly civil servants, but those were to be balanced by a cushion of excellent perks and opulent state banquets. It was supposed to be her opportunity to win the nation's respect in one of the UK's Great Offices of State, leaving her mark, righting some wrongs, making her parents proud. What she hadn't expected was a level of hatred that would have her likeness burned in outrage. They didn't know her, and yet they judged her so harshly as if she had become the people's enemy. Perhaps she should have stayed in the government's back benches, taking long holidays and writing many more letters on behalf of hard-done-by constituents. And yet… the allure of the bigger job of Home Secretary, offered to her following a reshuffle after yet another government cock-up, had drawn her like a cat to catnip, or maybe, she now thought, like a moth to the deceptive flame of a sweet-scented candle.

'They're asking for your head,' the Prime Minister said as they settled into their chairs in his office at Number 10 Downing Street. 'Should I give it to them?'

'That sly Peter Hammerson,' Nessa said.

'I have to tell you,' the Prime Minister said, 'I admire the guy. What a well-executed manoeuvre. And the mention of your dog…' He chuckled. 'An epic masterstroke. The man's a genius. Did you really say that?'

'Of course not. The dognapping was all Tom Smith. Sometimes he lets his mouth run away from him. Honestly, I could kill him. Could I borrow your firing squad?'

'I'd gladly oblige if I had one, but…' He tapped his finger on his cheek. 'Firing squads are unpredictable. Once you start using them, God knows who'll be next. Us, maybe? Well, all things considered, not so much us as you, and thank you in advance, by the way.'

She did her best to hide her irritation. 'I did what you asked, Robert. I kept your name out of it, but where does that leave me?'

He took off his glasses and held them by the tips of their temples, giving Nessa his warm, fatherly look, the look every minister in his government feared. 'It was the Cabinet's decision, and you are part of the Cabinet. That's what collective responsibility means.'

'I understand,' she said. 'I really do. Still…'

'Yes?' the Prime Minister said.

'You know very well I was against this strategy from the start. I told you the terrorism designation was a dreadful idea, *dreadful*.'

'And like the outstanding team player you are, you fronted it for us, performing your duty as Home Secretary with finesse and skill. A team protects its own as long as you play for the team, right?'

'Of course,' she said.

'Then I'm grateful for your loyalty.' He gave her his wide electoral smile.

She clicked her tongue and looked down, unable to smile back. Then, against her better political judgement, she shook her head.

'Aww, still sore?' he said. 'What will you have me do, Nessa?'

'Can I at least give you my perspective?'

'I'm sure you're going to.'

'We should rescind the designation order, and we should do it now before they kill the hostages. The wind has changed direction. We should adjust our sails.'

'Wind and sails, eh?' He shook his head. 'You know I hate U-turns. They make us look weak.'

'The payment deadline is in two and a half hours,' Nessa said. 'Then we'll have to defend televised funerals, and the kidnappers won't pay a single pound to charity. Everyone loses. We end up in the worst possible position – and that, Robert, won't make us look strong. It could sink this government.'

'Could it?' He brushed a piece of fluff from his shoulder. 'I hate to say this, Nessa, but sometimes you're as naive as my wife. The deaths will be a terrible, terrible tragedy, entirely of the kidnappers' making. The government will convey its deepest sympathies to the families. The world is a dangerous place, and we don't negotiate with terrorists.'

'You and I both know that's not true,' Nessa said, 'and so will the electorate.'

'Look at it this way,' he said, putting on an air of benevolent patience, 'suppose we rescinded the order. Four of the five hostages would die anyway, right? Charities are then given this tainted money. We'd effectively be paving the way for more abductions in the future. History will judge us as the spineless government that gave in.' He hardened his tone. 'It's the job of governments to help the poor and sick. It certainly isn't the purview of vigilante groups. What next? Militia replacing police, because their brand of tough justice is more effective?'

'That's Christmas cracker politics,' Nessa said. 'The public mood, it's… The BBC is interviewing professors about the Trolley Problem. The consensus in the polls is overwhelmingly in favour of saving the many and ideally a hostage too.'

The Prime Minister looked confused. 'You're an odd one,' he said. 'Trolleys?'

She cleared her throat but said nothing. She did not wish to risk alienating the Prime Minister further by explaining how the Trolley Problem was a thought experiment taught to first-year ethics students. It asks whether a bystander should intervene to divert a hurtling trolley car that is destined to kill five people onto another track – an act that would cause the death of only one. When it came to the kidnappings, the implied question was clear: *would saving the many justify allowing the death of a few?* The cocky PM appeared lacking in his knowledge of ethics, not to mention, Nessa decided, in their application.

'Anyway, consider the alternative, Nessa. No money is paid. This sorry saga ends in a few days. All we have to do then is stay on message: the greedy terrorists were never going to support good causes. We're already leaking to select journalists that we have classified intelligence to prove it. We'll say we called their bluff, and they reacted by showing their true nature: heartless murderers. Bottom line, by next year's election, the voters will have moved on. Have you read the asylum policy white paper? That should set the cat amongst the pigeons. The art of distraction. That's what accomplished magicians and politicians do.'

'They were burning my effigy, Robert.'

He crossed his arms over his chest. 'You're made of loyalty and steel. A strong Home Secretary who does what's required. That's why I chose you. Are you going to make me regret it?'

Nessa's eyes traced the intricate patterns on the room's Persian rug. Once more, she couldn't look him in the eye. 'So that's your final decision?'

'Final and conclusive. The Cabinet met earlier.'

'You met without me?'

'Scheduling conflicts. Your office said you'd take a while to get here. You'll be pleased to know that the Foreign Secretary praised how you've handled this. The Chancellor suggested we provide armed protection for your dog.'

Nessa felt the first flashes of an oncoming migraine and had to focus on her facial muscles to keep them in check. The sequence of events to come was clear. In fact, it had already started by excluding her from the Cabinet meeting. Once the crisis was over, the public will be unlikely to buy what the government planned to sell them: a show of force against callous villains. Peter Hammerson had seen to that with his interview. The only way to appease them would be a ritual sacrifice to cleanse the government of the whole affair. Blame, purge and move on. Nessa would find herself shuffled out of the Home Secretary's office. By the next election, she would lose her seat. The tabloids will forever refer to her as *disgraced* and *cruel*, as *the Nessa Thorns in the government's side*.

The Prime Minister rose from his seat, and Nessa did the same, feeling unsteady on her feet. He offered her his hand. 'Thank you for coming to see me, Home Secretary. Give my regards to your dog. What was his name?'

She shook his proffered hand and looked at him with unblinking eyes. 'He's a she. I named her Roberta, after you, sir. Turns out she's an obstinate bitch.'

The Prime Minister angled his head, his facial muscles

tightening, but only by a fraction. For a moment, he seemed like he was going to say something, but then he just gave another one of his winning, insincere smiles.

Nessa withdrew her hand and left him, working hard to look casual. She imagined the daggers of his unforgiving eyes stabbing her in the back.

EIGHTEEN

The last ditch

The meeting room in the Cabinet Office was small and generic, but it would have to do. Nessa had no time to waste. She had pulled rank to book it, waving aside the protests of a cigarette-scented civil servant with the manners of a Dickensian old fart who looked like he had been in his role since the Glorious Revolution. He gave her a scathing stare and a contemptuous click of his heels before strutting away.

Nessa took two migraine pills and pretended to read the topmost document in the pile of papers on the table before her, using a red fountain pen to add unnecessary underlines to random adjectives. From the conference phone speaker came the trickling sound of Tom Smith pouring water, or it might have been whisky. Probably the latter. Nessa couldn't blame him. But for her migraine, she herself would not have minded a double gin, or an entire bottle. Lucy Clifford MP was scrolling through her phone, looking untroubled.

In a clumsy entrance, all hands and apologetic gestures, Undersecretary James Lockerby burst into the room, the nostrils of his beak-like nose flaring in what Nessa hoped was embarrassment or a sign of respiratory distress. *I don't have time for this*, she thought. *Less than an hour to go before the deadline. Every minute counts.* She wished she hadn't invited him in the first place, but beneath his ungainly appearance and stuttering feebleness, James sometimes came up with nuggets that were worth listening to. She needed all the help she could get.

'Thank you for gracing us with your presence,' Nessa said.

'Apologies,' James said. 'The meeting about the free eye test benefit overran. Apparently, everyone in the Civil Service needed their eyes checked last quarter. We skidded well over budget.'

'Explains the sharp drop in the quality of their reports,' Lucy Clifford said without raising her eyes from her phone.

'Please sit,' Nessa said to James, holding on to a tiny semblance of patience. 'You know Lucy, and on the line we have my Special Adviser, Tom Smith.' James was barely in his seat when she continued. 'Lucy: kidnappings, do us the honour, brief. *In brief*, please.'

Lucy Clifford, the rising star Member of Parliament for Mid Derbyshire, reluctantly put down her phone and adjusted the sleeves of her black power-suit jacket. She addressed the room in an annoyingly competent voice, enunciating every word, speaking slowly and stretching Nessa's restraint near to breaking point. 'Police and security services are no further forward on locating the abductees. We're all aware of the prevailing public sentiment. Even the media outlets right-of-field are running stories about haves and have-nots. Looks like overnight we've turned into a socialist country. With the order designating the kidnappers as terrorists, we are seen as the villains of the piece. That said, the government's strategy is solid: stop any payments, meaning the Robinistas will have no benevolent hoods to hide under. The victims will perish and with them the public's sentiment against us.'

'You agree with this strategy?' Nessa said.

With perfectly manicured fingers, Lucy fondled her

necklace of overlarge pearls. 'That's the Cabinet's decision. When I spoke to the Prime Minister earlier, he was very clear about the line we're taking.'

'That wasn't my question,' Nessa said. She could see the political hunger in the woman's eyes. With her sharp mind and eloquence and her perfect shampoo-ad hair, Lucy Clifford was already making waves salty enough to catapult her from junior minister to a top job. Worse still, if the PM had met her today, it was clear the runes have spoken. She was the perfect candidate for Home Secretary, polished and presentable and ready to pounce at the very second Nessa was binned in disgrace.

'What's this meeting actually about?' Lucy said. 'In terms of next steps, our instructions are clear: condemn in the weakest terms and keep a low profile. I can't see there's much to discuss. And all the parents in this saga are new money, which makes the whole scenario twice as easy.'

'I beg your pardon?' James said.

She sighed as if having to indulge an overcurious child. 'Old money and landed gentry may be unpopular on the surface, but deep down the British public is deeply invested in them. The *nouveau riche*, on the other hand, are seen as uncouth, even by Mrs Muggins of Scunthorpe. The – soon to pass – sympathy you're seeing on the streets is for the terrorists, not the abductees. A few dead rich kids from the wrong class aren't going to draw too many tears. Works out so much better for our re-election prospects.'

'Is that what you really think?' James half said, half hissed at her.

'Calm down, dear,' Lucy said. 'You'll give yourself a heart attack.'

Nessa cleared her throat and turned to the triangular conferencing phone. 'Tom, any further thoughts about the backlash?'

'Well, there's campaign funding, for one,' Tom said. 'Four of the five billionaires are major donors to the party. Come the general election, our campaign budget will suffer.'

'Which one isn't a donor?' Nessa said.

'Dildo Davis,' Lucy answered for him, 'but the PM has considered this already. When this boils over, and no money is paid to charity, the backlash against the kidnappers will bury any sympathy for them. They'll just end up being terrorists who killed some moneyed heirs. Our government will prove itself strong and principled. The benefits will far outweigh any losses in campaign budget. The people will support us, simple as. All's well that ends well.'

'Are we really that callous?' James said.

'We send soldiers to war,' Lucy said, 'knowing some will die. Same principle applies. The country has to come first. If we give in to terrorists, the long-term effects are going to haunt us for decades.'

'Soldiers at war,' James said, his nose flaring again, 'are not civilians taken by force. For the life of me, I can't get my head around it. The news media was debating whether the sacrifice of a few was justified to save thousands or millions, and here we still sit, in our ivory tower, deciding to choose the worst possible outcome: blood on our hands. Our constituents who, may I remind you, voted us into government – they'll be justified to judge us for it.'

'Oh, give it a rest,' Lucy said to James.

'It's immoral, and it's wrong,' James said. 'Immoral and plain wrong.'

Lucy responded to his outburst with renewed composure. 'When we started this meeting, I asked the Home Secretary what we're here to discuss. With all due respect, James, I don't think it's helpful to relitigate a Cabinet decision that's firm and final. The government will not change its mind. The Terrorism

Designation Order has already been signed. If we're here for a philosophical debate, then–'

Nessa interrupted her. 'You're right. This meeting was a waste of time. I'm sorry to have dragged you in here. James, Lucy, thank you for coming. Could you leave me to wrap things up with Tom?'

Lucy Clifford stood to leave, a whiff of her expensive cologne filling the room. At the door, she gave Nessa a condescending smile, showing off her unnaturally white teeth. 'A pleasure as always, Home Secretary. The Prime Minister assures me you are loyal to a fault. It could have been his effigy being burnt out there. Make no mistake. He is grateful for your continued and unwavering support.'

James Lockerby muttered something in anger under his breath and nearly tripped over his feet while storming out with a slam of the door.

Nessa leaned forward and spoke to the phone. 'Tom, you still there?'

'Did Lucy Clifford just threaten you?' Tom said.

'Her master's voice,' Nessa said. 'I reckon she's already looking at fabric samples to replace the curtains in my office. I wanted to shove her in a canon and fire her from the battlements, but then…' She paused. In a thoughtful voice, she added, 'But then I listened, and things became a little clearer.'

'Yeah,' Tom said. 'I listened too. The PM's heels are dug in and cemented. I'm sorry, Nessa. We have to face reality. It's too late in the day to do anything. The brainstorming meeting was a good effort, but–'

'Actually, it was an excellent meeting.'

'I don't follow.'

'Lucy was good value. Without realising it, she might have just turned blood into wine.'

'How's that?'

'She said the Terrorism Designation Order has already

been signed.' Nessa rifled through her papers and found the order. 'I have it here in front of me. Nope. No signature. Not yet.'

'I hate to shatter your adorable delusions of grandeur,' Tom said, 'but your signature is just a formality. After Peter Hammerson's interview, the government was forced to make an official announcement. The order is effectively in place, whether you sign it or not. It's done, Nessa. It's out of your hands.'

'And I thought you were clever. Of course, I'll sign it. I'll sign it and time my signature: five minutes past one. Any payments sent before then will be legal. If the parents break the law in the second round, we can come after them, but by then, the kidnappers will have had their money. I know it's not a given they'll pay it to charities, but...' She laid her pen on the designation order and laced her fingers. 'If they do prove to be benevolent, the political picture will have changed completely.'

'Blimey,' Tom said. 'That is shrewd. Remind me why we never made a couple?'

'You're a drunken cad, Tom. I'm lonely, not desperate.'

'I've been called worse,' Tom said. 'It's a massive risk, you know.'

'I know.'

'When the PM finds out what you've done, he'll have kittens. But then... If this works, his position may well become untenable.'

'You'll tell the parents?'

'I will,' he said, 'even though they hate my guts.'

'They'll love you now,' she said.

'That may be so,' he said, 'but listen, Nessa. I hesitate to throw a hamster in the works, but there's only forty minutes left before the deadline. When I spoke to Nadia Sayal about, you know, the sensitive thing we discussed, she showed me the email she got from the kidnappers. Looks like they created their own cryptocurrency to avoid any limits on the amounts they receive. I don't know how sophisticated it is, but–'

'To the point, Tom. We don't have time for a TED talk.'

'You should know that with complex crypto systems, large payments can sometimes get delayed, very delayed, even. If the parents send money now, it's possible the kidnappers won't get it by the deadline. If their payments get stalled in the system, they could linger for a while. Result: all the hostages are killed by default.'

'Then make the call already,' she said, 'and Tom, after the deadline, please leak my late signature to the press. Do it off the record. *Sources close to the matter.*'

'All right.'

'Now go.' She clicked on the phone to disconnect the call, closed her eyes and lowered her cheek to rest on the cool table. Her migraine was back, shards of agony lancing through her temples, but there was also relief. With her focus solely on the pain, the cruel outside world had become imperceptive. She'll rest until five past one, and then she'll sign the order and call for her driver, vindicated and condemned by her actions, having to face whatever consequences followed.

NINETEEN

The masked executioner

Noah felt numb, dazed, his hand on his mouth, unable to move, staring with horror at the video feed from the beach, which was being streamed live to the basement's TV screen. They were not let out to watch the execution. The thought of Emily facing her death alone without a friendly face horrified him. He would have liked to see her in person, one more time, one final time, even if it meant being there for the horror that was to follow.

In the frame, they could see Emily bound to a wooden stake, her mouth gagged, the sea behind her. The high-definition video showed the details of the thick nautical hemp rope that encircled her shins, her thighs, her midriff and chest. In the grey nun's habit, she looked like a mediaeval martyr, awaiting her cruel, unjust death. Her face was devoid of emotion, lacking in fear. Noah focused on her eyes, which were soft with acceptance. Emily was the bravest person he knew. What would his reaction have been if they had tied him to the stake instead of her? He'd probably close his eyes, sink deep into his thoughts, and wait for it to be over.

Two of the guards arrived at the beach, pushing

wheelbarrows full of wood logs and kindling. They set the kindling at the base of the stake, then arranged the logs in a pyramid over it.

'Animals,' Ashleigh whispered.

Nobody else spoke. Noah felt like he was about to be sick, but he couldn't take his eyes off the screen. The revolting images paralysed him.

Two more wheelbarrows delivered longer logs that were added to the pyre, reaching Emily's waist.

Bill appeared at Emily's side. 'Are we all ready?' he said to someone out of shot.

The marine, Cody, came into view, holding a jerrycan. 'Just need the kero now, sir.' His voice came through clear and loud on the screen's speakers. He doused the wood and then encircled Emily, pouring liquid over her in rapid spatters.

Emily squirmed at what must have been the noxious smell of the accelerant, yet her expression remained peaceful. *My brave sister*, Noah thought. *My poor, brave sister.*

'Don't forget the props, sir,' Cody said to Bill.

Bill lowered a backpack onto the sand and rummaged inside it. He brought out Guy Fawkes masks, cloaks and Robin Hood hats. He handed one set to Cody, then donned the costume and threw his cane aside, out of the camera's view.

Cody disappeared, then reappeared clad in his costume. In his hand, he held a two-foot stick with cloth wrapped around its end: an executioner's torch. He raised the stick and put a lighter to the cloth. The fire took immediately. A thick plume of smoke rose from his torch to the heavens. He held it high, came to stand beside Emily and nodded to Bill.

Emily's face contorted. No longer calm, she seemed to be trying to speak, to shout, to cry out through her gag, but all the microphone picked up was desperate, muffled grunts.

Bill spoke to the camera, seeming to address the captives in the basement. 'As we have received no further ransom payments by the time of the deadline set for your parents, we will now sadly part ways with Emily Hammerson. Once we share the video of her demise, I can guarantee you this: the rest of your parents will reach for their digital wallets. I know you hate us now, but if you survive, you will understand. We do not take this action with glee. It is a sombre day indeed.'

'Bastard,' Noah muttered.

'Sometimes,' Bill continued, 'painful means are required for the greater good.' He seemed to think about this for a few seconds, then looked at the camera again. 'On reflection, we will not inflict unnecessary cruelty. You will not have to watch like your parents will. Cut the connection.'

The camera's feed ended abruptly, leaving only a black screen with the *Lorem Ipsum* logo.

Noah felt his feet buckle and his vision blur. He had a vague notion of falling, a sense of the coolness of the floor and then blessed oblivion. He dreamed of a picnic on a beach in Hawaii: Peter Hammerson serving cold bottles of beer, Noah's mother laying out a spread of artisan bread, cold meats and assorted cheeses. Noah picks up a bowl of Manzanilla olives stuffed with pimientos and offers it to Emily. She takes one, lobs it in her mouth and smiles as she chews. Her brother, Brendan – *my half brother* – is there, running around them, throwing sand in the air, laughing. Then, the dream corrects itself from Noah's memories. Brendan is in a wheelchair. Emily passes him the olives. Everyone smiles. A sunny day. A newly united family enjoying a happy outing.

TWENTY

Requiem for a nun

UNDISCLOSED LOCATION, 13 - 14 AUGUST

Noah's hand trembled as he held it over the back of his damp neck and gazed out from the villa's veranda. In the dark gloom of the sea, waves had become shadows, their frothy edges outlined by the meagre light of the rising moon. His eyes drifted to the right, but then he forced them back, away from the horror. At the furthest end of the beach, the flaming remains of the pyre still roared, sending occasional sparks and tentacles of smoke into the heavens, accelerated by the risen wind.

Standing beside him, like a line of sentries, were his three classmates, silent in the face of the unspeakable crime. Without the need for words, they each placed their arms around the person next to them. Noah stood stiffly between Zayn and Ashleigh's bony figure.

Jonny unlaced himself from the group and slumped to sit on the veranda's steps. Before long, he got up again, brushed the dust off his shorts and leaned his back on the veranda's handrail, facing his classmates. He placed his hands in his pockets and glared at them. 'I can't get my head around it,' he said. 'Why didn't they pay?'

'What?' Noah mumbled.

'Ashleigh's dad sent them ransom. If Davis Boroughs had the guts to stand up to the government, why didn't Emily's dad, or mine?' He looked at Noah, then Zayn. 'Or your mothers. What kind of parent leaves their kid to die? I mean, Emily's dad literally killed her – literally – and he's got more money than the rest of us.'

'Jonny, please,' Zayn said, 'now's not the time.'

Jonny ignored him. 'My dad, the eminent lawyer, Theo Salt, first of his name – he always finds a solution to everything, and yet, when it came to saving me…'

'You're still alive, you fat fuck,' Ashleigh said.

'So are you, miss skinny shrew,' Jonny said.

'For a week or two, if I'm lucky,' Ashleigh said.

'The cancer card again?' Jonny said. 'You got any others?'

'You know,' Ashleigh said, 'I'm feeling remarkably good for a walking corpse. They say that sometimes, before you die, you start feeling better again, just to give you a last chance to appreciate life, or maybe to sweeten the pill. That's how I feel today.' She gazed up to the sky. 'Emily, darling. I might just join you in heaven tonight.' She looked at Noah. 'You going to faint again? You look pale.'

Noah barely registered Ashleigh's words. The world around him had blurred, the night pressing down on him, like the avalanche of ice and snow in the scenario in which he sacrificed himself to save his mother. She would do anything for him. Why hadn't she? And why hadn't his father, the father who was also Emily's? A vision of his newly discovered sister flashed in his mind. *What a terrible death, fire.* He couldn't help but imagine the rising flames, the burning flesh, her gagged screams. He felt himself breaking, smashed into a thousand burning pieces, branded by grief and anger. A grunt of pain escaped him, and then he let himself go, howling breathy sobs, his face smeared with tears and salty snot. His feet melted from under him. If Zayn hadn't propped him up with his tree-trunk arms, he would have fallen, shattered into nothing.

Ashleigh let go of him, and Zayn took control, holding him close, patting his hair. 'It's okay, buddy. Let it all out.'

'She's gone,' Noah said.

'I know,' Zayn said. 'I know.'

'He loved her?' Jonny said. 'I mean, like that? I never knew.'

'Shut up, Jonny,' Ashleigh said.

Noah whispered into Zayn's shoulder, 'I'll kill them.'

'All right,' Zayn said, 'but first, let's go inside, get some food and water into you.'

Noah shook his head.

'Good idea,' Jonny said. 'The fuckers arranged a funeral spread for us. Might as well eat it.' He walked back into the house, his hands still in his pockets. Ashleigh followed.

Zayn cupped Noah's wet cheeks in his hands. 'Come on, chump. We'll go inside, we'll sit down, and we'll remember her, okay? She would have wanted you to eat.'

'She doesn't want anything,' Noah said. 'Not any more.' Still, he let Zayn guide him, his head lowered, his shoulders slumped, barely seeing, barely caring, stunned. They joined Ashleigh and Jonny at the dining table, upon which were sandwiches, bowls of smelly prawn-flavoured crisps and bottles of fizzy orange drink.

The basic meal had been there when they emerged from the basement. Cody had unbolted and opened the basement's heavy door, refusing to answer questions. Instead, he offered only a simple statement, 'It's all over, folks. You can come out now.' Then, he turned away and left them to stand at the bottom of the stairs, unsure, fearful of what they might find if they ventured up. When, a few dreadful moments later, they climbed back into the world, they walked out single-file to the veranda and witnessed for themselves the terror of the burning pyre.

At the table, Jonny poured drinks into plastic cups and handed out soggy cheese and tomato sandwiches. Noah refused both food and drink. Zayn placed a cup in front of him anyway.

Jonny devoured his sandwich, then added another to the plate before him. 'I wanted to say that I'm sorry,' he said. 'You all volunteered to go up there. I'm not proud of myself that I didn't.'

Ashleigh burst into scornful laughter that was much too loud. 'Hilarious,' she said and blew her nose into a napkin.

'No need to make it worse,' Jonny said.

'Oh, really?' Ashleigh said. 'I think there's every need.'

'I have a kid,' Jonny said.

'And a wife,' Ashleigh said. 'Don't forget your lovely wife. Makes your stupid argument sound better.' She dropped an octave, imitating him. 'I love my kid and my wife, so I decided I'm worth more than the rest of you. I couldn't die today.'

'It's not like you, Miss Boroughs, were ever at risk, all right?'

'Stop talking,' Ashleigh said.

'This isn't helping,' Zayn said.

'Actually, it is,' Ashleigh said. 'Trust my dad to pay the ransom so I can spend quality time away with my cancer, an entourage of schoolmates and a homicidal German prince.' She took a tiny bite of her sandwich, chewed, and swallowed. She cleared her throat, looked like she was going to say something more, but then seemed to think better of it.

Noah forced himself to drink some of the orange fizz. It tasted chemical and vile. He put the cup down but still squeezed it between his fingers. 'Evil bastards,' he said. The words came out with such anger that he bit his tongue, a second time that day. The welcome pain and taste of blood distracted him long enough to see reason and to remember Zayn's earlier warning about cameras. *They* might be watching, and listening. He stopped himself from saying what he thought they should do next: make a plan, attack their captors, avenge Emily, give the brutal killers a taste of their own medicine. Once again, as he'd done a thousand times that day, he imagined grabbing Cody's gun and spraying bullets into him – and into Bill and Marian – until they lay bloodied on the floor. Then he remembered the threat to his mother. He put down the plastic cup and covered his eyes with his hands. His head felt heavy. Waves of chills and bitter stomach churns made him feel ill.

'I'm sorry about Emily,' Jonny said to Noah. 'We used to hang out at school. She was a sassy one, a real rebel. Remember the school trip to Parliament? After it ended, she decided to take the Tube to Leicester Square. Mr Crampton-Hughes nearly had an aneurysm.' Jonny rounded his lips and made a passable impression of their former headmaster. 'Pupils at our school never take the Underground like plebs. It's unbecoming. Take a car, a helicopter, a horse-drawn carriage if you must, but not the filthy Tube. What would your father think, Miss Hammerson?'

'If we're doing eulogies,' Ashleigh said. 'Might as well do mine now, while I'm still around for a day or two.'

'Ashleigh Boroughs,' Jonny said, 'possibly an accomplished novelist, the voice of a generation. Sadly, we'll never know.'

Ashleigh's face blanched a ghostly white. She nodded and spoke in a tiny voice. 'I would have liked a stab at it, even just to finish the manuscript. That's all I wanted, to write *The End*. But there's no time left. It's run out on me.'

A sudden gust of wind rose outside, its whooshing sound blowing through the open door. A piece of cloth landed on the veranda's floor next to the entrance. Zayn rushed out and knelt to grasp it before it flew away. He raised it to the light. It was a piece of cloth from Emily's habit, its edges charred.

Noah caught his breath and held it.

Jonny stood, grabbed his plate, rushed to load it with two more sandwiches and a fist of crisps. 'I'll be in my room,' he said. Without looking at them, he escaped up the stairs.

When Jonny was gone, Ashleigh came to stand by Noah and patted his hair as you would a dog's. 'It should have been me,' she said. 'I'm so done with all this.' She, too, headed up to her bedroom.

Noah was barely aware of Zayn still sitting next to him. Time constricted and stretched. Hours and minutes were meaningless against his grief. He recognised the physical sensations, knew them well from the time of his father's death, the overwhelming depths of loss that cramped the stomach and tensed the nerves and made his body feel leaden.

At some point in the night, Zayn guided him up to his room, helped him into bed, took off his loafers and left him to stare into the darkness, to recall his memories of Emily's face, of their final conversation, of her look of pity when she spoke to him. *Was it pity? Does it matter now?* It mattered to him.

———

When dawn finally came, its nascent light brought no comfort. Noah was unsure if he had slept at all. He forced himself into the shower and stood under the steaming spray until his skin was lobster red. A thread of thought niggled at him, niggled and prodded and probed until he acknowledged it. *What if Emily hadn't died? We didn't go to the pyre. We didn't see her burnt body with our own eyes.* He imagined her greeting him downstairs. 'I was tired, so I went to my room to sleep. Didn't realise they'd let you out of the basement.' He imagined being angry with her. 'What were you thinking, letting us mourn you?' Then he'd hold her tight until she protested. 'I'm fine, Noah. Let go. I'm fine.'

With sudden, urgent purpose, he dressed himself in clean clothes, struggling with the shirt's buttons, rejecting the time it would take to put on shoes. Barefooted, he rushed down to the villa's front room.

Emily was not there.

He looked up at the bedrooms and recalled which room Jonny had gone into and which was Ashleigh's. Zayn had gone to his own room the previous day to fetch a clean shirt. The remaining doors were for his bedroom and Emily's. He sped up the stairs, nearly tripping, wishing, praying, hoping. With a sweaty palm, he grasped the doorknob to her bedroom, imagining her there, unharmed: 'Hi, Noah. You look disturbed. You thought what? They didn't tell you?'

He held his breath and slowly turned the doorknob. *Please, God!*

The room was identical to his own. Like his deflated spirit, it was bare of hope and bare of Emily. He thought back to the charred piece of her nun's habit, lying on the dining table like an executioner's confession. He shook his head and found himself on the floor, hugging himself and taking shallow breaths. *A foolish hope, that's all it was.* As his racing mind settled, another thought occurred to him. There was a twisted logic in what had happened. Peter Hammerson was the richest of the parents. If the kidnappers knew Peter had two horses in the race, two kidnapped children, they could afford to rid themselves of one. They'd demand of him the same ransom as they'd force out of Noah's mother. But then, wasn't it Emily who volunteered herself? And how could they possibly know she was his sister?

He walked down to the villa's front room, holding on to the handrail for support. When he reached the bottom of the stairs, the smell of toast distracted him. Jonny and Zayn came out of the kitchen with trays bearing breakfast: white bread toast, jams, spreads, a pot of coffee.

'Come sit with us,' Jonny said. 'Sorry to report, we're still on the same diet: bread and spreads. The coffee's instant.'

'Morning, chump,' Zayn said. 'What's that?'

'What's what?' Noah said.

On the table, held down by a vase, was a sheet of paper. Zayn grabbed it, turned it over and scanned its content. 'It's from Ashleigh, damn it!' He handed it to Noah.

Hi guys,

I've had enough. Might as well not wait for the inevitable. I feel well today and strong enough to end this stupid field trip on a high note while I still can. Might not be an option later. Cancer is an evil bitch. I won't wait to let her win.

Remember me from time to time. Not many will.

I hope you make it. Say hi to my dad. Tell him I died happy. Sometimes it's better to lie.

Ashleigh xxx

TWENTY-ONE

The constellation of Cancer

UNDISCLOSED LOCATION, 14 AUGUST

Noah and Jonny could barely keep up with Zayn's sprint-like pace, but they persevered, their breathing laboured, occasionally stopping to bend forward, their hands on their knees, wheezing for air. In the shadow of his grief for Emily, Noah had no capacity for more bad news.

Despite the exertion, running felt like a release. The brain fog that had engulfed him since the previous night lifted a little with every heave of his burning lungs.

They stopped to check the beach first, scanning the sea for any sign of Ashleigh. *Where could she have gone?* In the confines of their prison, between the beach and the electric fence that bordered on the jungle, it was impossible to wander far.

There was no sign of her in the sea, or if she had entered the water, they might have been too late. As Noah looked to his right, he noticed that the stake on which Emily had met her horrible death was gone. Bill's crew must have taken it away in the night. *No time to stop. We have to find Ashleigh.*

Zayn motioned with his hand for them to follow, once again racing ahead. Noah's leg muscles burned from the effort, and his lungs craved more air. A question briefly flitted through his mind: *will they give Emily a proper burial? Will they return her to her dad?* Then, the exertion refocused him. *Run.* Gasp. *Run faster.*

They circled the palms, sprinted around the house and mango tree, then checked under the trees in the sandy area where storm tides had left castaway plastic bottles, nets and a torn car tyre. Nothing. They jogged to the gate at the end of the beach. No sign of her.

Zayn led them along the fence-line, beyond which lay the dense jungle – green, damp, and foreboding – until, at last, they saw her.

They approached Ashleigh carefully, like a team of rangers, mindful not to scare an injured antelope. She was standing with her back to them, barefooted in a white summer dress and a *Lorem Ipsum* baseball cap. She was facing the imposing fence next to the sign that read *Electric fence. Danger of death.* Her hands were raised, fingers outstretched, so close to the chain-link wire, she had only to twitch forward to touch it.

'Ashleigh,' Noah said.

She turned her head and looked at the sorry state of the three of them, panting from the effort, their shirts drenched in sweat. In contrast to their strained faces, she looked calm and cool, as if resigned to what she was about to do.

'Don't be an idiot,' Jonny said, punctuating his words with wheezing breaths. 'Get away from the fence.'

'Shut up, Jonny,' she said with a smile. 'You saved my life once already. You don't get to do it again.'

'Don't be selfish,' Jonny said. 'Step away from the fence.'

'Not helping,' Zayn said to Jonny, then he turned to Ashleigh. 'Can we at least talk before you do this?'

'Thanks for coming,' Ashleigh said. 'There really was no need. Nothing you say will change my mind.'

'Listen,' Noah said.

'Like I have a choice,' Ashleigh said, 'but I'd prefer it if you weren't here, okay? Just leave. You don't want to watch my show, however *electrifying*.' She giggled. No one else did.

'People recover from cancer,' Noah said, trying to inject sincerity into words that sounded hollow even to his own ears. 'Miracles happen. New treatments.'

'Oh, Noah,' Ashleigh said, 'you're such a darling. If I had a twelve-carat emerald for every time someone used that line on stupid internet cancer forums, I'd buy a fleet of aircraft carriers, complete with jets and sexy sailors.' She licked her upper lip. 'Now there's a thought.'

Noah's instinct told him he should not sound desperate. He tried to steady his voice to keep it from shaking. 'We could be home in a few days. Why give up now?'

'I always wondered,' Ashleigh said, 'what if I ignored the invite and hadn't gone to the medical screening? I wouldn't find out I was sick, wouldn't know anything until just before... just before it was time to design my funeral invites. Instead, I got the diagnosis, went through the shock and awe phase, kept my oncologist happy by taking toxic drugs to keep me alive for another five minutes. They were vile, nasty infusions and then vile, nasty pills. Made me grumpy and sad all the time. What's the point, eh? No, really, what was the point?' She wiped her nose with one hand but kept the other within touching distance of the lethal fence. 'And you know the worst side effect? No mention of it on the packaging. I should sue them, really.'

'What?' Noah said, desperate to keep her talking.

'The devil pills kept me alive long enough to be kidnapped, to be here when they burned Emily, to feel so... whatever. If I hadn't taken them, I would have checked out by now. I could have skipped this horrible summer camp. And my dad – the only one who did pay the ransom, mind you – he'd be spared it too, the entire shit shebang.'

'Ash,' Jonny said.

'Don't call me Ash.' She turned to face the fence again.

'Not today. Not until I'm actually ash, which will be very soon.' She sneezed. As she did, her raised hand edged forward, nearly touching the fence. Noah caught his breath in fright.

'Pardon me,' Ashleigh said. 'Now, go away. Bugger off. Save your speeches.'

'I'm a dad,' Jonny said. 'If my son was sick like you, I'd want to be with him at the end. I'd want to hold his hand. Why not give it a few more days?'

'What did I say about speeches?' Ashleigh said.

'The electric fence isn't going anywhere,' Jonny said. 'You can die whenever you like, but please, for now, stop. Come and have a cold drink with us. You don't have to talk if you don't want to.'

Ashleigh looked back at Jonny. 'I bet you're imagining yourself in a Netflix feature,' she said. '*The Lorem Ipsum Five*? It's got a ring to it. You'll dress up in a sharp suit, look into the camera and tell them how you tried to talk Cancer Girl away from being zapped. "She'd made her mind up", you'll say, trying to impress the sexy American producer. "She couldn't bear what they did to Emily, thinking it should have been her instead".'

'I would never do that,' Jonny said. 'I always cared about you. I still do.'

'We respect your decision,' Zayn said to Ashleigh. 'You'll do what you have to do, but there's no rush. Can I tell you a joke?' He didn't wait for an answer. 'An academic, a playboy, a nun and a lawyer's son walk into a bar.'

'You left me out already?' Ashleigh said.

'All right. An academic, a playboy, a nun, an author and a lawyer's son walk into a bar.'

'That's a lot of people for a joke,' Jonny said. Noah shot him a warning look.

'So,' Zayn said, 'they walk into a bar, and the jukebox is playing a song by Nancy Sinatra, *My Baby Shot Me Down*. It's a

Wild West kind of place: cowboy hats, sawdust floor, ladies of the night with too much make-up. And the bartender says, "Guten tag, my friends. My name is Wilhelm. What can I serve you today?"

"'Beer for me and all my friends", the playboy says and tips his hat.

'After the bartender lines up the bottles on the bar, the playboy draws a gun and shoots him. Barely alive, the bartender says, "Why did you do zis? I have served you beer precisely as you required."

'The playboy smiles at him and says…'

Ashleigh looked nonplussed, impatient. 'Excellent set-up,' she said. 'Go on, hit me with your silly punchline.'

Zayn shrugged. 'Still working on it. Come back with us. I should have it ready by lunchtime.'

Ashleigh repaid him with a generous smile. She turned to the fence again, wiped her hands on the sides of her dress, gave them a shake as if casting off water and raised them again in preparation, tapping the air with her fingers.

Noah noticed Zayn taking small steps towards her while she faced away from them. He decided to distract her, give Zayn more time. 'What you're doing is selfish,' he said. 'Emily sacrificed herself. She's died the most horrible death. She did it for us.'

Without turning, Ashleigh said, 'For you. Not for me.'

Zayn was edging closer to her, tiptoeing. He gave Noah a signal, pointing to his mouth and circling his index finger in the air, which Noah took to mean *keep talking*.

'I want to confess something,' Noah said, speaking slowly, buying time. 'It's something I haven't told any of you. It's a little… shocking. It was a shock to me, anyway.'

'Yeah, whatever,' Ashleigh said. She shook her head and looked behind her for the final time.

Zayn was two paces away, not close enough to drag her back.

What followed felt to Noah like action captured in slow motion. Zayn leapt into the air, his arms spread wide, like an eagle in flight. He landed behind Ashleigh, at the same time encircling her with a bear hug that only managed to restrain her upper arms.

It was not enough to stop her from reaching out.

Ashleigh's right hand shot forward, and her fingers wrapped themselves around the fence's wire.

There was a high-pitched rasp, though Noah wasn't sure if it had come from Zayn or Ashleigh. He felt a ringing in his ears. The world came to a standstill. His entire body stiffened, and his hands rushed to his head.

Ashleigh fell back onto the sandy ground on top of Zayn. Zayn still had his arms wrapped around her. He was panting from the effort, panting and alive.

Ashleigh sighed. 'I hate this place. Even the fence doesn't work.' She looked up, wide-eyed, towards the empty sky. After a few seconds of silence, she roared out a crazed, hiccoughing laughter punctuated by words, 'Nothing works. Nothing. I need. To speak. To the manager.'

Zayn released Ashleigh from his grasp and gently pushed her to a sitting position. He got to his feet and pulled her up, though she was reluctant.

Ashleigh slapped Zayn in the face and then hugged him. 'You could have got yourself killed, you raving pot cracker nut twat. Electricity conducts through people, or did you miss that lesson too? Never the brightest spark, eh?' She covered her mouth, again hysterical with laughter. 'Spark, eh? Get it?'

'Jesus Christ almighty,' Jonny said, clutching his chest. 'I thought I was having a heart attack.'

'Well, that would've been unfair to Noah,' Ashleigh said, wiping tears from her cheeks, looking to have regained some of her poise. 'If Zayn and I got electrocuted, and you died of a heart attack, he'd be left all alone with a furious Wilhelm. You okay now?'

'No,' Jonny said, 'but I'll live.'

'Good for you,' Ashleigh said. 'Thank you all for coming to my one-woman show. My sincerest apologies for the slight technical difficulties. Won't happen next time.'

'That's not funny,' Zayn said.

'Actually, it's hilarious,' Ashleigh said. 'You know, Zayn, you and I never hooked up at school. I was pretty back then, wasn't I?'

'You're still pretty,' Zayn said.

She fluttered her lashes at him. 'You think you could do me one last favour?'

Zayn puffed out air but did not answer.

'You'd deny my dying wish? Ugh, men. Never there when you need them. Always there when you don't. Case in point, yeah?'

By now, Noah had had enough, more than enough. He sat on the ground, closed his eyes, hugged his knees and rocked back and forth, oblivious to the chatter around him. After a while, his breathing settled, but he felt broken, hopelessly broken.

'Well, that was a bloody waste of time,' Ashleigh said. 'Don't know why they'd bother putting the signs up about it being electric. It's still a twelve-foot prison fence with razor wire. It's not like we can climb over it. Is there anything for breakfast? I'm starving.'

As they walked back to the villa, through the mist of his overwhelmed thoughts, Noah could hear Zayn saying to Jonny, 'What did Ashleigh mean when she said you saved her life once already?'

'Oh, it's nothing,' Jonny said. 'Figure of speech. Exaggeration.'

TWENTY-TWO

Yet when we came back, late, from the hyacinth garden

Zayn suggested a picnic on the beach, away from any hidden cameras in the house. Noah was grateful for the idea. The inside of the villa felt intolerable to him now, with its oppressive basement where Emily had left them, where they had watched her final moments on the screen before the live feed died. He did not feel talkative, yet he dreaded being alone with his thoughts, with the images of the burning pyre on the beach and, later, the gut-punching fright of Ashleigh's would-be suicide. His university office seemed like a distant memory now. After all that had happened, he could not imagine himself reclining in his office chair, sipping coffee, reading T.S. Eliot, contemplating printed words. Some words still followed him though: *Yet when we came back, late, from the hyacinth garden, your arms full, and your hair wet, I could not speak, and my eyes failed, I was neither living nor dead, and I knew nothing.*

The four of them sat in a circle around plates of cold toast, half-empty spread jars and drink bottles, for what Jonny described as *the worst picnic ever*. Noah settled for the solitary apple that was left in the fruit bowl. It was too ripe and soggy to the bite. Jonny further complained that the bread was stale,

157

and they were running out of food. No one else seemed to care. Noah certainly didn't.

Jonny raised his plastic cup for a toast. 'To Emily.'

The others did the same, and for a long time they were silent. Noah's eyes moistened. A heart-wrenching sense of loss and misery tightened his throat.

At last, Zayn spoke, seeming keen to distract them. 'The sea's so blue. Not quite a six-star resort in the Maldives, but at least there's sand and sun.' He looked at Ashleigh. 'And no one else died.'

'The day's still young,' Ashleigh said.

Zayn shook his head. 'I'm working on a plan,' he said.

'An escape?' Ashleigh said. 'Your jokes are shit, but you're improving.' She placed three fingers on her chin. 'Let's see: high fences, electric or not, CCTV cameras, armed marines.' She turned to Jonny. 'Did I forget anything?'

'A prison island somewhere in a massive ocean,' Jonny said.

'Allegedly,' Zayn said. 'I'm not taking their word for it. We need to get in touch with the police or security services back home. There has to be a way.'

Ashleigh picked up a conch shell from the sand and examined it. She put it to her ear. 'Hello? Could you come get us?' She looked at Zayn and pretended to listen to the response on the other end. 'The Uber submarine is busy.' She handed him the conch. 'You talk to them. You'll do a much better job flirting with conch-centre mermaids.'

Zayn took the shell from her and inspected it. 'What if our parents don't pay the ransom? What if they can't? Wilhelm's militia will pick us off one by one.'

'I'm too fat for insurrections,' Jonny said. 'Ten minutes of cardio, and I'd be dead anyway. After the marathon to look for Ashleigh this morning, I don't think I'll survive another workout.'

'We need a plan,' Zayn insisted. 'I like to always have a plan.'

'You do?' Ashleigh said. 'How come you're here, then? Didn't plan for a kidnapping?'

For the first time, Zayn looked embarrassed. He put the conch down and took a moment to dig a hole in the sand. He placed the conch in the hole and covered it, smoothing the sand over it in broad strokes. 'A sexy actress in LA,' he said at last.

'You mean a female *actor*,' Ashleigh said, 'not *actress*.'

Jonny rubbed the back of his neck. 'Is that *really* the hill you'll die on when a man confesses his inadequacies?'

'Upholding standards to the bitter end,' Ashleigh said.

'Cancer doesn't make you queen of grammar,' Jonny said. 'Let him speak.'

Ashleigh stuck out her tongue at him.

'I met her at a party in West Hollywood,' Zayn said. 'Invites only. Supposedly, everyone was vetted, but Marky's system was rigged. Anyone with a heavy pair skipped the queue and got sent by special delivery straight to the poolside. She took me back to her place in Westwood.'

'An actress, eh?' Jonny said.

Zayn coughed to clear his throat. 'She gave an Oscar-winning performance, stripped to her lingerie and made me a Moscow mule: crushed ice, mint, just the right mix of ginger beer and vodka and roofie. It was going so well, and then... I woke up here.'

'You suffer from a condition called masculine poor judgement and an acute susceptibility to boob hypnosis,' Ashleigh said. 'Still, if karma brings me back, I'd love a chance – even for a little while – to live like you, like a filthy dog, always in heat.'

'That's harsh,' Zayn said.

'I was paying you a compliment,' Ashleigh said. 'Tell me, darling, did any of those girls ever stick?'

'Natalia did,' Zayn said.

'Was that her stripper name?' Jonny said.

Zayn ignored him. 'The goddess of romance and chic,' he said. 'The most beautiful woman I ever met. Her dad's a powerful man in Russia. Loves his daughter, treats her like a princess. They literally stop traffic on major roads in Moscow to let her car pass.' His face transformed to that of a teenager, the Zayn Noah remembered from school. 'One of the best nights of my life was when we went ice skating together on the rink near Paveletsky Station. The air was freezing but dry and so, so crisp. Everything was lit up. It felt like a fairy tale. And there we were, the two of us, together in our warm, fuzzy bubble of love. Nothing else mattered. When we were done skating, we stood in the soft snow by the limo, heavy coats and fur hats and scarves, and we drank marshmallow hot chocolate with vodka and coffee liqueur. It was magical.'

'What happened to Natalia?' Noah said.

'We lasted six months,' Zayn said. 'Then it had to end.'

'What did you do?' Ashleigh said. 'Or *who* did you do? You're such a sperm whale.'

'Wasn't like that. I know you'll think it's odd, but I'm actually a decent guy. I just… I didn't really have a choice in the matter.'

'Poor Natalia,' Ashleigh said.

'Don't make assumptions,' Jonny said.

'Hmm,' Ashleigh said.

Zayn's eyes appeared glassy and out of focus, as if his mind was wandering back in time. Then his mouth relaxed into its usual self-assured grin, showing his dimples. 'You should all come to Saint-Tropez with me,' he said. 'They have this party with dancers in gilded cages, amazing light show, great vibe.

The DJs are insane. It's VIP only. Jacques always has a table ready for me – and for my friends.'

Ashleigh smiled wistfully at him. She tapped his bicep with her fingers, the same way she had tapped the air before grasping the fence. 'It's a nice thought,' she said, 'but you're preaching to the doomed. If they don't kill us, which, let's face it…' The grim faces around her stopped Ashleigh's flow. She shrugged. 'Anyway, my parking ticket's almost up. Noah skulks in his university office most of the time, and Jonny… What are you, Jonny? Happily married?'

'More married than happy,' Jonny said. 'But don't tell my dad. We've got the façade down to an art form. Stage four misery. Sorry, Ashleigh. No offence.'

'Ooh,' Ashleigh said, 'I'll be very offended unless you tell us more.'

'The silver lining,' Jonny said, 'is section five of the prenup. If they kill me, she gets everything. At least this once, I'll make her happy.'

Noah's thoughts gathered to a conclusion that he found reassuring. If he made it out alive, he was going to accept Zayn's invitation. He'd go to the club, drink, even snort stuff if any powder was on offer. It was time for a change. Life was going to be different. It had to be. He opened his mouth to say so when something caught his eye behind Jonny's left shoulder. He tried to speak, but his tongue felt suddenly leaden, stuck to the floor of his mouth.

'What's wrong, Noah?' Ashleigh said. 'You look like you've seen a ghost.'

Unable to answer, he raised his hand and pointed. His three classmates looked to see what had stunned him.

'Emily?' Ashleigh whispered.

They all stared, wide-eyed, at the figure as it got closer. She was striding along the waterline, no longer in her nun's outfit but in yellow shorts and a white T-shirt, her hair blowing gently in the wind. She looked like a happy model in a brochure, the waves lapping at her feet.

'Well, fuck me,' Jonny said. 'Dead nun walking.'

They all got up, still staring. Noah felt an odd out-of-body sensation, as if he were watching the scene from afar.

'You guys all right?' Emily said as she approached them. The words were spoken in such a light, breezy manner that Noah, for all his relief at seeing her alive, felt an almost irresistible urge to punch her in the face.

'You're not dead,' Ashleigh said in a deadpan voice.

'I know,' Emily said. 'Hi.' Still appearing cheerful and untroubled, she came to stand with them, her hands on her hips. 'Our parents paid the ransom.' She met Noah's eyes. He stared at her with blank intensity. 'I'm sorry if…' she said, then faltered. 'There was no time for goodbyes. They took me away.'

'You took yourself away,' Noah said. '*You* did this.' Cold outrage crept behind his eyes. He felt dizzy.

'Martyrdom didn't work out,' Emily said. 'Seemed like a romantic idea at the time.'

'Romantic?' Noah said, the word spat out like a curse. 'You just stand there and you… you… you just… like nothing happened. Nothing. And we were left to–' He stopped himself before his rage would burst its dam.

Emily looked away, then back at Noah, her eyes sad and distant. Her next words came out flat and lifeless. 'They were getting ready to burn me. I closed my eyes and said my prayers. I made my peace with it. Fire was going to be really painful, burning, excruciating. I knew I'd scream, but then – but then – it'd be over. They soaked me in kerosine – the awful smell of it – and I kept thinking, that's a lot of fuel, a kindness, I'd burn quickly, but how long does it take for the pain to stop, until you don't feel anything? Cody, the marine, he lit his torch, but took his time. I kept telling myself: the pain, the burning, they'll only be temporary. Do you qualify for heaven if you're a novice? Will it wipe clean everything I've done before?' She rubbed her forehead with the back of her hand. 'And then, it all changed… I hear a woman's voice say something over the walkie-talkie, and Wilhelm shouts something at Cody. Next thing I know, they cut me down, and I fall to the sand. My habit was drenched in stinking kerosine. I had to take it off. They threw it on the pyre, added even more liquid and lit the logs. Massive flames. It was surreal, watching my outfit burn without me.' She shuddered.

'My dad paid,' Jonny mumbled to himself. 'He paid the ransom.' He looked up at them. 'They paid.'

'Yes,' Emily said. 'They were a little late, but they paid.'

'Why didn't you come back?' Noah said. 'Where were you?'

'I was dazed,' Emily said. 'I barely knew what was happening. I was in my underwear and bra, so they covered me with a towel and took me to this cabin, a bungalow, not too far from here. The kerosene made my skin break out in hives. I washed, and there was this woman there. She smeared me with emollient. Wilhelm didn't bother to show up, but he left orders for them to force me to drink jugs of ice tea. Apparently, he thinks it heals just about anything. They kept me overnight, and Cody brought me back just now.'

'Nuns wear bras?' Jonny said.

'Glad you dumped your God clothes,' Zayn said. 'Civvies suit you. They accentuate your–'

'Ignore Zayn,' Ashleigh said. 'He's a dog.'

'I think,' Emily said, 'it wasn't just the clothes that went up in flames. The burning of the habit was a sign. God saved me, but He doesn't want me back in the convent.' With galling cheer, she added, 'Anyway, how are things here? What's been happening?'

'Well,' Jonny said, 'as a matter of fact–'

Ashleigh cut him short. 'Nothing special to report,' she said. 'Just the usual gulag routine.'

'If you die again,' Jonny said to Emily, 'I'm not mourning you a second time, all right? Jesus!'

'Let's not make a big deal out of it,' Emily said.

Noah put his hands in his pockets and walked towards Emily. She opened her arms wide for an embrace, but he carried on past her, towards the villa.

Jonny called after him. 'Cheer up, Noah. They paid. We'll be on the first boat out.'

Despite the impression he must have given the others, Noah felt fine – better than fine. By the time he reached the house, he had let go of his anger, of his sadness, of his years of gloom after his father's death, of the helplessness he had felt since waking up in the hospital. It was as if the dark, surging river that had carried him through terrible rapids of dark, morbid thoughts now led him to a peaceful tributary. He smiled to himself. *We're all alive. Our parents paid the ransom. We'll go home soon. A new beginning.* Zayn's party would be a token start, like a declaration. He'll leave academia, travel the world and meet people, learn to live, *really* live. He would avoid plush hotels and stay in hostels instead, mixing with others. Maybe he'd come across a smiling backpacker and join her on the Inca trail. They'd kiss in the lost city of Machu Picchu. *I'm awake*, he thought, *awake after all these years, no longer a shadow struggling to cast a person.*

By the veranda, someone had left a wheelbarrow with provisions: mineral water, paper bags of oranges and peaches, more bread and crisps, jars of Marmite, honey, apricot conserve and red pepper spread, a box of Tsingtao lager. He used the edge of the wheelbarrow to pop the cap from one of the beer bottles, selected a peach, and sat on the veranda's top step, enjoying the beer's malty flavour, the coolness of the glass against his palm, the warmth of the sun on his face and the musty smell of the ocean. He rubbed the peach on his shirt, looked at it, uncertain, then placed it back inside the paper bag.

TWENTY-THREE

Comeuppance

Ashleigh came to join Noah on the veranda's steps. 'You all right?' she said and sat next to him, their knees almost touching.

He reached into the wheelbarrow, pulled out a beer bottle and offered it to her. She took it, removed the cap with her teeth and took a swig, closing her eyes in contentment. 'I missed booze. Wasn't allowed it with my treatment, but who cares now.'

'I'm a bastard,' Noah said.

'Oh, I wouldn't say that.'

'I mean, turns out I'm an actual bastard.'

'Please explain and cite sources,' she said.

He told her how he had found out from Emily that Peter Hammerson was his father.

She listened patiently, taking small sips of her beer. 'So, are you happy? Sad? Other? How do you feel about this bizarre revelation?'

'Other,' he said. They both seemed to be slipping into the well-worn paths of their old school's patter.

'That's an unsatisfactory response and misses depth and references.'

'Yeah,' Noah said. 'Any further questions or statements?'

Ashleigh shrugged. 'Not going to push you on it. I do have a statement, though.'

'Oh?'

'I've given up. I'm done. I'll just... go with the flow from now. No point moping about it. Won't be long anyway. Tonight's the night. I can feel it. I'll welcome death when it comes for me.'

He held back his instinct to protest. Instead, he said, 'That's brave of you.'

'Not brave,' she said. 'I was so angry all the time. With Emily back, somehow it feels different.'

'Yeah,' Noah said. He took a swig of his beer and looked out to the distance.

She raised her bottle to him. 'Let's enjoy the moment: a beer on the beach with a kind boy with arms like matchsticks.'

'You strike matchsticks against a strip of red phosphorus, and they ignite.'

'Take a metaphor and run with it, eh?' she said.

'It's a simile.'

'Yes,' she said. 'Yes, it is.'

She placed her bottle on the step, then picked it up again. 'Remember the bomb scare in English 2?'

He nodded. 'Everyone ran out excited, but then Mr Plough had his heart attack. Poor Mr Plough. Death by bomb scare. What a random way to go.'

'If we're confessing things...'

'You did that? You made the call about the bomb?' He paused and touched the bottle's rim to his chin. 'No, you didn't. You were in class. I remember. It couldn't have been you.'

'By proxy,' she said.

'Please explain and cite sources.'

'Jonny made the call. He had a free period, used voice distortion software.'

Noah looked at his feet, trying to find something to say. At last, he said, 'He was a brilliant teacher.'

'You think so?' she said.

'I understand school pranks, but this... And someone died. Mr Plough actually died.'

'You know these girls I used to hang out at school with? Marly and Fiona?'

'We called you the Hit Squad,' Noah said. 'The bullying, the name-calling, it was pretty toxic. And then you manipulated Jonny into doing *this*?'

'The other two girls only pretended to adore me so they could come on holidays with us. I was horrible, so they were horrible. Their parents were diplomats. They got shipped off to boarding school on public funds. Not much in the bank. They'd drink orange juice spiked with vodka on our yacht and parade around the deck in tiny bikinis to distract the crew. I didn't like them much.'

'I'm not sure I follow,' Noah said. 'I thought we were talking about Mr Plough.'

She met his gaze. 'I was a bitch. That's all.'

'But you weren't,' Noah said. 'Not always. You used to be shy and sweet, a proper teacher's pet. Then, year ten came around, and it's like you swallowed a demon. You started roaming the corridors and terrorising everyone with your evil sidekicks.'

She looked down at her knees. 'Teacher's pet,' she said. 'Yeah, that's the sum of it.' She hesitated, and then her voice became small and shaky, like a little girl's. 'The day of the bomb scare, I was meant to see Mr Plough for tutoring after class. Private tutoring, with the door shut and locked. He'd been at it for three years.'

Noah wet his throat with more beer. He chewed on his lip, unsure of what to say.

'One day,' Ashleigh continued, 'Mr Plough forgot to lock the door. Jonny came in unannounced and saw his hand in a place it shouldn't be. He didn't say anything, but the next day, he called in the bomb threat.'

'Bloody hell, Ashleigh. Three years? Why didn't you tell anyone?'

'I did, once. I went to the Head's office. Mr Crampton-Hughes told me it was unbecoming for a little girl to make up stories. And Mr Plough was married with two small children. He'd never do such a thing. I should never mention it again, not even to my dad. No one would believe me anyway. Textbook how these things work. Textbook. I was just another filthy statistic, except this statistic got her comeuppance. All Jonny wanted was to stop the pervert from touching me that day. No one could have predicted his prank would go so well. I'd never have to go into that smelly office again. Plough's breath was rank, like a sewer. I can still smell it. You know, I laughed at his funeral, had a fit of giggles, couldn't stop myself. Best funeral ever.'

'Ashleigh, I...'

'Look, Noah, I'm sorry I was a bitch to you. You weren't pretentious like a lot of them. You didn't deserve it. And the other thing... it's fine. Let's not make a big deal of it.'

'It is a big deal,' Noah said.

'I've rebuilt my life. Writing was my therapy.'

'Still, I mean, Jesus.'

'Jesus was your sister's catchphrase. Now I think about it, you do look alike. Your lips. It's all in the lips. Anyways, ancient history. I went off the rails, got back on them. Now, my train's hurtling to its final destination. The only person I feel sorry for is my dad. I was his princess.'

'And your mum?' Noah said, sensing she wanted to move on from the topic.

'My what?' Ashleigh said. 'This beer's strong, in a good way, or maybe I'm just out of practice.' She drank the last of it and hurled the bottle away with such force, it struck a palm tree. 'Mother married a wealthy restauranteur in Hong Kong. Three kids. *Dim sum*. That's all I know. We lost touch – or she lost touch. Dad says she wants nothing to do with us, or her new husband is possessive. Same thing.'

'Does she know, about your cancer?'

She shook her head. 'What's the point? I guess she might come to the funeral. Wouldn't that be lovely? Cremated Ash is best served cold.'

'You look better,' he said. 'Colour's come back to your face.'

'That's beer clouding your judgement. I only wish…' She didn't complete the thought. 'I'm sorry, again, about how I was.'

'Honestly, I barely remember it now.'

'Hmm,' she said doubtfully. 'When school was done, I became a hermit. All I wanted was a room of my own, to write and not to be disturbed.'

'That's easily done,' he said.

'You'd think so. My dad's house in Hampstead has enough rooms to hide a biker gang, and you wouldn't know they're there. But I felt uncomfortable with all the staff around, with people asking what I'd like for lunch or tiptoeing around waiting to clean. Big houses are like machines. They're busy contraptions, always ticking. Cooks, cleaners, fixers. You never feel alone. I'd fly out to our loft in New York and tell no one. Still, somehow, they always found out, and they'd show up like drone bees with their dusters.'

'There are solutions, you know,' Noah said. 'I got my own

flat in Covent Garden. No helpers. Just a fortnightly cleaning and cooking crew. They'd leave meals in the freezer.'

'You're way ahead of me. For years, I was too timid to ask, or I was worried my dad wouldn't agree. He's very protective. Then, just before my diagnosis, I bought a beachside cabin in North Wales: views of the sea, sandy beaches, stunning and simple. The plan was to go there and write. No staff. Online supermarket deliveries. I'd cook my own food. Come to think of it, it would have been the perfect place to die if we hadn't been *Lorem Ipsummed*.'

'I'll come with you to see it if you like, when we get back.'

'That's… thoughtful, but did you miss the part about solitude? Also, imminent death. Won't happen.' She placed her hand on his knee and squeezed it. 'You're a good man, Noah.'

'Is that a marriage proposal?'

She punched his shoulder and gave him a playful smile. 'You could do better,' she said.

'It's only a short-term commitment.'

'Get me another beer, will you? And no more marriage proposals. Definitely no marriage proposals.'

'Can I be your friend?' he said.

'That'd be nice.'

He handed her a beer and took a peach for himself. He brushed the fruit on his shorts to clean it. 'Do I dare to eat a peach?' he said.

'T. S. Eliot?' she said.

'You sure you won't marry me?'

TWENTY-FOUR

Confutatis maledictis

Alex set up the screen in the boardroom to show the website that had been emailed to the parents as the address of the kidnappers' next video. It displayed a version of the BBC's old test screen, *Test Card F*, but instead of the traditional central image of a girl playing noughts and crosses with Bubbles the clown, it showed the homeless girl from the previous day's video, clutching her one-armed Robin Hood doll. In the email, the kidnappers had also specified that the results would be announced an hour late, an extra hour of misery for the parents. The email did not give a reason for this delay, though Alex guessed it was because the payments would have reached their destination very close to the deadline, or even a little late.

In the few minutes before two o'clock, the five parents came into the room and sat in silence, avoiding eye contact and pretending to focus on their phones. The air felt charged with tension and anxious fear. They had paid the kidnappers whatever amount they had decided on. Now, like defendants in the dock, they awaited their judgements. *No, not the dock*, Alex thought. *More like reverse Russian roulette with four bullets in a five-chamber gun.* He had to keep reminding himself that this was only the first round of the kidnappers' "game". Things could still change in the next. At least the Home Secretary had come through for them in what was clearly a defiant move against the Prime Minister's plan. *Gutsy*, he thought, *or politically naive*. Either way, it gave the kids a chance and bought some more time to locate them.

At precisely two pm, the test image changed into dramatic flames, engulfing the entire screen. Alex realised, too late, that the monitor's volume was set much too loud. The occupants of the room were assaulted by a ferociously dramatic choral rendition of the '*Confutatis*' from Mozart's 'Requiem'. Alex knew the piece from Mary's choir days, and he shuddered at the Latin words: '*Confutatis maledictis, flammis acribus addictis, voca me cum benedictis.*' – *When the accursed have been confounded, and doomed to the searing flames, summon me with the blessed.*

'Dramatic,' Davis Boroughs said to the room, trying to look casual, yet his rigid posture was like that of a tortoise, hoping its shell would protect it from the smashing force of an oncoming rock.

The music faded out, and the now familiar face of the announcer in her Robin Hood hat appeared, looking like she was staring directly at them. 'We are Robin's Brigade,' she said. 'I come before you today to declare the results of our game's first round. I have to admit I am disappointed, *utterly* disappointed.' She frowned, then seemed to perk up. 'Before we get to the specifics of our billionaires' miserly contributions towards good causes, and their children's potential survival, I have a housekeeping announcement to make. It is aimed at the chief executive of the dementia charity, who made it his business to grace all the morning shows with his presence, explaining what he would do if his charity received some of our funding. To you, sir, I say this: thank you for your support, but we vet all good causes thoroughly. The Charity Commission may not mind, but our organisation would never contribute to a charity whose CEO earns £300,000 per annum. Dear viewer, don't you think that's an outrageous sum? Not only that, but only thirty per cent of this charity's funding goes towards its cause. The rest is used for,' she made quotation marks with her fingers, '*operational costs*. Seventy per cent! The regulator may be fine with this, but we encourage you all to follow our lead: do not donate to any charity that invests less than eighty per cent of its funding into the cause it is meant to support. No ifs, no buts.' She removed a stray strand of hair from her eye. 'Now that's out of the way,' she said, 'let us get to our purpose. Dear billionaire parents, clad in your suits and frocks and diamond jewellery, are you ready for the results of the first round of the game we call Heir Loss?'

She waited a beat, then said, 'We have a microphone in the room you're in, and none of you said yes. If you won't answer, we can just fast-forward to the end and not return any of your kids. Let's try this again: are you ready for the results?'

'Yes,' came the reluctant answers from around the table.

'That's better,' the woman said. 'We didn't actually bug your room, but it was a good gag, wasn't it? I'm fairly certain it worked.'

'Fuck's sake,' Davis Boroughs muttered.

The woman disappeared, to be replaced by the title *Heir Loss Results – Round One*. Under the title was an empty tabulated sheet with three column headings: *Name, Amount,* and *Points*.

'Our results, in no particular order, are as follows,' the woman's voice-over narrated. 'Jonny Salt, son of Theo Salt, £150,000. Wow, Theo! We'll calculate survival points shortly.'

Theo's lips formed into a tentative smirk.

'Zayn Sayal, son of Nadia Sayal,' the woman continued, '1.3 million.'

Theo pinched the back of his hand. His smile was gone, and his expression darkened.

'Next,' the woman said, 'we have a strange contribution,

which suggests you did not quite understand the rules of the game. Noah Gant, son of Cecilia, and Emily Hammerson, daughter of Peter, received exactly £1,165,000 each – as if they co-ordinated their donations. I want to make it very clear for the next round. These aren't the seventy-fourth *Hunger Games*. There will be no joint winners. If it happens again, they will both be disqualified from winning, no matter the amount paid. Am I clear? Good. And now to our final result.'

They all turned to look at Davis Boroughs, who had his head lowered and his eyes closed.

'Ashleigh Boroughs, daughter of Davis Boroughs,' the woman said, 'received a sum total of… Drum roll… £4.5 million. Congratulations on winning the first round.'

'Fucking retarded swine,' Theo hissed.

Davis opened his eyes. 'Don't be too hard on yourself, Theo,' he said with a pointed, unflinching glare. 'But I have to say, I'm surprised. The illustrious lawyer, you of all people. How could you be so naive and follow silly rumours?'

The rows on the screen filled with names and numbers. The scores read as follows:

Jonny Salt | £150,000 | 2 points
Emily Hammerson | £1,165,000 | 14 points
Noah Gant | £1,165,000 |14 points
Zayn Sayal | £1,300,000 | 16 points
Ashleigh Boroughs | £4,500,000| 54 points

Alex considered Peter and Cecilia's decision to pay the same amount. He understood the reason for it, but the strategy was only good for the first round. He didn't envy Peter the tough decision he faced. Would he choose the daughter he raised or the son he followed from afar? *Probably Emily, then*, he decided.

Everyone's faces, apart from Davis's, were crestfallen with a mix of shock and anger. Palpable tension rose in the room. Theo seemed like he was about to explode. Alex assessed it would only take a word to spur on violence. It was therefore lucky that the woman on the screen was ready to continue.

'I have to tell you,' she said, 'we were *very* disappointed with your tiny donations that are like a single tear in the vast ocean of your wealth. They tell a story, don't they? You have many billions at your disposal, and all you can spare to save the lives of others – and those of your firstborns – is eight million pounds and change in total? What a poor, poor show. Hashtag: ShameOnYou. Well, don't despair. This was just a warm-up. The next round is where you get the chance to make amends, shine brightly, make a difference.'

The woman leaned forward, widening her eyes. The words *Heir Loss – Round Two* appeared behind her. 'Now, listen carefully,' she said. 'We are good people. We'd like to be even-handed, fair and just, even when it comes to billionaire scum. That's why we have devised an equitable system, one which operates as follows. The next set of points will be awarded based on what proportion of your fortune you choose to donate. For example, if The Rich List says you are valued at two billion pounds and you donate one billion, that will be fifty per cent of your value, and so your child will receive fifty points. Are you with me? Do you understand? Good. And here's a sweetener for the bottom of the class. We don't wish you to lose hope just yet, even if you're already trailing far behind the others. The parent who contributes the highest proportion of their fortune will get forty bonus points. Are you following me, Theo? Keep up. You'll need to work the hardest this next round, you naughty, tight-fisted man. Only two points for your son, Jonny? Ashleigh Boroughs has fifty-four. I don't wish to sound folksy, but bridge the gap, Theo. Bridge the gap.'

Theo seemed frozen, though the tips of his ears were red as hot coals.

'All right,' the woman on the screen said. 'That's all for today's briefing. The deadline is three days from now, the seventeenth of the month, at 1pm. Dig deep for good causes! You can do it! Yes, you can! This is Robin's Brigade signing off.'

The test card screen reappeared along with a piercing, high-pitched beep.

'Turn it off,' Theo Salt said, then shouted, 'Shut the damned thing off!'

In his hurry to stop the noise, Alex kept clicking on the wrong buttons until he gave up, went across to the screen and turned it off at the switch.

Theo was first out of the room, with Davis Boroughs calling after him, 'Bridge the gap, Theo!'

TWENTY-FIVE

Killing with kindness

EWALD HOUSE, NORTHUMBERLAND, 14 AUGUST,
2.10PM

Alex stayed behind in the boardroom with Peter Hammerson, the other parents having left in a downcast, sober mood – except for Davis Boroughs, who sauntered out, a spring in his step.

'Please don't ask me why Cecilia and I paid the same,' Peter said.

'I know about Noah.'

'Brendan told you?'

'Don't be too hard on him.'

Peter waved the comment away.

'What are you going to do?' Alex said.

'I've always thought of Noah as my son, even if I wasn't part of his life, but I can't lose Emily. I just can't. But then… If I choose Noah, Cecilia and I can pool our cash and have a better chance of saving him.' He sighed, looking frustrated, bewildered by the intractable decision before him. 'If I choose Emily, she might stand a chance – or they could both die. I choose Noah, and another parent could still pay more than me and Cecilia combined. Either way, whatever I do, I don't know how I'll live with myself.' He shut his eyes and touched his temple. In a choked voice, he said, 'It's impossible.'

'I have two daughters,' Alex said. 'I can't begin to imagine having to choose between them.'

Peter sagged into his chair, playing with the pen in his hand. 'And you have to understand, Alex, being rich doesn't mean I can just go to the bank and withdraw billions. My assets are tied up in investments, in securities, in properties. To release them all would take months, years even – not three days. Most of my supposed money is held in Hammerson Oil, a public company with shareholders and a board. The board's duty is to the company, not me. I don't control them.'

'I'm not a finance expert,' Alex said, 'but can't you sell your shares?'

'Our share price dropped twenty per cent since the first video. Markets are sentimental like that. I'm the CEO and my likability fell off a cliff. The media isn't helping with their sanctimonious shouting. It feels like the entire country is baying for our blood and, at the same time, they're draining every pint of it. If I sell my shares at their current price, the result will be panic and a run on the company. Hammerson Oil would fail before I've had a chance to raid the stationery cupboard. Fifty thousand employees could lose their livelihoods. There will be suicides. There always are when you go under on such a massive scale. These kidnappers talk about us like we're some rich vampires, sucking everyone's blood, but that's not true. I've built a successful business. I created jobs. A lot of people depend on me. How can it be right to punish them like that?'

'I hadn't thought of that,' Alex said.

Peter didn't look at him. 'Even if I manage to sell all my shares, which is a big if, I have no idea where it would leave me compared to what the other parents raise. I'll have to see if I can leverage any other assets.'

'Do you know where Cecilia stands?' Alex said.

'She's in the same boat in terms of access to cash,' Peter said, 'and she's got her own challenges, or at least that's what I think. The others can still outmanoeuvre me. What if Nadia raises eighty per cent? What if Davis does? Their companies are private. If they want to sell, they'll sell. They aren't accountable to anyone.'

'Again,' Alex said, 'not an expert, and correct me if I'm wrong, but you can't just sell a company overnight. There are legalities to go through, details to iron out. Your shares seem much more liquid.'

'Maybe,' Peter said. 'Nadia is one of the smartest operators I know. She might just succeed in structuring some sort of financial vehicle that would release the money to her on the promise of a sale. And, it gets worse.'

'How?' Alex said.

'The kidnappers said they'll score how much we pay compared to our Rich List value. That list is just a bunch of estimates, which means every parent's real worth could be higher or lower. Good for some. Bad for others. Fair, it isn't – not when it's used to decide if your child lives or dies. They don't care, of course. They just want us to pay, and the truth be damned.' He shook his head, then put the pen's cap-end into his mouth and bit on it. 'But look, that's for me to figure out. Any news on locating our kids?'

'As a matter of fact, yes,' Alex said.

Peter's mouth slackened. He put down his pen, looked at Alex and squared his shoulders.

'I don't want to raise any hopes yet, but my team's identified a mobile device that was present in both Noah and Emily's kidnappings. They were taken from locations that are very far apart – Inverness and London – so this is a good, reliable find. We're waiting for the device to ping again and tell us where it is now. If it does, we're in business. The extraction team is on alert in a hangar in Sussex, ready to mobilise within ten minutes. Again, I don't want to oversell this, Peter. The device only helps us if it reappears, and we can trace it.'

Peter nodded but said nothing. After a moment of silence, he got up, turned on the TV at the socket and clicked on one of the remotes that were lined up on the table. A newsreader appeared on the screen. Peter reclined back in his chair and stared at the picture with vacant eyes.

'Thank you for watching Sky News,' the presenter said. 'Our main headline today: sources close to Home Secretary Nessa Thorns have revealed that she had defied the Cabinet and delayed the signing of the Terrorism Designation Order that would have prevented the billionaire parents from paying ransom for their five kidnapped children. Those payments have now been made, with the father of Ashleigh Boroughs contributing the highest amount, four-and-a-half million pounds. Sky News can confirm that the entirety of the £8,280,000 received from the parents was immediately given to charitable causes. We are now joined by Enzo Wakefield, CEO of the homeless charity Street Assist and Davina Roe, Director of Child Medicine International. Welcome to you both. Davina Roe, we'll start with you. I understand you have some news to share?'

The charity director's face filled the screen. Her expression was soft and friendly, like an advertisement for sympathy cream. Her voice came across as warm and caring. She looked jubilant. 'I'm still pinching myself,' she said. 'This afternoon, we received a donation of one million pounds from an offshore account. The transaction was marked "Robin Hood". In addition, documents were delivered to us, which we have verified with the issuing bank, confirming an annuity trust set up in our name with a value of a little over three million pounds. It will pay us an annual sum.'

'And what will be the impact of these donations on your work?'

'Millions of vulnerable children in developing countries die every day because they lack simple life-saving medical care, the kind of care we take for granted here in the UK: essential vaccinations, antibiotics, simple medical procedures that could mean the difference between life and death. The million pound donation will be used immediately to supply local doctors with essential medical equipment, vaccines and life-saving drugs. The annual trust money will do the same on a longer-term basis. We estimate they will save thousands of children who would otherwise have died, at least thousands.' She hesitated, tugged on her ear, then added, 'We are grateful for the kindness of those who sent the donation. Despite the circumstances, it would be impolite not to thank them.'

The presenter turned to the UK homeless charity CEO, who relayed a similar story. A million pound donation and a trust set up to support the charity in years to come. At the end of his interview, he said, 'I would like to reiterate something Robin's Brigade has said. The initial eight million pounds they received, even if it were given to us in its entirety, is a drop in the ocean compared to the desperate need on our streets, right here at home in the UK.'

'That's a fair point,' the presenter said, 'but do you feel the donation you received justifies the kidnapping and potential killing of four innocent people who have done nothing wrong, with only one coming back alive?'

'We are, of course, very concerned for the welfare of those kidnapped,' the CEO said. 'I run a homelessness charity. It's beyond my remit to comment on matters that are better put to others.'

'Let's suppose for a moment,' the presenter persisted, 'that it was you who built a successful company, and it was your daughter or son being bargained for. Would you still think their lives were worth sacrificing for donations to charities?'

'I don't think it's helpful to comment on hypotheticals,' the

CEO said. 'I am not the police or a politician. Perhaps you should ask the government. I hear they had intelligence that none of the ransom would go to good causes.'

Peter Hammerson stiffened but remained silent.

'Thank you both for joining us today,' the presenter said. 'I've just been told that the Home Secretary will be making a speech, tomorrow at 4pm. We will carry it live, here on Sky News.'

'What do you think she's up to?' Alex said.

Peter took a moment to think about this. 'When her man, Smith, called you to tell you about her signing the Order late, did you happen to record the call?'

'You think she'll recant?' Alex said.

'Well did you, record it?'

Alex shook his head. 'It's all over the media. I don't think she'll do that.'

'The Prime Minister is a browbeating bully,' Peter said. 'I wouldn't rule out him leaning on the Home Secretary to claim her late signature was a clerical error or that it didn't happen. Watch out for a gang of police hoodlums showing up to arrest us right after Ms Thorns makes her speech.'

'Let's not jump to conclusions,' Alex said. 'She struck me as a formidable woman.'

'She's a politician,' Peter said. 'They only care about their backsides.'

TWENTY-SIX

The power of magic

LONDON, 15 AUGUST

'You see, Evan,' Theo Salt said to the boy as they both stepped out of the lift onto the seventeenth floor of Salt-Lather-Reese, 'this is where grandad works. It's my law firm. And now we're going to see Justine Klein. She knows everything there is to know about money and the law.'

'She'll give you money for Daddy?' Evan said.

'Unfortunately not. She'll give me numbers, and words.'

The boy angled his head and held up his toy magic wand. 'You mean words like spells?'

Theo smiled. 'The only wizard in this building is you. You're the only one who can *really* cast spells. But not right now, okay? In this meeting, I'd like you to sit quietly and hide your powers. Here, this is Justine's office.'

Justine Klein wore jeans, a T-shirt that read *Carbolic smoke junkie* and the offhand nonchalance of a lawyer who mainly dealt with emails, spreadsheets and corporate documents. Not many client meetings for her. She was top of her field, having built a successful practice that mostly avoided the nuisance of people and courts. Theo had headhunted her from a competitor over a decade ago, and he still considered her to be one of his best hires.

Justine was on the phone but waved at him to come in and pointed to the two chairs in front of her desk. Evan was hesitant but followed his grandfather and took the seat to his right. Justine ended the call and pressed the intercom button. 'Niall, hold my calls.' She turned to Theo. 'You came by helicopter?'

'Some meetings are better taken in person.'

'And you must be Evan,' she said to the boy. 'I don't like children, but I guess I'll have to make an exception for the boss's grandson.'

'I'm here to cast a spell,' Evan said.

Theo squeezed Evan's shoulder. 'It's the only way for me to spend a little time with him. The partner meeting's in an hour. Then I'm heading back to the misery of my victim support group at Peter Hammerson's place. You've done the analysis?'

She nodded, swivelled in her chair to the metallic filing cabinet behind her, pulled out a bundle of documents from a drawer and swivelled back to place it on the desk. She drew a BIC pen from behind her ear and toked on it as if it were a cigarette, tipping imaginary ash onto the pile of papers.

'Best pro-bono work I've done in ages,' she said, 'if I say so myself.'

'Aren't I paying you enough already?' Theo said.

'Good thing I only had to use threats with my sources. I know how you hate signing off bribes as hospitality expenses.'

'Justine!' Theo said.

'Kidding,' Justine said. 'For the benefit of the tape, I was making a humorous comment. Salt-Lather-Reese is a respectable, upstanding law firm. We would never bribe anyone.' She jabbed the blunt end of the pen into her cheek. 'Except that one time… What was it?'

Theo shook his head. It was his steadfast view that some

things should never be joked about: bombs at airports, bribes at a law firm. He guided Justine back to the purpose of their meeting. 'What have you found out about the other parents and what they can raise?'

She tapped her pen on the document bundle. 'On the face of it,' she said, 'there are disparities between the sort of sums the different parties – I mean parents – can put together, but dig deeper, and the picture is a little less clear. The media seems to think the clear winner is either Davis Boroughs or Nadia Sayal if either of them initiates a fire sale of their companies. But… I'm not so sure. I managed to get my paws on their latest internal P&L reports. Nadia's company is on solid ground, but the price of her raw materials and transportation costs have shot up recently. Davis Boroughs is embroiled in a class action lawsuit in the US, something to do with…' She cleared her throat and glanced at Evan, who was playing with his wand, mouthing words. 'Let's just say one of his products may have had some unsavoury chemicals mixed into the rubber, causing nasty rashes in nether locations.'

'What's a nether lo-cation?' Evan said.

'It's a complex of caves in America,' Justine said without a moment's hesitation.

Evan giggled. 'A cave with rashes? You mean, on the walls?'

Justine nodded and faced Theo again. 'With his clear lead in points, and at the right price, Boroughs is in a sound position. Same thing for Sayal, though it's evenly balanced and depends on them being able to somehow leverage a sale in such a short timeframe. If I were their lawyer, I'd say it's impossible, but…' she shrugged, 'there are ways and means, like raising the money from a shadow sale. If a buyer is keen enough, it's a great deal to have, and they'd snap up these companies for a bargain. Definitely worth cutting some corners for.'

'What about the other two?'

'Hammerson Oil stock is spiralling down, and Peter Hammerson hasn't sold his shares yet. The big question is what other holdings he might have. My gut tells me he's trailing behind, but I can't confirm it. Cecilia Gant is also in a spot of bother. You owe me one. I left the hallowed peace of my office and went on a date with her CFO.'

'I appreciate your dedication,' Theo said. 'I hope he was a gentleman.'

'She was,' Justine said, 'though we did go back to hers for drinks, and we…' She cleared her throat.

Evan looked up from his wand. 'You did S-E-X with a Seefo?' He giggled. 'What's a Seefo?'

Justine ignored the comment, but her cheeks reddened. 'Bottom line,' she said to Theo, 'Cecilia's been negotiating a deal to sell her company for the last six months. She's more ready than all the rest of you, but her position is not as rosy as it seems. The company did some fancy footwork on their accounts to inflate profits for last year's prospectus. Her ranking on the Rich List is too high. It's spiked her chances. She'll have to negotiate an exceptional deal to get ahead.'

'To summarise,' Theo said, 'we know nothing for certain about who could win the highest percentage, except that Hammerson might be behind unless he has other fat assets he can dispose of. You know my next question.'

'Yeah, well,' Justine said. 'I couldn't possibly comment on that one. That's between you and the other partners.'

'From what your spreadsheets tell you,' Theo said, 'assuming I convince Jim and Avery to sell at a reasonable price, where do I stand against the other parents?'

She busied herself scribbling circles on the top document in her pile. She wouldn't look at him.

'The truth, Justine,' he said.

She shook her head. 'There's a thin margin between success and failure, but it's there for the taking. I wouldn't bet against you, but the horses in this race appear evenly matched.'

The two partners were already waiting in the boardroom when Theo and Evan entered. Theo could not shake the feeling that he was walking into a well-orchestrated trap.

'Hello, handsome,' Jim Lather said to Evan. 'I heard you came to help your gramps.'

'I'm not allowed to tell you,' Evan said and jumped onto the seat at the head of the boardroom table. He had hidden his wand under his shirt, held in place by his trousers' elastic band.

'We've been monitoring events from here,' Avery Reese said. 'We're so sorry, Theo. It's terrible – absolutely terrible.'

'I can't begin to imagine how–' Jim started to say when Theo interrupted him.

'Try to imagine, Jim. Do me a favour and try to imagine what it's like, what you'd do in my shoes if it was your Hilary.'

'We understand,' Jim said. 'We're as upset by it as you.'

'As upset as me?' Theo said.

'We're here for you,' Jim said, 'not just as colleagues, but as friends.'

'Yes, as you said in our last meeting, along with the worst advice you've ever given anyone. You were one hundred per cent behind me.'

'I'm sorry. Beth Grisham was our best shot. Maybe she didn't deliver her best performance. With people like her, these things, they can sometimes…'

'Yeah,' Theo said. 'Sometimes, but not this time. Not today. What you'll do today is help me climb out of the hole you've dug for me. You'll buy my share of the firm, all of it.'

A nervous glance passed between Jim and Avery.

Jim crossed his arms and cleared his throat. 'I'm not going to patronise you, Theo. Let's be lawyers for a minute, go back to first principles, play this out calmly and logically, look at probabilities and outcomes. That's exactly what Avery and I did before you joined us today.'

'I built this company,' Theo said.

'We respect you immensely,' Jim said. 'You know that.'

Theo turned to Avery. 'You're very quiet.'

Avery leaned forward, his usually imposing frame looking small, like he had shrunk into his seat. Before he could speak, Jim interjected. 'We discussed it between us. Of course we'd like to do anything we can to help you save your son, but let's suppose for the sake of argument that we could even somehow, *somehow*, buy you out in such a short timeframe. Odds are you'd be throwing away everything: your fortune, this law firm – everything – and still you won't help Jonny. We've seen the numbers. Your chances against the other parents are slim. See sense, Theo. I'm sorry to say it, but someone has to: Jonny is as good as gone if his life depends on this fanciful sale happening.'

Theo's face tightened. He stared at each of his partners in turn. 'You will buy me out,' he said, speaking slowly, deliberately, with the menace of a man holding a pinless grenade. 'You'll do it at a fair price, and you'll do it today. And let's avoid tiresome discussions about challenges with the regulator and challenges with timeframes and challenges with clients – I don't have time for it. We have hundreds of associates. We can create a legal vehicle to make it happen. I don't care if the official sale has to wait months. I don't care if I have to go in front of the regulator after the event. I don't care about any of that. The only thing that matters is that the money moves first. The rest can follow.'

'Look, Theo,' Avery said. 'I know Jim can be direct, and maybe his… phrasing was a little crude, but he's right. Of course we'd like to help you. Of course. But how do we even value your share of the firm? It will take weeks, not days. We'll need an external firm to come up with a valuation.'

'Remember when we went out for drinks at the Crown last month?' Theo said. 'Remember how we discussed how rich we were?'

'Yes, but–' Jim said.

'You were very specific, weren't you, Jim?'

'Back of an envelope in a time of hubris,' Jim said, 'nothing more.'

'That's the valuation,' Theo said. 'I'm selling my share to you two at a four per cent discount, and you will raise the money to prepay me on account, and you will prepare the documents, and we will all sign them, done and dusted by tomorrow. We're pretty liquid, but what you can't find in liquidity, you'll get from short-term loans. Is there anything I said that's not crystal clear?'

Avery got up, walked over to the window and stared out to the London skyline. He turned around and leaned his back against the glass, his hands in his trouser pockets. 'Hammerson Oil pulled their business away from us,' he said. 'Dream Cave Entertainment and Jude-Cornice Cement did the same as soon as the kidnappers released their second video. Overnight, someone spray-painted the front of our building with the words *Deworm the country. Kill rich lawyers*. It's tough for me to say this, Theo, but I don't think we're able to leverage so much cash. It could sink us.'

'He's right,' Jim said, a look of finality on his face. 'He's right, and you know it.'

'So, you won't do it? You won't give me the slightest chance to save my son?'

Avery looked down at his silver cufflinks. Jim stared ahead and half-nodded.

Theo let the thick silence hang in the room for a moment, then turned to his grandson at the top of the table. 'Evan, remember what we talked about, how you can save Daddy?'

'The spell?' Evan said. 'Now?'

Theo nodded.

Evan stood on his chair and then stepped on top of the conference table.

'What's this?' Jim said with an edge of a smile.

Evan reached under his shirt and drew out his toy wand. He circled the wand's tip in the air and pointed it at Avery, then at Jim. In a loud, confident voice, he called out, 'Alexis Brice, Alexis Brice, Alexis Brice!'

The two partners froze. Jim's hand rushed to cover his throat. Avery seemed to breathe harder.

'You can't,' Jim said to Theo, enunciating his words as if he were in court. 'Her case was settled. We shut it down and locked it tight. This is serious, Theo. It can't come out now. It'll bring the company down and you with it.'

'I have the dossier ready,' Theo said, 'to submit to the police, to HMRC and a very special copy for the IRS. It details how, in the curious case of Mrs Brice's multimillion dollar estate disposal, we deceived the tax authorities on both sides of the pond and crapped all over our fiduciary duties with a dollop of, ahem, what might even be construed as a bribe. How you, Avery, lied in a sworn statement, and how you, Jim, used that lie to sweeten things with the Internal Revenue Service. I hear they're less forgiving than our own guys. And then there's the shady transfer on October 2nd. Your fingerprints are all over it, Jim. Prison for you, I'd wager. Avery and I will just end up destitute.'

'You'd burn the house down with you in it?' Jim said.

'I'd burn the entire city, the entire country if I have to.'

'Did my spell work?' Evan said.

'It was spectacular,' Theo said to him. 'Why don't you come down from the table and go outside. See if Astrid, the lady at the desk over there, can get you some biscuits and milk. Every magician needs to fuel up after casting a difficult spell.' He turned to his partners. 'Now, let's nail down the details. Time is of the essence.'

TWENTY-SEVEN

Secrets

'Well, that's a plush-looking bathrobe,' Mary Czerniak said to Alex. 'Looks so soft. How's the high life treating you? Is it true billionaires put gold leaf on every course?'

Alex couldn't help but grin at his wife, who was sitting at her desk in London, her Met Police uniform looking stiff as ever. 'You should see this place. They have so many rooms, I could smuggle you and the girls in, and we could all live here happily ever after, and no one would ever notice. Maybe we could move into the wine and cheese cellar. They have these massive cheese wheels they imported from an artisan producer in Spain. Enough for a lifetime. How are the girls?'

'Acting up without their father figure. Rose arrested Poppy yesterday. She used her unicorn tail as handcuffs. Poppy was not best pleased.'

'Well, now I know why you didn't just call me,' Alex said, 'but don't you think it's overkill to use the encrypted Met Police video app to tell me my daughter's impersonating a police officer? She's too young to be arrested.'

'It's not overkill for what we have to discuss. I have some information for you, but you can't share it with the parents. It's a bit delicate, and I didn't want to risk anyone tapping our calls.'

'That sounds ominous,' Alex said.

'It… complicates things a little, but before we go into all that, anything on your end to share?'

'Tease,' he said with a smile.

'You're the one in a bathrobe.'

'The boot print on Emily Hammerson's vow of silence card is a dead end. Army surplus. Too many of those around. The emails from the kidnappers were untraceable. I'm pleased to say Peter Hammerson is happy for me to co-operate with the Met's investigation, especially after I explained we have more to gain from exchanging information.'

'Like a non-disclosure ever stopped you before,' Mary said. 'Anything about the phones? I'm still buried in red tape to get records.'

'We might have a lead,' he said. 'All the victims' phones became inactive at their abduction points, except for Emily Hammerson who didn't have one, but we know where she was taken. I got my tech guy to crunch triangulation data. He was looking for patterns, adjacent handsets, et cetera.'

'You found a phone signature that was present in the abduction scenes?'

'Not a phone. The kidnappers are pros, but even pros can slip. There's one device, a Samsung watch with a SIM that links two of the locations. We find the watch, we find the kids, or at least someone who knows where they are.'

'I hate to say it, husband, but that's stellar work. You sure I can't convince you to join the Met?'

'Thanks, but that's a no to triplicate forms and salutes and shiny shoes, not to mention the pay. My wife has expensive tastes, and I need to save for two huge dowries. I want good husbands for the girls, not some civil servant at the Department for Environment, Food and Rural Affairs.'

'Tracking a watch isn't easy,' she said thoughtfully, 'and it might not be in the country any more.'

'Yeah, it's a tough ask, but we're lucky to have unlimited funds here, and I found exactly the right people to help us.' He looked away, then back at her. 'We might be bending a few rules with this one, hon. Probably better I don't tell you too much about it.'

'Fair enough,' she said. 'How are the parents doing?'

'Avoiding each other. Eating in their rooms. Strategising, I expect. Are you going to tell me about the top secret thing?'

'I'm not supposed to,' she said, 'but I think you should know, even if it puts me in breach of… well, anyway, you never heard it. It dies after this call.'

'Now you have me worried,' he said.

'What do you know so far about Zayn Sayal?'

'Zayn? Really?' He reached behind him on the bed and grabbed a stack of files. He riffled through them, extracted one and tossed back the rest. The file had Zayn's name written on it in black marker. He opened it and showed his laptop's camera the picture that was attached with a paper clip to the inside cover. Zayn looked like a glamorous boy band member with a smile that could melt plastic.

'Zayn Sayal,' he said. 'Good-looking, dumb, popular. Abysmal grades at school once hormones kicked in, but from what I gather, even those were higher than what they should have been if not for his mother's generous donations to the school. Just as well he never went to university, although I'm sure they, too, would have benefited from a new library or a science wing to make sure he passed.' He turned the pages in his file, scanning their content. Most of it he already knew by heart. 'Since graduating school, he's been wasting his life in jet-set parties of the sort you, my love, could only dream of.'

'Just me?'

'Oh, I've been dreaming about them incessantly since I got

here. Outrageous soirées with exquisite drinks and canapés and – your favourite – gold leaf on everything.'

'When you interviewed his mother? Did anything she said about him sound off?'

'Not sure what you mean. In her mind, he's just taking his time to grow up. Once he finds his inner dolphin, he'll become a responsible member of the moneyed elite. If our girls behave like that, I think we should disinherit them.'

'You'd let them marry the man from Defra?'

'What's going on, Mary? Are you going to tell me what got you so interested in the vacuous heart-throb? Come to think of it, the Home Office rep asked me questions about him too. Can you shed any light?'

'Turns out,' she said, 'he's not as vacuous as he looks.'

'Oh?'

'I sent two officers to his school to interview the headmaster. Mr Crampton-Hughes is exactly what you'd expect from someone in his elevated position: superior, condescending, greasy hair and greasy attitude. He ran rings around them or thought he could. Jenny and Lei are two of my best officers. They dug deeper, asked to see Zayn's student files. He was unco-operative, so they threatened him with a court order. If there's one thing public school heads are terrified of it's a scandal, so he folded. In hindsight, he really shouldn't have, but that's by the by.'

'What could possibly be significant about Zayn's school file?'

'His grades.'

'We already assumed they were doctored to be better. What's new?'

'Not better. Zayn's original sixth-form grades were straight A's. He's highly intelligent, would have been a model student. His certificates, however, were changed to C's and D's, and in one instance, an F.'

'I'm not following. His mother wanted to lower his grades? Why would she?'

'She knew nothing about it. The only people at the school who were in on the secret were the Head and Zayn himself.' She cocked her head. 'All right, Mr Top PI, show me your beautiful mind. What reason could anyone have to bury a brilliant student's achievements at the bottom of the heap?'

'Hmm,' Alex said and winced. 'I give up. Don't laugh at me.'

'I'm not,' she said and laughed. 'While Jenny and Lei reviewed Zayn's files, the Head made a phone call. Ten minutes later, I was ordered to remove my officers from the premises. A man in an anorak – an actual anorak – came to see me. I had to sign a fifteen-page document, and I'd probably be hanged, drawn and quartered for telling you about it.'

'I love you so much,' he said.

'When Zayn was seventeen, he was summoned to the Head's office to meet with two gentlemen. Before the meeting, the Head was ordered to sign the Official Secrets Act. A plan was put to Zayn, and he agreed, enthusiastically.'

'You're joking,' Alex said.

'After the meeting, Zayn's grades dropped off a cliff. By the time he left school, it was clear no decent university would have him. After that, no one was surprised this suave, good-looking guy became a top-tier socialite, jetting off from party to party, mixing with the rich and powerful, daughters of oligarchs, sons of tyrants, arms-dealer wives. His mother didn't know, of course. The man who came to see me was his MI6 handler.'

'Yeah, okay, but… I still don't get it. Why go to all that effort? He could have finished school with good grades and then join the spooks.'

'Anyone else, and you'd be right, but Nadia Sayal is a rich, powerful woman, and she had Zayn's future mapped out. He was meant to go to a top university, get an MBA, prepare to take over the business. She would never have allowed him to join the Service. The Service, on the other hand, was in great need of Zayn's skills. Even at seventeen, he was showing great promise at being a socialite, a seducer, someone who could mix in circles that the men in grey suits could only ever wet-dream of. His handler said he was easy to recruit. Zayn had no interest in taking over the Sayal food empire. Young Zayn and the Service, his handler said, had a meeting of the minds. Both sides weren't too keen on Nadia's plan.' She gave him her tough police officer look. 'Do you understand the implications, Alex?'

'Of course I do,' he said, 'by which I mean…'

She raised an eyebrow.

'Maybe explain it to me like I'm Poppy.'

'At first, I thought this was good news,' she said. 'With the security services having skin in the game, the chance of these kids being found would be a higher priority, but then…'

'Politics?'

'Every time. You told me the Home Secretary's rep had a private chat with Nadia Sayal. My guess is he wanted to check if Zayn had, at some point, confided in her about his job. If she knows he's an agent, she might spill the beans about her son to the media, Official Secrets Act or not.'

'I doubt that would move the needle much,' Alex said.

'Maybe not now when the kidnappers are popular,' Mary said, 'but if he dies, there could be serious recriminations. Members of the Intelligence and Security Committee will be furious. Even without publicly acknowledging the truth about him – which they can't – tough questions could be raised in Parliament, questions about what was actually done to find and save these kids, which, between us, is not a lot. Being unable – or unwilling – to rescue one of our own would be seen as a damning failure. There might even be a public inquiry, under one excuse or another. The government could find itself in the firing line.'

'So,' Alex said, 'you think if Nadia knows, Tom Smith would have tried to lean on her to keep quiet? I have to say, that's a heap of conjecture.'

'At the very least, they'd want to know if she's a risk to them. My sense is this government is more interested in its survival than anything else.'

'Governments usually are. Thanks for telling me. To be honest, hon, I'm not sure what to do with this information.'

'I didn't want you to be blindsided by it if it came to light. The parents trust you. You should be playing with a full deck.'

'And that, there, is why I love you so much. By the way, is Zayn trained? Can he fight his way out of a bind?'

'I did ask. Apparently, he's had some combat training, but mostly, he's very good at being pretty and getting people to underestimate his intelligence. We hope this, at least, will give him an edge.'

'Well, that's something,' Alex said and exhaled a loud sigh. 'I think I'll go to the orangery now and drink some expensive champagne. A couple of bottles should do it.'

'And Alex—'

'I know. This conversation never happened.'

'Since it's an encrypted line, I was going to say I love you too.'

TWENTY-EIGHT

The missing scholar

'Time is running short,' Nadia Sayal said to Alex as they sat together on the comfortable red leather chairs facing each other. They had been served tea in the south wing sitting room, where the décor was a strange mixture of Americana and Victoriana, lit by the warm light of an artificial candle chandelier. Nadia's face was no longer glowing with friendly warmth the way it had before. Now, she looked strained and exhausted, perhaps even defeated. 'I have a bad feeling,' she said, 'here, at the pit of my stomach, like something terrible is going to happen. I keep telling myself it's me, I'm a worrier, but then, isn't a mother connected to her child, no matter where he is?'

'I appreciate how difficult it is, and–'

She raised a finger to stop him. 'How can I help you, Alex? Is there anything you'd like to ask me? Anything I might help you with? Please, go ahead. Except for the money. I won't talk about the ransom money.'

'Understood,' he said. 'When was the last time you saw Zayn?'

'About a week before they took him. We had dinner

together. It was so lovely to see him. I can barely keep track of the boy. One week he's in Okinawa, the next in Sydney. I think he was en route from Moscow to LA this time. He complained that I force-feed him. I mean, I'm all for him keeping fit, but a bit of fat won't go amiss on top of all that muscle.'

'What was he doing in LA?'

She raised the teapot and poured tea into the two porcelain cups. 'Milk? Sugar?' she said.

'Black.'

She reached for her tea, raised the saucer, brought the cup to her lips and blew on the steaming liquid to cool it. Her tired eyes locked with Alex's. 'You're tiptoeing,' she said. 'I can sense there's a subtext to this meeting and it's not about my son's movements. So, are you going to ask your question, or are we going to drink tea and dance around it?'

'If I ask,' he said, 'will you answer?'

'You do your profession credit, Alex. Mr Smith of the Home Office wished to ascertain, delicately, if I possessed certain information. He thought he was being clever. His type often does.'

'And did you, possess this information?' Alex said.

'I'm not allowed to say.'

'Thank you,' Alex said and relaxed back into his seat. 'That's helpful. We're still hoping to have a breakthrough with the extraction team. It's good to know there's someone resilient on the ground.'

'When I learned, a while ago, about the way he… the way he lives now, it came as a surprise but not a shock.'

'Did you worry for him?' Alex said.

'Of course. That's what mothers do. Zayn is good-natured, kind, driven. He experiences life deeply. It's like he sees things in brighter colours than the rest of us. And that, Alex, is what keeps me up at night.'

'It doesn't strike me as a disadvantage,' Alex said.

'I assume you collected background information about us. Every detail helps, you said.'

'I did,' Alex said, 'and it does.'

'What did you uncover about Zayn's father?'

Alex picked up his teacup, leaving the saucer on its tray. He took a sip, intrigued by Nadia's question. 'I admit, I found nothing at all about your husband, which was a little odd. There are mentions of him in the early days of your success, magazine profiles, interviews. You seemed like a happy couple. He's no longer in the picture, so I assumed you were estranged.'

'It's a fair deduction, seeing as our little group of parents marched into this awful event single file. Can I trust you, Alex? Is everything between us spoken in confidence?'

'Nothing leaves this room,' Alex said. 'I promise.'

She took a moment to look at him as if inspecting his face for a sign. At last, she spoke. 'Money isn't always enough to hide things, but if the exalted private detective Alex Czerniak hasn't found my husband, there's hope for us yet.'

'What are you trying to tell me?' Alex said. 'Has he run away from his family? Disappeared? What?'

'He's buried in my back garden,' she said, 'next to the sycamore tree.' Then, for the first time since they entered the room, she gave him a reserved smile. 'Oh, the look on your face, it's precious. Of course he's not dead. I love my husband, Alex. I love him with all my being. We are not estranged.'

'Where is he, then? And why isn't he here with you?'

'Taj is the kindest man you'll ever meet.'

'Okay.'

'Ten years ago, we flew to Sicily for a long weekend. We go there to get away from things, recharge, spend time together without the niggles of my work. There's a Four Seasons in Taormina, and the local airport is convenient for private jets.'

Alex looked at her and waited for more. In his mind, he

was still baffled by how he hadn't been able to find any information about the man's whereabouts for the last ten years. Dr Taj Sayal was a scholar in his younger days. According to an interview with the couple in *Vanity Fair*, after he married Nadia, Taj focused on helping his wife with her empire, a man undeterred by living in the shadow of a successful woman. In the interview, he appeared supportive of Nadia, happy with his lot. A rare man indeed. Or was it all for show? Alex laid down his tea, leaned forward and listened.

'Taj hadn't slept well the previous few nights,' Nadia continued, 'and I was a bit worried for him. He was behaving strangely, and not communicating much, but I thought he was just tired. Anyway, we're in our jet at cruising altitude, and Taj starts whispering in my ear that we're in danger. Something about the crew wanting to kill him. His face, it was changed, like he was suddenly a different person. Then he starts mumbling gibberish, and by this point I became scared, not of him, but for him. You see, Taj would never hurt another person.' The teacup shook in her hand.

'He had a breakdown?' Alex said softly.

'Believe me, the last place you want this to happen is mid-air. Poor Taj. He got up and started shouting, "I have to get out. Out, out, out." He kept repeating this, and nothing I said helped. He couldn't see reason, like logic had left him. Then he rushed to the front of the plane and tried to open the door.'

'Good God,' Alex said.

'The crew was exceptional. They wrestled him to the ground and bound him to a seat. We turned around, of course.'

'What did the doctors say?'

'I argued with them, and I argued with myself, but in the end, I had to accept the diagnosis: schizophrenia. There were no signs before, or maybe there were, and I ignored them.

These were dark times for us, the worst. It took a while to figure out what to do.'

'I'm sorry,' Alex said. 'That must have been tough.'

She waved away his sympathy. 'He's in a private facility that I arranged for him in Shetland. On the outside, it looks like a private house, but he has twenty-four-hour professional care, the best of the best, and he's safe there. There's a small indoor pool, a library, a chef, everything he needs. We can land a helicopter in the field.'

'Why not keep him at home and treat him?' Alex said. 'Isn't there medication for schizophrenia?'

'We tried,' Nadia said. 'Every time he feels better, he stops taking his pills. Staying away was his idea. He's terrified he'd hurt someone, even though I keep telling him he never would. Taj wouldn't hurt a fly.'

'Well, he did try to open an aeroplane door,' Alex said. 'At thirty-five thousand feet, he could have hurt more than a fly. You'd all be dead.'

'That's a crass comment and also ignorant. He wasn't himself, and you can't actually open an aircraft door at that altitude. There's too much pressure. I looked into it.'

'I apologise. Do you see Taj?'

'Every opportunity I get. We go for walks on the beach, have delightful meals together. It's like a sweet, long-distance relationship. They make sure he takes his pills, so he's almost entirely himself. He's gained some weight, but it looks good on him. Zayn goes there whenever he's in the country long enough to visit.'

'Does Taj know about the kidnappings?'

'He doesn't follow the news, and I've asked the staff not to tell him. It could unsettle him, and I have too much to deal with without having to worry about Taj. I feel terrible about it, but if he relapses, I'll have to go to Shetland. Right now, I need to focus on raising the funds for Zayn.'

A thought that niggled at the back of Alex's mind rose to the surface. 'Nadia, when you told me you were worried about Zayn experiencing life deeply, did you mean…'

'Yes,' she said. 'It can be hereditary. There's about a ten per cent risk. I used to panic whenever Zayn was in a mood, but so far my worries have proved to be motherly angst, nothing more. As far as I can tell, he doesn't fit the profile. He's sociable, warm, maybe a bit immature, but not too much. He's not neurotic, which is a common trait for sufferers. Apparently, they do regular psych evaluations at the, er… the fitness programme he's a member of, so that's reassuring.'

'I see,' Alex said. 'Have the people from the fitness programme been supportive?'

'They were supportive, in a threatening way. I told him – I mean them – that I was grateful and that my lawyers would send a thank you postcard if they don't pull their finger out.'

'A quiche best served cold,' Alex said.

Nadia nodded. Then, without warning, Alex saw the powerful, dignified woman crumble before him. She managed enough composure to replace her teacup and saucer before covering her face with her hands.

'There-there,' Alex said as she sobbed, debating with himself whether to put a comforting hand on her shoulder but deciding against it. 'It's not over yet. We could still find them. Please, Nadia.' He handed her a tissue and thought back to his meeting with Davis who had also shown him the depths of his anguish. Being billionaires seemed to force the parents to hide themselves behind ten layers of masks. When it came to their children, this restriction must have been unimaginably tough. At least Alex could act as a kind of confessor, letting them be their true selves for a few precious minutes.

As her crying subsided, Nadia looked at him with a deep desperation that brought a lump to his throat. 'Two weeks ago,' she said, 'I made a large donation to a mental health charity.

They came to me, and I simply couldn't turn them away. You may have heard from your sources that the race for our kids is tight. As far as my people can tell, we're neck and neck in our chances. I may still make it, but the fifty million pounds I gave away could be the difference between life and death for Zayn. Please, Alex. I'm begging you. If there's any way to find him… If there's anything… Please help him.'

'I swear to you,' he said, 'we're doing everything we can. Everything.'

She wiped her eyes. 'I believe you,' she said, 'but swearing may not be enough. Our chances look so desperate. I feel so little hope.'

TWENTY-NINE

We regret any loss of life

WESTMINSTER, 15 AUGUST, 4PM

Nessa Thorns stood straight-backed behind the lectern and pretended nonchalance in the face of the journalists, the TV crews and the constant click-click-clicks of cameras. She had chosen a masculine dark suit over a bright white blouse, large pearl earrings, precise make-up and a perfectly cut political bob hairstyle that had cost a fortune but helped her feel a little less unready. A carefully placed leak had tipped off the media that this press conference was *a big one*, a potential source of front-page headlines.

At precisely 4pm, when she was confident the cameras were broadcasting live, Nessa silently cleared her throat and started speaking, trying for an authoritative tone with only an occasional glance at her notes.

'This afternoon, I met with the Prime Minister. We discussed the Terrorism Designation Order applied to the kidnappers of the five UK nationals held to ransom, an order that would criminalise the payment of funds to them. In our meeting, the PM asked me to explain to you today that any suggestion I approved the order late was, in fact, entirely wrong, and that reports to the contrary were misquoted or misconstrued.' She glanced down at her notes, paused, and then looked straight into the cameras. 'I'm afraid I cannot make such a statement, as it does not accord with the truth.'

An excited murmur rose from the crowd of correspondents. Cameras clicked and flashed.

'The Prime Minister has also asked me to repeat the mantra you have all heard from his office over the last few days: *we regret any loss of life*. Politicians will often use this well-worn phrase to mask their true position. It means nothing of the sort. It is spoken by apologists who condone amoral actions; apologists who defend the indefensible. Make no mistake, these words are duplicitous. If one truly regrets the loss of life, then surely one must take action to avoid it.' She paused and gave this statement ample time to bed. 'I have always stood firm in my unyielding commitment to preserving life, even in the face of tough decisions. I explained to the Prime Minister that I could not, in good conscience, utter these weasel words to you today.'

Nessa waited for another wave of clicks and whispers to subside. 'I'd like to make it clear: I do not support the kidnappings. I believe the methods used to extract money from the parents of these five individuals are abominable and cruel, *abominable and cruel*. However, by the same token, we must listen to the parents. We must consider their plea to give their children a chance of life, even if that chance is reduced and requires that they donate their fortunes.' She cleared her throat and surveyed her audience. They were devouring her words like hungry vultures. 'I therefore say this to you today: we must not stand in their way – especially since we have now seen that the ransom does not end up in the pockets of those who demand it and instead contributes to good causes.'

She counted to five, reminding herself to take her time, let her words sink in. 'The mark of good leadership reveals itself when the going gets tough, when hard choices must be made –

not for political reasons but for what would *genuinely* be the best possible outcome. I know the Prime Minister is steadfast and firm in his position. For my part, I am steadfast and firm in my belief that he is entirely wrong.'

Nessa relaxed her gaze in what she hoped projected a mixture of regret and determination. 'When I expressed these views to the PM, he asked me to wait while his staff prepared a resignation letter for me to sign. There was no need. I came armed with my own version, one that states exactly what I have shared with you here. Copies are now available on my website.' She straightened the microphone and loosened her shoulders, trying to appear personable. 'It wasn't easy. My decision to stand in front of you, as I do today, risks my career, my seat and my position in government. I do, however, hold an unflinching belief that we should all make our choices, even the hard ones, based on what's right, not what serves our political agenda. Not only do I stand by these convictions, I am proud of them.'

Some journalists in the audience looked ready to bolt, to file copy, to provide their commentary in front of their camera crews, but Nessa was not finished.

'Here we go,' Tom Smith whispered behind her. 'Good luck.'

Nessa steeled herself. She looked at her notes, then held her head high to speak the words she calculated could spin the political wheel off its axle. 'I've said enough about the past. What matters now – what really matters – is the future. Our country deserves better. *We* deserve better. I therefore call on our Prime Minister to resign his post with immediate effect and for the appointment of an interim leader. In the last few hours, I have canvassed my parliamentary party colleagues and expect to have the signatures of a majority calling for the PM to step down. As you would expect, there are processes to follow to bring about such a change. However, I hope our PM will do the right thing, rather than wait to be removed in disgrace. I know my actions are unusual and unprecedented, but these are unusual and unprecedented times. The country and its will must come first. Thank you.'

'Ms Thorns,' called out the political correspondent for BBC News, 'Are you putting yourself forward as interim leader?'

'That is a matter for the parliamentary party,' Nessa said. She turned around and walked through the open glass door, Tom shielding her from further questions.

Once they were inside, Tom placed a hand on her shoulder. 'Excellent delivery,' he said.

'You don't know Robert,' Nessa said. 'He's a brute, and he won't go down without a fight.'

'Yes,' Tom said. 'He might still win this scrap, but we are sumo wrestlers, you and I. Let us wax our hair and prepare to throw salt into the dohyo circle.'

'I think I'm going to be sick,' Nessa said and covered her mouth with her hand.

THIRTY

The Ides of March

The summons to Number 10 came within the hour. Nessa and Tom were ushered in, then made to wait for an hour in a stuffy room where the resident cat's litter box was kept. When the Prime Minister finally deigned to see them, he was all plastic smiles, but his eyes were tense and hostile.

'Sit down, Nessa,' the Prime Minister said without preliminaries or niceties, ignoring Tom who nevertheless took his seat next to Nessa to face the PM. 'All this commotion for the sake of five rich kids who probably won't make it anyway. Honestly, I have a country to run.'

Lucy Clifford came in from a side door and joined them in the chair to the Prime Minister's right.

'You look positively radiant, Lucy,' Nessa said. 'Are congratulations in order?'

'I have just offered Lucy the position of Home Secretary,' the Prime Minister said.

'A good choice. A safe pair of hands,' Nessa said and turned to Lucy. 'Have you accepted?'

'She's playing coy,' the Prime Minister again answered for

her. 'Told me she needs time to think about it. I gave her until 7pm, but we all know she'll accept.'

'She demurs,' Tom Smith said. 'How interesting.'

'I called you in here, Nessa,' the Prime Minister said, 'not to admonish you for the juvenile stunt you pulled in front of the media. That would be beneath me, though by the end of this meeting, I dare say you'll reflect on your choices.'

Nessa uncrossed her legs and rested her palms flat on her thighs, projecting a calmness she did not feel. She intended to follow Tom Smith's advice, and say as little as possible until she knew the PM's position.

'I wanted to hear an explanation from your own mouth,' the Prime Minister said, 'as to why you came out with those unedifying lies.'

'I don't know what you mean,' Nessa found herself saying.

'In your *riveting* statement to the press, you announced that you've canvassed our party's MPs, and they'd like to remove me from office. We both know that's not true. Unlike you, my other MPs are loyal. They've told me so. We called almost all of them.'

'They would though, wouldn't they?' Tom said. 'It's called hedging.'

'If this is your feeble attempt at whipping up a political storm,' the Prime Minister said to Nessa, 'thinking it will gather momentum when there is none, I can tell you right now, it won't work. You've made yourself look like an amateur with your Hail Mary move.'

'Blessed art thou amongst women,' Tom Smith said to Nessa. To the Prime Minister, he said, 'If you weren't rattled by Nessa's statement, why have we been summoned?'

'You, sir, have not been summoned, nor invited,' the Prime Minister said with undisguised contempt. 'Nessa will answer me, and you will remain silent.'

'She doesn't have to respond to spurious accusations,' Tom said.

The Prime Minister looked sideways at Lucy Clifford, then fixed his angry eyes on Nessa. 'You won't answer me?'

Nessa angled her head in defiance and said nothing.

'All right,' the Prime Minister said. 'You've made your position clear. In years to come, when you wonder where it all went wrong for you, you'll come back to this defining moment, to this meeting where you've treated a sitting Prime Minister and the leader of your party with contempt. I've given you fair warning and a chance to row back. You haven't. You leave me no choice.'

'The suspense is killing me,' Tom said.

'Quiet, Tom. Please,' Nessa said to him.

'Thank you,' the Prime Minister said without warmth. 'I take no joy in saying this, but I've misjudged you. I saw great promise in you. Yes, you were politically naive, a baby politician, but I believed that with the right direction, under my tutelage, you could grow into a real political operator. I can see now how that belief was a regrettable, fucking mistake.'

'You wanted a reverse Pinocchio,' Tom said, 'but then she didn't become a puppet?'

The Prime Minister offered Tom a vacant smile but again spoke to Nessa. 'The untruths in your press conference,' he said, 'not to mention your spiteful act of defiance when you signed the designation order late – these actions show that you are no more than a rebellious little girl playing at politics. You have neither the gravitas nor the nous to warrant being anywhere near government policy, anywhere near public service, actually. I wouldn't hire you as a secretary.'

Tom opened the notebook he had brought with him and scribbled two words in it, saying them out loud as he did, 'Gravitas and nous.' He looked up from the page at the Prime

Minister. 'I'm sorry. Don't let me distract you. Just writing up the highlights.'

'Childish,' the Prime Minister said with a shake of his head. 'Nessa, before you ruin your life, I'm going to give you one last chance. I only do it because I feel partly responsible. You were my appointment.'

Nessa felt her gut sinking. First, he'll make demands. Then, the threats will follow.

'You will call another press conference,' the Prime Minister said. 'You will show humility. You will say you misspoke and that you support me fully and unequivocally. In fact, we'll draft the speech for you, so there are no… infractions. I expect every word of it to be spoken, every punctuation mark to be obeyed. My office will then issue a statement saying we are grateful you have seen the light after what must have been a momentary lapse of judgement, an episode resulting from, well… You have been under a lot of stress lately. After that, you will scuttle to the back benches, and I never want to hear from you again. At the next general election, you will step down as a Member of Parliament.'

Nessa made a show of thinking about his demands. 'Thank you for your kind offer,' she said.

'It's agreed then,' he said. 'You'll renounce your statement and make a quiet retreat?'

Nessa lowered her chin, pretending she was going to nod, but then she looked up and met the Prime Minister's eyes. 'Not for all the kimchi in Korea.'

The Prime Minister ran his hand through his hair and muttered something inaudible under his breath. 'Very well,' he said. He pointed a finger gun at her and pretended to shoot. 'I wish you all the best in the rancid fish factory.'

'What does that even mean?' Tom said.

Lucy Clifford's phone buzzed. She glanced at it and quickly typed something in while speaking. 'What the Prime Minister means,' she said, 'is that he intends to remove the whip, expel you from the party. Once you're on your own in the Commons, he plans for his office to trickle-feed the media with damaging stories about you.' Her phone buzzed again.

The Prime Minister shot a warning look at Lucy. 'You're overstepping, Ms Clifford,' he said.

'I shouldn't have said that,' Lucy replied. 'Sorry. It's unwise to tell people you're going to smear them.' She turned to Nessa. 'I was at the brainstorming session. That's why you were kept waiting. They'll start by planting hints about bribes, then move on to a series of racy stories about unseemly relations, sleazy liaisons, that sort of thing.'

'Lucy!' the Prime Minister said in a threatening voice and glared at her.

Undeterred, Lucy continued. 'Someone suggested we invent an investment you supposedly made in Jonny's Brothels, the soup chain. Big headline on the front page, *MP Invests in Brothels* followed by an explanation no one would bother to read in the inside pages. Obviously, this will also tangle you in a conflict of interest. They'll claim you could not be objective about the kidnappings whilst being an investor in Jonny Salt's business.'

'That's enough,' the Prime Minister said to Lucy Clifford through gritted teeth. 'Please leave us.'

'Of course,' Lucy said, but remained in her seat. 'There's only this update. This one update…'

'Your phone's been buzzing,' Tom said to Lucy.

'I've added my vote,' Lucy said.

'I'm grateful,' Nessa said, 'if a little surprised.'

'Blessed art thou amongst women,' Lucy said.

'That's very gracious of you,' Tom said to Lucy.

Lucy put her hand on the Prime Minister's knee in an overfamiliar way. 'Let me explain, Robert. I just got word. An overwhelming majority of the parliamentary party has called for your immediate resignation. They disagree with your position on the kidnappings. In fact, they are so aggrieved by it, they're prepared to join the opposition in a no-confidence vote if you do not step down, today.'

'That's preposterous,' the Prime Minister said, 'and I don't believe you. Sitting members of a ruling party would never be so foolish. A vote against themselves? I don't think so.'

'Your MPs have concluded,' Tom said, 'that keeping you on board would cause a landslide defeat in the next election, a landslide so devastating it will consign your party to the political desert for the next decade. Most of them would lose their seats.'

'I'm afraid, Prime Minister, there's more,' Lucy said.

'I'm sure there is,' the Prime Minister said. 'I'm telling you now, it won't wash.'

'Another canvass is doing the rounds,' Lucy said. 'Nessa may not be aware of it, but she has the support of a majority, requesting that she stand in as caretaker PM until we can elect a new party leader, which, all things considered, is likely to also be her.'

The Prime Minister rubbed his temples. His bravado was gone. He seemed deflated, smaller, like a punctured wheel tube leaking air, held together by the tyre's rubber skin.

'Thank you, Lucy,' Nessa said. 'If I become caretaker, will you accept the position of Home Secretary?'

Tom smiled. 'That is certainly an offer that shows gravitas and nous.'

'I'd be delighted to,' Lucy said.

'Prime Minister,' Nessa said, 'I know this has been a distressing meeting, and I'm sorry to have put you in this position. If you leave without a fight, I promise I will sing your praises and recommend you for a peerage. You can serve the public with all the trappings of the House of Lords. But my offer expires at 7pm.'

'Gravitas and nous,' Tom said. 'The sumo wrestler bows at fight's end.'

'What on earth is he talking about?' Lucy said to Nessa.

'Robert,' Nessa said. 'I'm asking you to think of the party and the country. Make this a seamless transition, and we can pretend this meeting never happened.'

The Prime Minister huffed through gritted teeth, barely containing his irritation. 'You will call me by my title, Prime Minister, and as Prime Minister, I'm telling you, the schemes of a Barbie MP and a subversive understudy won't wash. You have no idea who you're dealing with.'

'Which one's the Barbie?' Tom Smith said.

'I think he means me,' Lucy Clifford said.

'Ah, makes sense,' Tom said.

Nessa touched Tom's arm and shook her head to signal that he should stop. The meeting had gone better than she could have hoped, yet she felt no joy, only apprehension. For all his bluster, the Prime Minister was a savvy politician. Once he spoke to his advisors, he'll know he was done. By the next day, the baton could be passed on to her and with it a grave responsibility. She may have dreamed of one day leading the country, but not so soon, not tomorrow. What if she had a migraine tomorrow? What if she wasn't up to the task?

As they walked out of Number 10, Tom Smith seemed to sense her trepidation. 'You'll make a great PM,' he said. 'There's just one thing that makes you, dare I say, a lesser leader.' He wiped his mouth with the back of his hand. 'It's nothing, really. I shouldn't even bring it up.'

'I'm listening.'

'It's all in the optics. What I mean is… Well, you're an impressive woman. You'll do a great job, especially with my sage advice.'

'And yet?'

'Well, you see,' he said, hesitated, then spoke again. 'What would round you up to perfect is a devoted husband.' He cleared his throat. 'Will you, perhaps, consider marrying me?'

'For the sake of optics?'

'For the sake of optics.'

She burst out laughing. 'You'll make a brilliant comedian one day, Tom. Thanks for cheering me up.'

THIRTY-ONE

The secret agent

The hammock croaked like a toad each time it swayed, with Noah pushing the ground with his hand to keep it swinging at a pleasant pace. In the shade of the palms, serenaded by the sound of the waves, he felt at peace, ready to go home and start a new life. In his mind, he drafted his resignation letter to the university, with immediate effect, before the start of the autumn term. As much as he hated leaving the department's faculty in the lurch, the university wouldn't dare object to his departure. His kidnapping was international news. They could hardly deny him a respectable exit. And if that didn't work, Noah could always get his mother's bulldog lawyers involved.

He heard the patter of flip-flops and lazily turned his head to see Zayn, who came to sit on the sand beside him, just outside the hammock's trajectory. 'All right, chump? Enjoying your holiday?'

'It's growing on me.'

'Don't be alarmed, but I have a question for you.'

'You can have Emily if you like,' Noah said.

'She really did a job on you, didn't she?'

Noah felt a new warmth towards Zayn. *Is that what having a friend feels like?*

Zayn shuffled forward, held the hammock's edge and steadied it to a stop. He touched Noah's cheek with the back of his hand. 'Poor boy,' he said. 'We'll have to hook you up with some classy women. I have an idea or two in that department.'

'You said you have a question?' Noah said.

Zayn arranged himself into the lotus position and gave the hammock a gentle push. 'If you had to find your way from here to Wilhelm's cabin, could you do it?'

Noah pointed in the general direction of the gate at the far end of the beach. 'Up the trail, about ten or fifteen minutes that way. Why?'

'I'd feel more comfortable if you came with me.'

Noah sat up awkwardly in the hammock, supported by his elbows. 'What?'

'Something's not right,' Zayn said. 'It's been two days since they told us our parents paid the ransom. I'm not buying the story that there's some boat that comes once a week. Wilhelm and his outfit had enough funds to fly us at least halfway around the world. They could have sent us back yesterday, but they didn't. Every day they keep us here is risky for them, makes it more likely they'd be tracked down. My gut tells me we should do something tonight, before it's too late. You said you saw computers in that cabin. We should make a move, go there and try to access them, send our location to someone.'

'That could get us shot a lot quicker,' Noah said.

'Maybe,' Zayn said. 'Or we're sitting ducks for whatever they're planning. They never hid their faces from us. We've seen Wilhelm. We know enough to identify Cody and probably some of the other men. Why would they risk sending us back?' Zayn gave the hammock another push and a tug. 'Come with me. You've seen the trail to Wilhelm's cabin, and you know the layout there.'

'Yeah, sure,' Noah said. 'Do you plan to fly over the fence?'

'I've already dug a way out under it. The fence's base wasn't set too deep under the surface. They didn't expect us to try, considering it's supposed to be deadly. I spent hours last night digging with a coconut shell. Didn't want to risk them seeing me in daylight.'

'Good thing Ashleigh tested the fence, eh?' Noah said.

Zayn chuckled. 'I actually touched it before her. On our first day here, when I was walking the perimeter with Jonny. A real electric fence will have insulators, cable boxes, wires. This one has nothing. I saw through the lie straight away. It's just a fence.'

'You knew?' Noah said. 'You actually knew that Ashleigh was never in danger? Why didn't you say?'

'Was better for her that way. I reckoned she needed to get it out of her system.' He shrugged. 'So I played along.'

'And Jonny?'

'Innocent. He didn't see me test it, and I didn't tell him.'

'You're a lot more clever than you–'

'Nah, and I would have liked to start digging earlier, but on day one, they sent us to the basement, and then the thing with Emily happened, and after that, well, it looked like they might send us home.'

'And now you don't think they will,' Noah said. He bit his lip, drew in air and eventually relented. 'Fine. I'll join you on your suicide mission. Nothing better to do anyway.'

Zayn patted him on the shoulder. 'Meet me here after sunset, about ten minutes after you see me go. We'll just slip out separately and join up here. I don't want to worry the others. Wear long trousers and sleeves. The plan is to navigate out of the jungle in the dark. Luckily there'll be a bit of moonlight later. One question though, Wilhelm's dog, the pit bull, was it there when you visited?'

'The Marines took him away. Wouldn't want to see him again. What if he's back?'

'One problem at a time.'

The ominous jungle on the outer side of the fence was a wall of sound: crickets chirping, frogs croaking, animals shuffling in the undergrowth. As they marched in the near dark, branches broke under their step, and Noah did his best not to think about venomous spiders and snakes.

Zayn's original plan was to bank further left and away from the enclosure, reducing the chance of them being seen, but the wall of trees and bushy vegetation was too thick to enter. They had to stick to the perimeter and hope the fence was not guarded.

By the time they reached the trail that led to Bill's cabin, they were covered in sap and dirt. Noah's arms felt itchy and hot. Something had bitten him on the back of his neck, producing a sore lump. The meagre moon was shielded by clouds, the dim light forcing them to watch their step and advance slowly, mindful of the sheer cliff to their right. Halfway up the trail, they stopped for a drink from the bottle of water Zayn carried with him.

'What will we do when we get there?' Noah said.

'You're only asking me now?' Zayn said. 'I like it. Blindly following the fool.' Zayn made a show of sighing, but it was a light-hearted sigh. 'We'll get to old Wilhelm's cabin, see what's what, especially how many people are there. If there's more than one, you might have to create a diversion while I go in. If it's just him, we'll tackle him together. I'm pretty confident I can take his old bones out of commission. All that time I spend at the gym should count for something. If the dog's there, well, we'll see how it goes.'

They approached the cabin from the back, crouching low, treading lightly to avoid making any noise that would announce their arrival. The sea's usual hum had quietened. The wind had died to nothing. Noah felt as if even his breath was too loud. They were close now, almost at the cabin's back window. Soft light emanated from within.

Noah took a step forward, and his shoe hit something metallic, a watering can. The bang reverberated into the silent night like a cymbal being struck. 'Shit,' he whispered. Zayn dropped to the ground and signalled for Noah to do the same. They both lay flat on their fronts, looking up from the wild grass. What felt like a line of ants crawled over Noah's arm, but he dared not move.

A face appeared in the window above them. It was Bill, a cigar in his mouth. He looked out, coughed, shook his head, and then disappeared.

Zayn signalled for Noah to stay where he was and edged himself to the side of the window. He looked into the cabin for what felt like forever. Then, in the dim light, he held up one finger, signalling that only Bill was inside, *one person*. He pointed to the side of the cabin, mouthed 'front,' and motioned for Noah to follow him.

They tiptoed to the cabin's front door. Zayn stood to the right of the doorframe and Noah to its left, readying to barge in and surprise Bill.

Then came the sudden blinding whiteness of powerful LED torch lights. Noah felt a rush of adrenaline.

'Down on the floor!' A cacophony of shouts came from every direction. 'On the floor, now! Down! Now!'

As if out of nowhere, they were surrounded by six or seven soldiers; guns pointed at them. 'On the floor, I said!' It was Cody's voice.

The shock paralysed Noah. He didn't move, couldn't move.

Someone kicked him in the knee pit, and he squirmed to the ground, falling on his side, hugging himself.

'Hands behind your backs! I said, behind your backs. Jono, zip ties, double quick.'

Within seconds, they were bound and rolled onto their backs, their hands digging into their spines.

'Sorry, Noah,' Zayn said. 'That was a crap date. I'll take you on a better one next time. Do you like sushi? I know this little place—'

'Quiet,' Cody barked and kicked Zayn in the stomach.

Zayn squirmed in pain. 'All right, dude, chill!' Cody kicked him again, harder this time. Zayn rolled on his side, bringing his knees to his stomach.

Bill opened the door and stepped out, still puffing on his cigar. In his German accent, he said, 'Well, well, well. Mr Gant, Mr Sayal, if you wished to see me, you should have made an appointment. We have sensors and cameras along the route and night-vision drones at the ready. We followed you from the moment you thought you escaped.' He pressed his shoe over Zayn's face and pushed down until Zayn growled in pain. 'It is unacceptable,' Bill said. 'Entirely and thoroughly unacceptable, and for this you must pay the ultimate price, a shot to the head. Do not say I did not warn you, yes? Well, I guess the warnings did not work.'

'Do what you want to me,' Zayn said, 'but—'

Cody kicked Zayn again.

Bill looked down at Zayn and angled his head. 'I wager what you were going to say, Mr Sayal, is do what you like to me, but let Noah Gant live, correct? Bloody Hollywood films. Everything you young people utter is like some bad script.' He looked up. 'Cody, we'll start with Mr Sayal. Point to his head and on my mark, shoot.'

'Yes, sir,' Cody said. With his boot, he rolled Zayn onto his back and positioned the barrel of his Mini-Uzi an inch from

Zayn's mouth. 'Open wide, pretty boy. I wouldn't want to smash those beautiful teeth with my bullets. They must have cost a fortune.'

'Oh, you're so tough, aren't you,' Zayn hissed at Cody. 'I bet you make your meth-head parents really proud. Go on, be a man, shoot. I'm bored of your threats.'

Cody looked up at Bill. 'Permission to blow this mofo's head off, sir. He's earned it.'

'Please,' Noah pleaded. 'Please don't shoot him.'

Bill toked on his cigar and blew sweet smoke into the humid night. 'I hate the tropics,' he said. 'It looks so good in pictures – beaches, jungle, all that – but the heat and mosquitoes are hell. Next time I arrange a kidnapping, I shall want full air-conditioning and appropriate mosquito netting on all the doors and windows.'

'Sir?' Cody said.

'Hmm,' Bill said. 'I have decided to be benevolent. We shall let them enjoy our hospitality a little longer. The lesson, I think, is learned.'

'But sir,' Cody said.

'If they do it again, if they set foot even an inch outside the fence, I give you permission to shoot on sight, okay?'

Cody's shoulders fell. 'Yes, sir.'

'You were never going to shoot me,' Zayn said. 'I can see the pattern. You need us alive.'

'Why provoke him?' Noah said to Zayn.

'Best listen to Mr Gant,' Bill said to Zayn. 'Some things are better not gambled upon.' He turned to Cody. 'Take Zayn Sayal back to the villa. I wish to interrogate Mr Gant further. I think he is more likely to give answers. Leave one of your men outside here for when I am done with him.'

After Zayn was dragged away, Noah was helped up to his feet by the guard. He hobbled after Bill into the cabin. Bill searched a cabinet drawer and brought out a pair of scissors, which he used to cut Noah's hands free from the zip tie.

'Would you like some iced tea?' Bill said in his English accent.

Noah shook his head.

'You did well, mate,' Bill said. 'Your mother and I are grateful. Are you sure no one saw you nipping out to the intercom in the afternoon?'

'They were all inside the villa.'

'You're a top recruit.'

'Blackmail is not recruitment.'

'Spy agencies the world over would beg to differ.'

'Why are you still keeping us here? If our parents paid the ransom, why aren't you sending us home? That's why Zayn wanted to come here.'

'Pretty boy's right. We've set up an instalment plan. Only two payments. The second one is due tomorrow. I wouldn't worry too much. I'm sure most of them will pay.'

'Most of them?'

Bill waved his hand dismissively. 'Bah!' he said. 'Don't worry. Here's the message to take back to your mates. There's no need to make any trouble. We'll be throwing a goodbye party for you tomorrow night at the villa, bubbly and burgers, music, dancing, the lot. Dress code is black tie and dresses, strictly enforced, no exceptions or feminism. You don't want to upset Cody. He's hot-headed and a sucker for dress codes.'

THIRTY-TWO

Herding Sallies

Nessa sank into her chair in the Cabinet Room, closed her eyes and took a tentative sip from the steaming cup of coffee brought to her by an aide she did not recognise. The drink was too bitter, probably the way her predecessor liked it. She made a mental note to update Downing Street staff on her beverage preferences, a note that would sit near the top of the endless list of tasks slotted in for her first day on the job. Coffee, meetings, more coffee, flasks and flasks of it.

Only two hours earlier, Nessa had travelled to Buckingham Palace to see the King for her official appointment as Prime Minister. She did her best to appear unfazed, prime ministerial, keeping her excitement in check. Following a briefing from the Lord Chamberlain, she was led to meet His Majesty. After managing a passable YouTube-learned curtsy, her nerves settled a little. She could have opted for a handshake but knew her father wouldn't approve. The King was pleasant and informal, offering congratulations and small talk. When Nessa commented on how the nation was gripped by the kidnappings, he simply said, 'It's a tough one, isn't it? I suppose we ourselves will appear on some rich list or other. Do you think we should tighten protection for the royal heirs? Yes, perhaps that should be looked at.'

Nessa opened her eyes to the sound of footsteps. Tom Smith had entered the Cabinet Room, wisely holding two coffee shop paper cups. Nessa hushed him before he could speak and pointed to one of the wall-mounted TV screens. Sky News was interviewing trade union man Robbie Sage. She turned up the sound.

'It's an outrage,' Sage said, 'An absolute outrage. The way Hammerson Oil employees have been treated is nothing less than a travesty of justice, losing their jobs like that from one day to the other. Families will be left destitute, unable to feed their children.'

'Mr Sage,' the presenter said, 'I am a little confused by your position. Didn't you call on Peter Hammerson to pay the kidnappers as much as he could? Was it not you who said, and I quote, "He should pay – and pay generously. What are a few million to him, a few hundred million, a few billion?" Isn't it true that the only way for him to dig deep, as you demanded, was to sell his shares in the business? You effectively pleaded for him to do exactly as he did. The run on the company that followed was a direct result of those actions, was it not?'

'I don't accept the premise of your question,' Robbie Sage said. 'I didn't mean that he should ruin the company and send Hammerson Oil's workforce into jobless misery. What kind of man does that? Common decency–'

Nessa clicked the remote to turn off the screen.

Tom Smith tutted with relish. 'Cattle petitioning for slaughter, then moaning they end up in Yorkshire pies.' He sat down, sliding the coffee her way. 'Good morning, Nessa.'

'We're not doing that,' she said.

'My apologies. Good morning, Prime Minister.'

'Better. In this job, I can't be seen to–'

He raised a hand to stop her. 'Say no more. What's on the sheet?'

'This morning, I had meetings with ministerial colleagues and others. In addition to my duties in this house, I shall have further such meetings later today.'

'Had any breakfast?' he said.

'That's scheduled for Wednesday, if I find the time.'

'How can I assist?' Tom said.

'For starters, I need you on this next meeting. We're a day away from the kidnappers' second deadline, so it will weigh heavily on people's minds. If we can rescue the hostages, it'll be a massive win, especially if the ransom's already been paid. Win-win. I'd like to make sure our security services are doing everything they can to locate them. Whatever Robert knew, he never shared, even when I was Home Secretary. There's always a chance we know where they are but haven't acted on it for political reasons. If that's the case, I'll put a stop to the dithering. I want my selection for PM to matter. I want to save them if I can.'

'Who's attending the meeting? The usual shadows?'

'Bertram and the two Sallies.' She was referring to Chief of the Defence Staff, Bertram Grieves, MI5 head, Sally Summers, and MI6 head, Sally Smithfield. It had become common practice to refer to the two women, even to their faces, as *Sally Five* and *Sally Six*.

'A trio of swinging dicks,' Tom said. 'Actually, except for Sally Six. I find her solid and effective.' He reached into his pocket. 'Oh, I almost forgot, the girl with a cravat, the one that looks like a duck, she gave me a note for you.' He handed her a folded square of yellow paper.

'It's not a cravat. It's an ascot,' Nessa said while reading the note, 'and the "girl" in question is Moira Sands, my new chief of staff. Black belt in karate. She could geld you with a single kick.'

'Karate is so sexy in a woman,' Tom said.

She flashed him a warning. 'Let's tone ourselves down a little, all right? As befits.'

'Yes, Prime Minister,' he said through a subversive grin, 'as befits.'

'For goodness' sake, Tom.'

'Sorry.'

Nessa drew in a deep breath for calm. 'The National Security Adviser was also meant to be here. Called in sick. That's what the note from Moira says, but he already phoned me earlier. He's worried what I might think.'

'Should he be?'

'Most definitely.'

'People get sick,' Tom said.

'His so-called illness came from losing several rounds of gin pong. They were having leaving drinks for my predecessor last night.'

'Ah,' Tom said, 'the long shadow of Robert's gin pong regime.'

An intern opened the door and ushered the three invitees into the room. The two formidable women carried almost identical tan leather briefcases, which they placed on the table, unclasped in tandem, and then brought out folders and pens. The head of the army, clad in full dress uniform and a scowl, came with only a thin stack of papers.

'I've read your briefing notes on threats, et cetera,' Nessa said once they were seated. 'However, in this meeting, I only have one item on the agenda. I'd like to get up to speed on the kidnappings – any information, progress, intelligence, anything we know.' She turned to MI5's Director General. 'Sally?'

Sally Five raised an eyebrow. 'The billionaire kidnappings?'

'This isn't a trick question,' Tom Smith said. 'The Prime Minister would like an update on a matter that has been spinning the nation's news cycles like a blender with our hands in it.'

Nessa shot Tom another warning look, which he made a show of ignoring.

Sally Five stroked her chin. 'I… Well…' She cleared her throat, fidgeting with her Cross pen. 'I have nothing to tell you at this time, no breakthroughs.'

'Nothing at all?' Nessa said.

Sally Five shook her head and dropped her pen onto the stack of files.

'Six?' Tom said.

'Obviously, there's a complication for us,' Sally Six said, 'and we're grateful you've probed Nadia Sayal, but otherwise, I'm afraid I'm in the same boat.'

Bertram Grieves, the Chief of the Defence Staff, looked at her with interest. 'What complication?'

Tom Smith answered for her. 'That's for another time, Bertram. Now the army, what say you?'

Bertram Grieves did not hesitate. With confident, almost cocky, finality, he said, 'This is not an army matter.'

'Explain it to me like I'm your Prime Minister,' Nessa said. 'Suppose we locate the five victims and need to extract them. Wouldn't an elite unit like the SAS be the right tool for the job?'

'That's one view,' Bertram Grieves said. When he saw the look on Nessa's face, he quickly added, 'Of course, if intelligence is available and instructions are issued to us, we will act as required. My hesitation was entirely about how it looks. Our special forces have rescued civilians in the past. However, you wouldn't like the public to think we swung into action because rich party donors made a fist.'

'What we'd like the public to think, Bertram,' Tom Smith

said, 'is entirely above your pay grade. If we say march, you march, like the good soldier you are.'

'Who are you again?' the army chief said to Tom.

Sally Six clasped her hands over her document bundle. In a soothing tone, she said, 'Prime Minister, let me try and clear up the mystery. It's your first day, and obviously some developments have, how shall I put it… Well, you've not been fully briefed yet.'

'I'm about to fall off the edge of my seat,' Nessa said.

'Your predecessor was quite clear on the matter. Robert told us – and these are his words – to twiddle our thumbs and practise mindfulness. Finding and recovering the five hostages was designated a low priority or, to put it bluntly, a *no priority*. Our instructions were to focus on other threats, of which there are many. The Met Police have been allowed to carry on with their investigation but without help from the security and intelligence services and no additional resources. The previous PM's view was that this crisis, such as it is, will run its course in just a few days and is not worth the bother.' She drew her lower lip between her teeth. 'We're not stonewalling you, Nessa. If the Cabinet's position has changed, we will, of course, adjust our approach.'

'I see,' Nessa said and looked around the table. Bertram Grieves's shoulders were squared, his lips even. Sally Five was playing with her wedding ring, slowly turning it around her finger, avoiding eye contact.

'Well,' Nessa said, 'at least I know now where we stand.'

'We stand,' Tom said, 'haunted by the consequences of doing not a miserable, tossing thing.'

Sally Five looked up from her hands. 'Not quite nothing,' she said. 'We've been keeping an eye on the private operation run by the parents.'

'You're tapping Alex Czerniak?' Tom said. 'Jesus wept. Our spooks are reduced to copying someone else's homework?'

'Thank you, Tom,' Nessa said. 'Sally, Sally, I know it's late in the game, but as of this minute, this becomes a high priority, *the highest priority*. Any leads, any discoveries, brief me immediately, day or night. We still have about twenty-seven hours. Let's make the most of them.'

The two women looked relieved to move on from the grilling.

'We'll get right on it,' Sally Five said while Sally Six dipped her chin in agreement.

'Bertram,' Nessa said. 'I want a response force ready for an extraction the very second we have reliable intelligence, be it here in the UK or abroad. Thank you all for coming to see me.'

Bertram Grieves looked nonplussed but gave her an obstinate nod. The two Sallies made their exits first, each offering the standard line Nessa had already heard two dozen times that day: *We look forward to working with you, Prime Minister*. When the head of the army reached the door, he stared at it for a moment, seeming to hesitate. Then, he turned back to face Nessa. 'Prime Minister,' he said, 'I didn't mean to appear uncooperative earlier. My doubts have nothing to do with you personally.'

'Of course,' Nessa said and waited. Bertram appeared to have something on his mind.

'You've risen to your new position with tremendous support from the people and from Parliament, and I congratulate you on your... tenacity.' He tapped his fingers together under his chin. 'The thing of it is, I can't help but wonder: the public's support for the kidnappers and by association for you – what does it mean for our country? In the coming days, this incident will end. Charities might be handed large sums. Maybe a hostage will come back alive. But what then? How will it affect our politics, our society? If the state is beholden to people who think their cause justifies any means, that they're so right, killing becomes an acceptable price… What then?' He shook his head. 'I've said enough.'

'More than enough,' Tom said.

Bertram cleared his throat. He gave Nessa a tiny bow of the head and left the room. When he was gone, Tom said, 'What a windbag.'

'He has three daughters and five grandchildren,' Nessa said. 'I know his eldest, Clare. We worked together at the FCO. Deep thinker. I can see where she gets it from.'

'And?' Tom said.

'He has a point. The events that got me here – it's like I'm part of a design.'

'It's an excellent design if it made you PM,' Tom said.

'Is it?' Nessa said. 'I'm not sure how I feel about being the rubber stamp for what will happen if we don't find the hostages first.'

'You're having one of your deep Buffy moments,' Tom said. 'It's natural. Then, you'll smile and become a cheerleader again. I'm sorry, obscure reference.'

'All right, Tom,' she said. 'You're my Special Adviser. Advise me. What do you think happens next?'

Tom drank the last of his coffee and crumpled the paper cup in his fist. 'By the deadline, 1pm tomorrow, Five and Six will barely have time to tie their laces, let alone trace the piggies. I hate to say this, but my sense is they'll make the right noises, send you a memorandum or two to show they care and wait it out. Bottom line, the rich kids are buggered unless the parents' useless PI chances on something. Don't hold your breath.'

'And then?' Nessa said.

'A hundred years of peace,' Tom said, 'with purges and guillotines and student politics.' He shrugged. 'Or brutal martial law.'

Nessa wiped her nose with the back of her finger. She felt a little dizzy.

'Either way it pans out,' Tom said, 'you'll need a skintight leather outfit with sharp pointy shoulder pads. Maybe a live snake for public appearances?'

'I need some air,' Nessa said.

'I'll come with you.'

'No,' Nessa said. 'I need to be alone.'

THIRTY-THREE

Collateral damage

'You got sunscreen on? They have it in the rooms,' Noah said to Ashleigh, who was in her bikini again, lying on one of the fluffy room towels on the beach's golden sand. She had been spending a good deal of her time on the beach while the rest of them lazed around in the hammock, on the veranda or in the shaded areas under the trees, reminiscing, playing word games, drinking bottled water and eating without set mealtimes, almost accustomed to the bland food that was delivered to them by wheelbarrow once a day. Noah and Zayn had gone for a swim in the morning, chatting and making plans for the days after their release, their friendship evolving into an honest closeness – honest other than Noah's betrayal of Zayn's plan to venture to Bill's cabin the night before. He couldn't tell him – not yet – but he was certain Zayn would understand. Noah had no choice in the matter if he wanted to keep his mother safe.

The final hot and humid days in their beach enclosure felt like a holding pattern, but at least their time in captivity was nearing its end. The next day, they will be heading home, and it looked as though Ashleigh would make it home with them.

Everything will be fine, or as fine as it can be considering Ashleigh's condition.

'Don't fret,' Ashleigh said to Noah. 'Sunscreen's the last of my worries.' She sat up and patted the sand beside her. 'Join me?'

He hesitated.

'You can't catch cancer. It's not contagious.'

'You spurned my marriage proposal,' he said, 'and now you taunt me with your scantily clad posing?'

'Yeah,' she said. 'Come, sit next to my rotting body. Enjoy the dimming glow of my stupid karma.'

'Karma?'

'Figure of speech. We live. We die. That's it. There's a party tonight. If I get that far, I'm going to treat it as my pre-mortem funeral service. But no eulogies, please. Just fun.'

'Fine,' Noah said and cleared his throat. 'I don't like parties anyway. Funerals, well, that's a completely different vibe. I totally dig those.'

She searched his face. 'I never told you how sorry I was, about your dad.'

He looked away. 'Thanks. It was a long time ago.'

She looked up at the sky and shaded her eyes with her hand. 'There's a pretty ball gown in my wardrobe, sparkly and white. It's perfect.' She looked at him. 'Sorry, I know I keep talking about death. I can't help it, but I'll stop now.'

'Everyone needs a hobby,' Noah said.

'Fuck off.'

'Ooh, prickly,' he said with half a smile.

'Look who's come out of his shell,' she said. 'Did you a world of good, this kidnapping, and I mean that in the nicest possible way. Oh hi, Jonny. You're standing between me and the sun.'

Jonny loomed over them both. 'You mocking the size of my shadow, Ash?'

'It's huge, and I want a nice tan for my imminent demise, so if you don't mind…'

Jonny took a step sideways, clasped his hands behind his back and looked at Noah. 'Have you recovered from last night? Zayn's got some impressive bruises.'

'Zayn answers back. He's got balls. I'm more of a peaceful protestor. Mine are more like mothballs, in every respect.'

'You actually believe it's our final night here?' Jonny said.

'Dare to hope,' Noah said. 'What's the first thing you'll do when you get home?'

'See if my wife takes me back,' Jonny said. 'Being here gave me a certain… perspective. I didn't appreciate how important my family is to me, and I–'

Ashleigh's hand rushed to her mouth. 'Oh no. Oh shit.' She made a low guttural sound. 'I feel ill.'

Jonny's face fell with worry. 'You shouldn't be out in the heat. Want us to help you inside?'

Ashleigh made a retching noise, then uncovered her mouth to reveal a teasing grin. 'Sorry, Jonny, your twee emotional moment made me sick.'

'Damn you, Ash!' Jonny said.

Ashleigh pouted at him. 'You can't say that to a poor dying girl.'

Jonny chuckled. 'Oh really? Can't I?'

'Fair enough,' she said. 'I'm sorry, *again*. I know I get a bit much. Every day, I convince myself it's going to be my last, which is funny because science and statistics say I won't be wrong for too long. Shouldn't complain, though, right?'

'Are you in pain?' Noah said.

'Not at the moment. I was in agony for the last few weeks. Everything hurt, but the past few days have been better. Like I said, if you're near the end, you sometimes get a good phase. It just means the end is nigh. That's why I'm being such a bore, which I'll stop, at once, I promise.'

Jonny looked at her, then lowered his eyes to the ground. 'I'm glad you're feeling better. I know it's selfish, but I'm grateful we got a chance to know you properly, as an adult.'

For a long time, they remained silent, enjoying what Noah felt was a certain closeness, a bond. Ashleigh was scanning the gentle waves and the waterline, looking as though she was lost in a dream. Then, all of a sudden, her lower lip fell lax, and her eyes grew wide. Her breathing quickened. 'Oh fuck,' she rasped. 'No, no, no. Not now. It can't be. Not now, please… my mind… I think I'm hallucinating.' She started crying, rubbing her eyes with her fists. 'Make it stop, please. I'm not ready.'

'What's happening?' Jonny said, looking unsure. 'Are you messing with us again?'

Noah didn't think it was another trick. *Was this it? The rapid deterioration after a short period of feeling well?* 'Ashleigh,' he said, 'do you want us to call for help?'

Ashleigh didn't answer. She looked overcome, no longer able to speak. Somehow, she got to her feet, looking unsteady and frail, as if the slightest gust of wind could blow her away in tiny fragments of flesh and bone.

'Ash, maybe you should sit,' Jonny said. 'Sit down.'

She didn't seem to hear him. She was staring forward with horror, her whole body shaking. Noah followed her gaze. A figure was pushing a wheelbarrow loaded with boxes of beer and champagne bottles along the beach. It was Marian. Instead of heading straight to the villa, she came towards the three of them. A couple of feet away, she lowered the wheelbarrow's handles and stood up straight, cracking her knuckles.

Noah checked himself. His hatred towards her had mellowed to disdain. She was an employee of whoever was holding them. Ashleigh needed help. Maybe they had some medicine for her, something to ease whatever was coming. He nodded at Marian, hoping to appear civil.

Marian ignored him. Instead, she locked eyes with Ashleigh. Ashleigh was hugging herself, her hands balled into fists, her face pale as a shroud.

'She needs help,' Noah said to Marian. 'She's not well. Please, can you help her?'

'You can see her?' Ashleigh whispered. 'She's here?'

Marian gave Noah a nod but returned her gaze to Ashleigh, crossing her arms and waiting as if she needed Ashleigh to speak for herself. Noah felt his patience waning. 'Marian–' he started to say.

Ashleigh interrupted him. 'She's my oncologist.'

'Your what?' Jonny said.

Noah looked from Ashleigh to Marian. 'Oh shit,' he said. 'Oh shit. For heaven's sake.'

Ashleigh turned to Noah. 'You know her?'

'I came to give you the good news,' Marian said to Ashleigh. 'Congratulations, you're cancer-free. If you survive our hospitality, you'll live to write that novel you couldn't shut up about.'

'What are you doing here?' Ashleigh said, looking as though she hadn't heard a word.

'Noah, darling,' Marian said, 'could you help us out here?'

'She's not an oncologist,' Noah said. 'There's no cancer. There was never any cancer. Right, Marian?'

'But the hospital, the scans, the blood tests,' Ashleigh said. 'I saw them. The second opinion. The other oncologist, Dr Drummond, Eliza Drummond.'

'We intercepted your annual health check letter and sent you our own. Eliza is many things, but not an oncologist. She works for us. Right, Noah? Your blood tests are fairly normal. You're a bit anaemic, but nothing that can't be fixed with a balanced diet. More B12 and iron. I'd load up on spinach, shellfish, liver if you like it and red meat. A good bloody steak once a week. That should see you right.'

'You're lying,' Ashleigh said. 'Why would you say that? I've been so ill, fucking puking my guts out. I could barely get up in the morning. My skin, it's—'

'All expected symptoms,' Marian said.

Ashleigh placed her hand on her stomach and looked down at it. She swallowed hard, swallowed again, grunted, looked wide-eyed at Noah and Jonny and then at Marian. 'The pills,' she finally said. 'The fucking pills you gave me.' She squeezed her eyes shut for a moment, then opened them. Her frailty had evaporated into anger. Her face turned wild with rage. With a low growl and a screwed-up face, she lunged at Marian, fists forward.

Marian moved aside, expertly avoiding the attack. She grasped Ashleigh's wrists and used the momentum of her attack to haul her forward until she fell on the sand, face first. Then she held Ashleigh's hands behind her back and pulled them up by the wrists.

'Ow!' Ashleigh cried.

Marian pulled harder. 'Are you done?'

Ashleigh didn't answer.

'I said, are you done?'

Ashleigh finally relented and nodded. Sandy spittle had stuck to her chin. Marian let go of her and took a step back.

Ashleigh spread her arms wide to her sides, lying prostrate as if crucified. She started sobbing, moaning, mumbling out words. 'How could they? How could you?' She rolled onto her back and covered her face, her chest rising and falling, growling as though in unbearable pain, as though she was dying.

Jonny remained rooted where he stood, his hand over his mouth.

Noah looked at Marian and shook his head. 'The cruelty of it. Do you even have a soul?'

Marian gave him a bright, carefree smile. 'I've just saved

241

her life, haven't I? She's cured. Praise the Lord! Surely you're happy for her. Anyway, can't stop. Have to put the booze in your fridge. Big party tonight.'

She raised the wheelbarrow's handles, banked right and headed for the villa, walking breezily away.

Jonny and Noah came to kneel beside Ashleigh. 'Come on, Ash,' Jonny said. 'It's all right. You're all right. Up you get. Let's take you inside. Everything's going to be fine now.'

They helped Ashleigh to her feet, supporting her on either side. Jonny knelt to pick up her towel and used its clean side to wipe the sand from her cheeks in gentle dabs. She started crying again, without sound, her lips trembling, tears streaming down her face.

'Let's wait until Marian's gone,' Noah said. 'Then we'll take her inside.'

'You're all right now, Ash,' Jonny said. 'You're all right.'

THIRTY-FOUR

Conspiracy theory

After leaving Ashleigh to rest and recover in her room, Noah and Jonny sat on two wicker chairs on the veranda, a bottle of water between them.

'I can't believe…' Jonny said.

'Oh, I can,' Noah said.

'Why would they do that to her?'

Noah cursed under his breath but then said nothing.

'I was in love with her, you know,' Jonny said, 'at school.'

'Aren't you still?' Noah said. 'By the looks of it–'

'I'm a married man.'

'So, hypothetically, notwithstanding your marriage…'

'Wife and child very much withstanding. Otherwise, I'd be in there in a flash. Not that she'd take me. Ashleigh will always be out of my league.'

Noah chuckled. 'Yes, I suppose she would be.'

'You've changed,' Jonny said. 'I like this new, acidic version of Noah.'

'Everyone keeps saying that.'

Jonny reached for the water bottle, took a long swig, and then wiped his mouth with the back of his hand. He passed the bottle to Noah. 'You know, the five of us should stay in touch after this. It's nice to get to know everyone, now life's weathered us a bit.'

'You're going to cater an annual get-together?' Noah said. 'Brothel broths and artisan bread?'

'Nah,' Jonny said. 'I'll be closing down the brothels. Leila hates the brand. Or maybe I'll keep them, but call the chain something pious, like Mother-Soup-erior: *Mary Magdalene chicken soup*, *Aquinas's minestrone*. Servers dressed as nuns. A tale of redemption. The best little nun-house in Camden. I'll ask Emily for advice on uniforms.'

'Sounds way too clever,' Noah said. 'Not sure your customers would approve.'

'And that, my friend, is my problem. It was never about the money. I just woke up one day and thought: brothels, yeah, that could be funny. So, I hired a team and opened a chain. I know my dad's not as rich as the rest of your parents. His law firm's massive, but he just skirts over the billion mark. Still, I only ever needed a few million here and there for my crazy ideas.' He laughed. 'If anyone except you guys heard me say that, they'd think I'm a right twat.'

'You are,' Noah said, 'but it's nice that your dad supports you.'

'Tell you a secret,' Jonny said. 'The best way to milk a rich man's wallet is to give him a grandchild.'

'I'll bear that in mind,' Noah said.

Jonny tapped his fingers on his knee. 'Yeah, so, I've been thinking about the kidnappers, about their motives.'

'It's not that complicated,' Noah said. 'They wanted ransom. Probably a lot of ransom. It costs a fortune to requisition an island and then transport us here – planes, boats, mercenaries. The whole operation smells of someone with means. Someone who's after a lot. They'd want a return on their investment.'

'I have a theory,' Jonny said, 'but it's a bit out there.'

'Aliens?' Noah said.

Jonny chuckled. 'Old money wanting to take new money down a peg. It's a tale as old as time.'

'That's very flat earth and fake moon landing,' Noah said. 'You're basing your theory on Wilhelm's aristocratic claims?'

'I did initially,' Jonny said, 'but then, even without him, it just makes sense. They hate us.'

'They don't hate us that much. Zayn slept with half of their daughters, and probably their sons too.'

'And you think they love him for it?' Jonny said.

'All right,' Noah said, 'so a group of moneyed cigar smokers gathers in a room in some castle in Bavaria, and they hatch a plan? I'd imagine it in black and white, with subtitles.'

'Why else the five of us?' Jonny said. 'Why not the daughter of the Marquis-of-Something or the Duke-of-Other?'

'Could be organised crime,' Noah said, 'or oligarchs. Maybe the path of least resistance was our pupil records at school. They keep our addresses up to date for their annual begging letters. My money's on the headmaster. Someone as uptight as Crampton-Hughes must be hiding some serious skeletons in his closet. Wouldn't take much to blackmail him. Or they offered him a bribe. When you're used to getting large donations from parents to admit their child, what's a personal backhand for a sheet of paper with some addresses?' Noah paused a moment, then added, 'Also, I don't think many titled people are actual billionaires.'

'Still doesn't rule out my theory,' Jonny said. 'Blue bloods with enough government and media connections to cover it up.'

'I see,' Noah said. 'And the moon landing was faked.'

'Go to Mauna Kea in Hawaii, and you'll see,' Jonny said. 'They've identified the exact rock formations that match the ones in the Apollo 11 footage.'

Noah put down the water bottle and swatted a mosquito that was feasting on his arm. 'Are you being serious now? I can't tell.'

'Absolutely,' Jonny said, then slapped Noah's knee and laughed. 'You gullible clown. My dad's an international lawyer. He's dealt with the US government. Ask him, and he'll tell you. They couldn't manage a competent cover-up if they tried. The rest is bunkum for the masses.'

'So you did ask him?' Noah said.

'Checking all angles, as one does,' Jonny said. 'Keeping an open mind. My problem is my education. It's tough to maintain gullibility when you're taught to think for yourself.'

'And yet,' Noah said, 'you still believe aristocrats in smoky rooms got us, and they have enough influence to hide it.'

Jonny shrugged. 'That's my hypothesis. Like I said, the idea started with Wilhelm, but now I think he's pretending. His claim to be noble is bullshit.'

'Please explain and cite sources,' Noah said.

'Our family has properties in Berlin and Vienna. I've spent a lot of time there. Even had an Austrian nanny for a while. I know what German speakers sound like when they speak English. When I listen to Wilhelm, it's like he's a caricature of a German speaker. He might as well be American, or Welsh.'

'I don't think so,' Noah said out of caution. They were on the veranda. Bill might be listening.

'When we get back,' Jonny said, 'I'm going to have security around my family twenty-four-seven. No one's ever getting close to Evan or Leila.'

'A proper family,' Noah said. 'I'm jealous, notwithstanding the other thing.'

'All it takes to make a kid is a prenup and sex,' Jonny said. 'Finding the right wife, though, that's a tad more difficult. Women are complicated.'

Noah rested his chin on his fist. 'Didn't Wilhelm say

something about them being good people? About saving millions of destitute people?'

'Did he?' Jonny said.

'When we first met him.'

'Probably just making shit up,' Jonny said.

Emily and Zayn walked towards them from the direction of the hammock. The large bruise on Zayn's left cheek from the night before had turned black and blue, but he was smiley as ever.

'Taking the air?' Jonny said to them.

'Enjoying the last day of our holiday,' Zayn said, then mimicked Wilhelm's German accent, 'One must enjoy his days on this earth, for one never knows if they are his last, hmm?'

Noah shuddered at the foreboding words, but then he reassured himself. *We're going home tomorrow. This will all be over. And Ashleigh's fine. We're all going to be fine.*

THIRTY-FIVE

Heir Loss

EWALD HOUSE, NORTHUMBERLAND, 17 AUGUST

Alex asked the parents to gather in Ewald House's boardroom ten minutes before the results of the second round were to be announced. Based on what he'd heard and gathered, they had all done their best to pay the kidnappers the most they could. Their mega-financial moves could not be undertaken without creating ripples. Businesses being sold made announcements about their new owners. Trade unions decried the "cost-saving" layoffs that followed. Details of properties leveraged to secure funds were leaked to the press by publicity-hungry brokers and estate agents. There was no shortage of rats delighted to be interviewed about their sinking ships or the ones they had jumped to.

The news media, for its part, obsessed over charts, rumours and speculations. The BBC's esteemed financial editor, Laura Gunter, summarised the consensus amongst analysts: the race between the parents to secure the highest ransom compared to their Rich List value was too close to call. Gunter praised the parents for valuing the lives of their kidnapped children above money. She did, however, surmise, perhaps a little unkindly, that if one of the parents would have decided not to pay any ransom, the jury of public opinion would forever judge them as evil. Being seen in public or doing business would become impossible after such a betrayal of both their child and the kidnappers' popular cause.

Interviewees on news and talk shows referred to *a paradigm shift* and *the new zeitgeist*, using the terms *socialism*, *Marxism*, *bolshevism, communism* and *Robinism* as interchangeable currency. Left-leaning columnists were basking in thinly veiled glee at the parents' misfortunes. Students marched with banners bearing hammers and sickles. Robbie Sage, the trade union representative for Hammerson Oil's employees, jumped to his death in front of the 9.23am train to Reading following the collapse of the company. His call for Peter Hammerson to pay as much as he could had made him a pariah in the eyes of the people he represented, tens of thousands of whom had lost their jobs.

The parents shuffled into their seats, their faces drained of emotion. Nadia Sayal somehow carried herself with dignity, impeccably dressed in a flowing sari, clasping her hands in poised anticipation. Theo Salt's customary sharp suit was pressed, but he was unshaven and sported an angry spot on his nose. Davis Boroughs smelled like he had drenched himself in vodka. Cecilia Gant and Peter Hammerson both wore T-shirts and deeply grooved worry lines. Alex felt for them all, for their anxiety and fear. At least he had some news to share.

As soon as everyone was present, Alex stood. 'I know this might sound like terrible timing,' he said, 'but I have an update. Overnight, we got a hit on the device we identified as present in both Noah and Emily's kidnappings.'

'A phone?' Peter Hammerson said.

'It's a smartwatch with a SIM, which is probably why they overlooked it. People dump their phones, but forget they're wearing watches. We've traced its location. We know where it is.'

'Where?' Davis Boroughs said.

'A tiny unnamed island in the South China Sea, in the Spratly archipelago. Satellite images of the island show buildings and a floating access pier. The signal came from two of the buildings, which will become the focus of our operation.'

'Too fucking late,' Davis Boroughs said. 'They announce the results in ten minutes. Most of our kids could be dead in twenty. For all we know, they're already gone.'

'Let's not jump to conclusions,' Nadia Sayal said. 'Any hope is better than no hope.'

'Put that in one of your fortune cookies and eat it,' Davis said.

'If you want to be racist,' Nadia said to Davis, 'at least be accurate.'

'That's not what I meant,' Davis said, 'and you know it.'

'Do I?' Nadia said.

'This island,' Theo Salt said, 'which country does it belong to?'

'Vietnam,' Alex said, 'but it's a sensitive area. We've also had to coordinate with China and the Philippines to get there. The Foreign Office was useless, but we approached the countries involved directly, and they've been surprisingly eager to help. The kidnappings have been top of their news cycles for days.'

'How long to get there?' Nadia said.

'Our people travelled overnight and should land in Cebu in twenty-five minutes. From there, the Philippine Air Force is ready to help with two long-range helicopters. That's another two to three hours.'

Davis Boroughs thumped his fist on his forehead. 'Gawd! That's the stupidest thing I ever heard. Criminally stupid. I understand you want the glory of a rescue, Alex, but why on earth would you wait for *your* people to travel to the other side of the world? If you knew about this last night, why not get the Philippines or Vietnam – or whoever – to send their troops to this island the second you heard? They could have got them by now. Or China. China would do a good job and take no prisoners, shoot the bastards dead where they stand.' He huffed in frustration. 'Stupidest, stupid, stupidity. And why didn't you tell us as soon as you knew? We would have had the chance to tell you about this *little* thing you missed, this detail that could have saved our kids. They'd be safe by now.'

Alex waited patiently for Davis to finish. 'I didn't tell you,' he said, 'because my team and I were busy making sure the operation could go ahead. You have no idea of the complexity of what we've achieved. I haven't had a minute to spare since last night. It was a finely balanced thing that we got our forces there.' He took a breath to keep himself calm. 'And you're right. The ideal solution would have been to mount a rescue from the region. However–'

'However, what?' Davis barked.

Alex did his best to respond in an even tone. 'Six countries lay claim to islands in the area. It's a heavily disputed region. China and Vietnam were extremely generous in allowing our people to go in armed on Filipino choppers. If any other military personnel were to fly onto the island with weapons, it could trigger an international incident and potentially a war in the South China Sea. I'm sorry, but that was never an option.'

'So say you,' Davis said. 'If anything happens to my daughter, I'll hold you personally responsible. I'll have you castrated, then shot.'

'I might not be too technical, Alex,' Nadia said, injecting her measured tone into the conversation, 'so please humour me. You're telling us a device, a smartwatch, was active in kidnapping locations. It was then, what's the word? *Pinged*? The device was pinged on an uninhabited island in a distant archipelago. How is that possible? Presumably, there are no mobile masts there, no communication networks.'

'That's correct,' Alex said. 'There's no mobile reception as such, so you can't pinpoint the device using mast location.'

'How, then?' Nadia said.

'Wifi. It looks like the kidnappers set up satellite internet on the island, and this particular smartwatch connected to it. Our surveillance partners use military-grade systems. They were able to hack into the watch's mapping application and show us where it is. It seems to move between the two buildings I mentioned.'

'Two to three hours until they're there?' Theo said and shook his head. 'I wish we'd found them earlier. No. Say nothing, Alex. Please say nothing else.'

Davis huffed. He was about to speak again when the monitor screen came to life, and the familiar presenter appeared. All heads turned to stare at her glib, AI-generated glare.

'Robin's Brigade welcomes you to this, our final Heir Loss video message. Before we get to the results of our fun game, I would like to take the opportunity to thank all our supporters around the world. Your demonstrations and hashtags were a sight to behold. Keep them coming. They send a message to the elites, to world governments, to everyone: we must help those less fortunate than us.'

'Fuck's sake, fuck off,' Davis said.

'She can't hear you,' Theo said.

'Really?' Davis said.

'I am pleased to report,' the woman on the screen continued, 'that our funding drive has raised just over fourteen billion British pounds. This amount, in its entirety, has already been distributed to deserving charities and organisations, either immediately or in annuity trusts that will pay them an annual sum. The breakdown of this redistribution will be available online after my message ends. As before, we take nothing for ourselves. We only used justified, proportionate violence to achieve a noble goal. And to you, the parents, I have this message. You paid a high price, and I'm sorry, but what we plan to do to your children is necessary. We have to follow through, or our threats will have been hollow. All I ask of you is this: think of the millions of lives they'll save. Think of how they'll make a difference. They should be thanked for their legacy, for their sacrifice, you and them both.'

'They haven't killed them yet,' Theo said. 'She said *what we plan to do to your children*. They're not dead yet.'

Alex, who had also noticed the wording, allowed himself a hopeful out-breath.

'Now, forgive me for taking a few moments for logistics before we announce the results of our game. Dear parents, in six hours' time, we will dispatch your children to you. As promised, four will unfortunately leave us in coffins. Their current location is a long way from home, so it will take a while to transport them. Once they reach their final destination, we will email you the coordinates. Their sacrifice will not be forgotten.' She paused, then continued. 'And now to the breakdown of the results, starting with the person who paid the least, compared to their net worth…'

The woman then read out the final list at an excruciatingly slow pace, each syllable pronounced fully, each pause extended until the screen updated to include the hostage's name, corresponding payment and points, each name eliciting a gasp, a fallen face, an emotion held back or frozen or shouted – until the "winner" was announced.

THIRTY-SIX

The best guys for the job

NORTHUMBERLAND AND THE SPRATLY ARCHIPELAGO
(SOUTH CHINA SEA), 17 AUGUST

The parents seemed as though their emotions were in suspended animation, the implications of the announced results temporarily set aside in favour of a fleeting glimmer of hope. If all their kids were to be rescued, everything would turn out differently.

'I hope they kill these bastards while they're at it,' Davis said. 'Spray them with bullets until they're human sieves.'

'What are we looking at here?' Nadia said, her bangled hand pointing at the boardroom's screen.

All eyes in the room turned to Alex. He had no first-hand experience of military operations, so he was forced to rely on the briefing email he received, coupled with his thorough repertoire of action films. The background noise was of helicopter rotors. The grainy green image came from a helmet-mounted night-vision camera. The caption at the top-right of the screen read *Team Two*.

'It's night over there,' Alex said. 'We'll be watching the operation in real time. You can't see much yet. They're still in the choppers. Team Two, the one on screen, will access the smaller structure we identified on the satellite images. It's where the watch spent the most time. Team One will focus on the bigger building that's close to the beach. The leader of Team One, Glen, is also the operation's commander on the ground.'

A clipped voice with a mellow Welsh accent sounded on the audio feed. 'Team Two to Commander. T-minus one minute to target. Requesting permission for immediate deployment on landing, over.'

There was a crackle of noise. Then, the response came back on the comms audio. 'Commander to Team Two. Owen, this isn't Fallujah. You're clear to proceed, no formalities. CBeebies talk is fine.'

'Roger that, Commander. Clear to proceed.'

'Tread carefully, Owen. Assume they're armed. With all the rotor racket, they'll know to expect us. Follow the plan, and may the Force be with you.'

'And you, sir,' Owen said. 'Our Filipino friends have confirmed. Landing spot is circa two hundred metres from Structure Two. Approaching ground now... Tell your wife I love her.'

'You can have her, Owen, and I'll throw in the kids two-for-one. Hyper scowling rascals the pair of them. You sure they aren't yours already?'

'Only thing I gave her was the clap, honest, guv. Get yourself checked.'

'Touché. God, you're good.'

'Everything I know I learned from you, sir. Okay, confirmed landed. Ready to rock and roll.'

'Godspeed. We're about four minutes from our target. And Owen...'

'Yes, sir?'

'I'm having some trouble with my video uplink. Looks like Team Two is the only show in town.'

On screen, the fighters of Team Two could be seen

assembling on the ground from the viewpoint of what Alex assumed was their commander Owen's helmet camera. They all wore body armour and helmets. Their faces were obscured by camouflage paint. In their hands were assault rifles.

'After me,' Owen said, and the grainy green video image turned about. He marched forward into thick vegetation. From time to time, a machete was visible in Owen's hand, clearing a path. A few short minutes later, they stopped at the side of a small cabin.

'All dark,' Owen whispered. 'Stevie, with me. Front door. The rest of you, sides and back, as drilled. Cover all exits and remember there may be hostages. Watch your fire. Go, go, go.'

The camera's view saw them dashing forward, accompanied by heavy breathing. It panned quickly to the right and left, then focused on a closed door. Owen's hand could be seen, counting down with his fingers: three, two, one. Then, a kick to the door. It flew open without resistance. Once inside, the camera pointed this way and that. The cabin was empty, except for the broken remains of what might once have been furniture. Owen rushed through to the cabin's second room, gun pointed forward. It, too, was empty other than what appeared to be a shattered chair.

A shrill scream could be heard. At that moment, Alex played out worse-case scenarios in his head. *Did they find bodies? Were the fighters in the other room being attacked?*

'What's going on?' Davis said. 'What the fuck is going on?'

Owen's camera view panned as the green night-vision picture swam unfocused. He ran to a defensive position at the side of the door. 'Molly?' he shouted. The sound of laughter came through the speaker, then some muffled speech.

Owen raced back to the main room, gun pointing, seeking targets.

The rest of the team was there, their guns lowered. One of

the fighters raised a hand to placate him. 'Whoa, whoa, whoa. Don't shoot, Cap!'

A monkey was hanging from the open window, looking at them curiously.

'Meet the locals, Captain,' the woman said.

'Jesus, Molly,' Owen said through laboured breathing. 'I could have shot you. Say something next time. Where's your training? All of you.'

'Sorry, Captain,' came the responses from the group. 'Sorry.' Then, a few more giggles.

'Briefing said nothing about monkeys,' Molly said. 'It's not even supposed to be here. Maybe the people who used to live here–'

'Shut up,' Owen said. 'Just shut your mouth.' He drew breath, then removed the helmet from his head and pointed it so the mounted camera showed his face. 'This is Team Two, reporting. Nothing but dust mites and a primate. All clear here.'

'Team One reporting,' came the response from Glen. 'Regret to report, same here. Target on the beach is just a ruin. Looks like an old army post. I'd say no one's been here in years.' There was a brief pause, then Glen continued. 'Op Commander to HQ, I assume you heard all that?'

An older voice, full of authority, responded. 'Affirmative, Op Commander. Clearly lousy intel, but had to be checked. Good job, both teams. Get yourselves back to Cebu, wipe the cam off your faces and await further instructions. Over and out.'

The feed from the teams on the ground was cut and replaced by a clear video image of the deep-voiced man. He was wearing a dark pinstripe jacket and tie. Behind him were maps with pins and markers. 'I'm sorry, Alex,' the man said. 'Looks like these guys pinged us a decoy. It would have taken a good bit of effort to make a watch signature show up in such a remote location. I reckon they faked it, planted a location into the device without it ever being there. They're savvy bastards, pardon my language. Unfortunately, we had no way of knowing. It had to be checked out.'

Alex nodded. 'Let me introduce you,' he said. 'These are the parents.' He pointed to the screen. 'And this is Bill Drake. He's our security contractor. The extraction and surveillance teams are his. Thanks, Bill. Keep your guys on alert in case we hear something new.'

'I wish we had better news,' Bill Drake said. 'I hate to say this, but if they pointed us to this region, they're probably on the other side of the world. We'll be on alert, though. If anything else comes up, my guys are ready for it. I wanted to take this opportunity to say how sorry I am for the situation you find yourselves in. I know it's devastating. You have my sympathies.'

THIRTY-SEVEN

And then there was one

UNDISCLOSED LOCATION, 17 AUGUST

The music from the four speakers set in the villa's front room sounded to Noah like it was selected by an easy-listening fan from the eighties, including hits by George Michael, Elton John, Dire Straits and Tracy Chapman.

Bill's men were an odd sight. There were four of them, dressed in their usual camouflage fatigues but with white clip-on bow ties, their submachine guns hanging by their slings over their backs. Three acted as waiters, circulating with trays of mini hamburgers, cocktail frankfurters and assorted canapés, or at the ready with bottles of champagne to refill any wanting flute. Cody stood behind a trestle table loaded with beers in ice buckets, observing the event, looking like he was counting and recounting the five partygoers. He seemed even more alert when Queen's 'I Want to Break Free' came on. *As if we would run on our last night here*, Noah thought. *As if we could run.*

In a jolly voice, Zayn was telling tales of his conquests to Jonny and Ashleigh, who were laughing and groaning with delight, drinking up his anecdotes and sipping their champagne. Zayn himself was caressing a bottle of Tsingtao

259

beer. 'Two expressions you never want to hear,' he said, 'I'm pregnant and marry me.'

'I bet the world is full of little Zayns,' Ashleigh said. 'One day, they'll all come home to roost. You'll have to set up a foundation to look after them.'

'Or a modelling agency,' Jonny said.

Noah had to admit the event felt like a real party. The perfect fit of the ball gowns and tailored dinner suits made his four former classmates look glamorous. He wouldn't have been surprised if a high society photographer suddenly appeared to snap them relaxing and enjoying themselves. He was relieved to see Ashleigh looking radiant in her sparkly dress. Whatever she felt under her cheerful façade, she was hiding it well, though she seemed to ask for more champagne refills than the rest of them. *We'll be home soon*, he thought. *It's over.*

Emily sat quietly in the corner, beer in one hand, a mini burger in the other. She bit off half the burger, chewed, and then shoved the other half into her mouth. Noah steeled himself and walked over.

Emily finished chewing and took a swig of her beer. 'You're speaking to me now?' she said.

'It's a party,' Noah said. 'That dress looks lovely on you.'

'Thanks. The best in island fashion.'

'Why are you sitting by yourself?'

'Said the man who hates parties.' She raised her beer bottle and toasted the air. 'I guess we both inherited the antisocial gene from dad.'

'I'm working on mine,' he said. 'Zayn's offered private tuition.'

'Follow the lizard people at your peril,' she said.

'You look sad,' Noah said.

She nodded towards Ashleigh. 'I'm fuming. The cruelty, the fake cancer. Makes my blood boil. They shouldn't have done that.'

'People think we're fair game,' Noah said. 'We didn't ask to be born rich or to become, you know, *Lorem Ipsums*.'

He sat on the chair beside her, and they were quiet for a while, observing the trio of their classmates having tipsy chats, laughing and seeming jolly.

'Am I forgiven?' Emily said.

Without looking at her, Noah said, 'Of course not.' He gave her a humorous grimace, and she looked relieved. He took her hand in his. 'I've recovered from my feelings for you.'

'So quickly?' she said. 'Should I be insulted?'

'Your nun costume helped. It wasn't very attractive and, well, the smell of incense…' He nearly said *incest* but stopped himself.

'Praise be,' she said, and they both laughed.

Sitting with his half-sister, seeing his other former classmates chatting, swaying lightly to the music, relieved of the crushing stresses of the week, Noah felt a new sense of peace. Jonny was right. They should keep in touch. Their shared experience had forged a bond he had never experienced before: closeness and friendship and a sense of belonging. 'Get you another beer?' he said to Emily.

She shook her head. 'But don't let me stop you.'

Noah left her to nurse her bottle and walked towards Cody's bar. He was about to ask the marine for a beer when Marian showed up at the door, wearing a red sequin ball gown. Noah hated to admit it, but with her cropped bleached hair, startling black eyes and giant silver hoop earrings, she looked attractive, sexy even. He pushed away the thought, but Marian had already caught him looking. She came to face him, standing close, too close. He could smell her breath, stale with a hint of sweetness. 'Impressed?' she said.

'If looks could kill, maim and psychologically damage,' Noah said.

'Listen, Noah, I need you to come with me for a minute.'

'I'd rather stay,' Noah said.

'Wilhelm wishes to speak to you. Something about your mother.' She slipped her arm around his waist, trying to guide him outside. He pushed the arm away but reluctantly followed her. The mention of his mother made him worry. Was it another trick? Marian couldn't be trusted.

'Where is he? Where's Bill?' Noah said.

'Just a bit further,' Marian said as they walked down the veranda's steps. 'Were you enjoying the party?'

'The army-themed waiters were a bit of a downer, but the mini burgers were decent.'

'You need to learn to let your hair down,' Marian said, 'live in the moment.'

'Another nugget of unsolicited psychobabble?'

'Don't be so cynical,' Marian said, 'and all this pent-up negativity…'

'Do you mind if we just, you know, not talk?'

They were halfway to the beach when Marian stopped and turned to face the villa. Noah did the same. A foreboding sense of dread made his stomach lurch. 'What are you up to?' he said.

'So we're talking now?' she said.

'Where's Bill?'

'Looks like he's indisposed. It falls to me to break the good news. Great news, actually.'

'The suspense is boring me,' Noah said.

'Your mother paid a considerable amount of money to free you, as did your father.'

'My father's dead.'

'That's not really true, is it? Your mother and Peter Hammerson pooled their resources. Out of all our guests, your ransom was the highest.'

'How delightful,' Noah said flatly. 'Do I get a gold star?'

'Something like that,' Marian said. She unclipped a walkie-talkie from her belt and brought it to her mouth. 'Cody, Mason, you're clear to proceed.'

'Roger that,' Cody responded.

'Roger, clear to proceed, Mason out.'

From the trees behind the house, another group of Bill's soldiers emerged, six of them, holding up their guns and aiming them forward like they were attacking an enemy house in an urban warfare game.

As the men approached the villa, Noah felt a stinging prick in his neck and glanced to his right. Marian was holding an empty syringe, looking amused. 'Don't worry. It's just a sleeping drug. You should be used to those by now. Your parents paid for this one. Oh, and one more thing: when you get back, don't even think of saying a word about Bill, about me or our soldiers, about what happened: not to your mother, not to anyone. This isn't an empty threat. We'll be watching. A sniper will be ready to take out your mother first and then you. No warning. Remember, we have infinite resources, and we're very, very good at this.'

He swallowed hard and looked at her, shaking his head.

'We're not asking for much, Noah,' Marian said. 'Live your life, enjoy it, for once. Forget any of this ever happened.' She held his cheeks between her palms and gave him a long, wet kiss on the lips. He tried to resist, but the effects of the drug slowed him down. *I should have seen this coming,* he thought through the thickening haze. *Why are they going into the house with their weapons drawn?*

Marian held him upright a little longer and whispered in his ear. 'Goodbye, Noah Gant. We won't meet again. Congratulations. You survived. Now rest, sweetheart. Your parents did well.'

Marian kissed him again, this time on the forehead. Then, like a mother gently putting her child down to sleep, she helped him to the ground, where he lay, his back on the sandy trail, his eyes to the stars. He tried to speak but managed only slurred vowels. With effort, he turned his head to the right. The last thing he saw before closing his eyes were four coffins, laid symmetrically next to each other, their lids balanced against their sides. A single tear ran down his cheek. Before he blacked out, he summoned all of his will and mouthed four names: *Emily, Zayn, Ashleigh, Jonny*, and then again, *Emily, Zayn, Ashleigh, Jonny*. The name of his sister. The names of his classmates. The names of his friends.

THIRTY-EIGHT

Lorem Ipsums

NORTHUMBERLAND AND SUFFOLK, 20 AUGUST

For three days that seemed as long as an eternity, nothing was heard from the kidnappers. After the announcement of the final results and the failed rescue attempt, Ewald House felt to Alex like a haunted mansion. The distraught parents wandered its halls like tormented ghosts, or they hid away in bedrooms and offices. Sometimes Alex spotted them, their eyes on the ground, going for walks in the gardens when the weather was tolerable, which it rarely was during an unseasonably rainy August.

Alex made a point of having his breakfast downstairs, in case any of the parents wished for company. None did. Instead, meal trays were delivered to them by soft-footed staff, though these were often left untouched at their doors. Mealtimes felt like a series of unanswered knocks. Willow the Labrador was taken for walks by house staff three times a day, with Cecilia sensibly trying to avoid the other parents' wrath.

That morning, as Alex ate his bowl of muesli and oat milk, he once again reviewed the notes he had taken of the final scores. He had scribbled the names of the five hostages alongside the total points each had received from both rounds.

That total alone determined who the "winner" was, the one person to be returned alive. For completeness, he also noted each parent's ransom in the second round, expressed as a percentage of their Rich List wealth.

With Peter contributing his ransom to Noah's account, Emily Hammerson received no payment and was therefore disqualified, though Alex resented the cruel use of such a technical sporting term for what was essentially a death sentence.

Emily Hammerson: **14 points** (from first round) | 0% of wealth
Jonny Salt: **78 points total** | 76% of wealth
Zayn Sayal: **94 points total** | 78% of wealth
Ashleigh Boroughs: **133 points total** | 79% of wealth
Noah Gant: **202 points total** | 148% of wealth (joint contributions from Peter and Cecilia. Points include a winner's bonus of 40 points).

The list told a miserable tale of *what-ifs*. Had Peter Hammerson not added his funds to Cecilia Gant's, Davis Boroughs would have been in the lead after gaining fifty points in the first round. By the time Peter had cashed in his Hammerson Oil shares, they were at an all-time low, and if he had allocated the proceeds to his daughter, he would not have come close to the scores of the other parents. In fact, Peter was lucky to be able to sell his shares at all. The run on the company had caused it to collapse.

Alex felt sorry for Peter. Seeing his daughter at zero per cent was heartbreaking, even if logic had forced his hand. Every one of the parents, apart from Davis, would be kicking themselves in frustration over their performance in the first round, yet all hindsight could offer was the torture of regret. If they had paid more in the first round, their chances would have been much improved. Then again, Peter and Cecilia

266

coming together to rescue Noah made the odds of beating their joint funds remote.

Tempers ran high in the house the morning after the results were announced. At breakfast, Davis exploded, shouting at Peter and Cecilia that they had killed his daughter, that they had cheated. Cecilia made a valiant effort to defend Peter and explained the reason for his choice, but her confession was rebuffed by a wall of seething anger. Peter, for his part, said nothing. He may have saved his son, but at Emily's expense.

After that excruciating breakfast, the parents no longer spoke to each other except when absolutely necessary, though they all remained at Ewald House. Perhaps their sense of closeness to those who shared their agony was more powerful than their need to escape it.

To make things worse, overnight, the five billionaires had become people of no tangible means. Alex heard murmurs from the staff at Ewald House, anxious as to whether they would get paid at the end of the month. Peter was in no condition to speak to them, so Alex took it upon himself to explain. Peter Hammerson could mortgage one of his properties until he could sell some of his assets. It might take a little longer, but Peter was not poor by any stretch of the imagination. His latest unsold yacht was rumoured to be worth more than a hundred million pounds. 'Bear with him,' he had told them. 'Bear with him, and I'm sure he'll repay your loyalty.' Despite this, one of the cooks and two of Ewald's cleaning staff were spotted slithering off into the night in a taxi.

As Alex was drinking the last of his coffee, he heard a sudden commotion, like cavalry riding down steps, doors slamming, raised voices, and even an urgent shout. In less than three minutes, all five parents had entered the dining room flushed with anxiety. Theo was out of breath as if he'd run a marathon. Davis hadn't tied his shoelaces. Nadia was still arranging her sari over her shoulders. Peter and Cecilia came last, both looking haunted and drained.

A message had appeared in their mailboxes, short and to the point. The kidnappers had clearly decided the time for bluster and rhetoric was over. *Shipping container, to be found in the following location.* The next line contained numbered coordinates and the code words to authenticate the message's validity: *Lorem Ipsum.* Alex took the printed email from Peter, opened his laptop and checked Google Maps. The location was on the edge of a field in Suffolk, some three hundred miles away.

While the parents took care of travel arrangements, Alex called the Prime Minister's office and then his wife at the Met Police. The two women would hopefully bypass any delays and help send support to tackle whatever was waiting for them deep in Suffolk's countryside.

The helicopter charter company, influenced by sensationalist media reports, was reluctant to be engaged by its former clients, now supposedly fallen on lesser financial means. After a few choice words and an uncompromising threat from Nadia Sayal, it relented and provided two of its crafts on credit. Alex travelled with Cecilia Gant, Peter Hammerson and Brendan along with a folding wheelchair. The other helicopter took Davis Boroughs, Nadia Sayal and Theo Salt. As the helicopters took to the air, Willow the Labrador barked at them from the ground, comforted by estate manager Darren.

'Well, this is all very cosy,' Brendan said into his headset's intercom. 'The three of us, travelling like a family to collect my half-brother, the winner who takes it all. Is Noah going to inherit from you now, Dad, seeing that he's the older brother, or am I still the heir to your shrunken empire?'

'We don't know your sister is dead,' Cecilia said. 'We don't know anything.'

'Easy for you to say,' Brendan said. 'Emily's not coming back. I felt it. I know it. You can take delivery of your bastard son and celebrate. Honestly, after this is done, I never want to see you again.' For the rest of the flight, Brendan was silent, gazing out of the window, on his face alternating clouds of anger, sadness and distress.

At last, the helicopter was over Suffolk. The pilot pointed a finger to the terrain below them. Alex followed his direction and saw a convoy of police cars and ambulances, their blue lights flashing. 'The A14,' the pilot said, 'and over there is Stowmarket. We'll be landing shortly. They'll probably get there just before us, assuming I can land in that field.'

A few minutes later, they were hovering over their destination. The field was barren, and the pilot announced it safe. They landed a short distance from a rusty blue shipping container that had been left by the field's drystone wall. Next to the container was a gate that led to a dirt road. Three cars and two vans with police stripes and insignia were already parked in the field, their blue lights flashing. Ambulances were lined up along the dirt road outside the gate.

By the time Brendan was safely lowered to his chair by Alex and Peter, the party from the other chopper had landed.

'Can you be the one to push me?' Brendan asked Alex. 'It looks fairly level. I'd like to avoid my new nuclear family as they prepare for a joyous reunion with their love child. Honestly, they make me sick.'

The field was dry, though Alex still struggled to pilot the portable wheelchair, having to bypass rocks and grooves in a kind of left-right dance. When he and Brendan finally arrived at the cluster of apprehensive parents, they had already been stopped by a surly police officer, who held up her hands in the air as though she was miming an invisible barrier.

'I'll ask you again. Stay back,' she said. 'Let us handle this.'

'Our children,' Nadia Sayal said. 'Please. We need to know.'

'I understand this is difficult,' the officer said, 'but we have to be careful.'

Nadia took a step forward.

'Madam, please – all of you – stay where you are. For all we know, the container could be rigged with explosives, or there could be armed people inside.'

Nadia shook her head but did not go further. The rest of the parents came to stand beside her.

'Shitshow,' Brendan said to Alex. 'We should have got here earlier, before the swarm of jobsworths swooped in.'

The back of a police van opened, and a group of armed police in body armour and helmets poured out. They spread into a semicircle in front of the container's door, pointing their guns at the ground but at the ready. An officer in a thick bomb disposal suit approached the door. He took short, slow steps, hunching forward, in his gloved hand a sturdy pair of bolt cutters.

'For goodness' sake. Seriously?' Davis muttered.

The man laid down the bolt cutters and took his time, inspecting the container's door and its hinges. The door had two sides, opening to the right and left, held closed by a bar with two padlocks. The man knelt and lowered his head to look up at the bolting mechanism. Finally, he stood again, removed his gloves and took the bolt cutter in hand. With swift movements, he cut the two padlocks and turned the locking bar's handle. He looked back at his fellow officers and nodded. Then, he put on his gloves, faced the container again and retracted one of the door's twin sides a few inches back. With a thin torch, he looked in from top to bottom. Finally, he took a step back, grasped the two doors, and, with all his force, pulled them towards him, rushing to the side of the container while the momentum swung them fully open.

The armed team moved towards the open container, their guns now aimed forward. Alex struggled to see what was inside, the container's contents hidden by the officers approaching it. The armed team's torch lights probed the dark space, and then a voice came over the radio. 'All clear.'

This time, the police officer's warnings fell on deaf ears. The parents ran forward like sprinters, ignoring the officer's protests, Alex pushing Brendan's chair behind them as fast as he could. When he got close enough, what he saw made him dizzy.

At the front of the container, facing the door, was a single aircraft seat bolted to the floor. In the seat was Noah Gant, fastened in place by a dual-shoulder seat belt. A drip was hanging above him from a metal bar. Behind him were four coffins.

The parents stood frozen in place in front of the container's entrance, except for Cecilia, who rushed to Noah's side. She touched his cheek with the back of her hand, and he stirred. 'Noah?' she cried. 'He's alive. Noah, can you hear me, darling?'

A silver-haired police officer came to stand by Cecilia. 'Medics!' he called out to the ambulance crews standing to one side. 'Get this one out. I'll check the coffins.' To Cecilia and the other parents, he said, 'My name is Gerald. I'm in charge of this operation. Please take a step back and let us do our jobs.'

Cecilia looked at him as though he was speaking a foreign language, and then her eyes returned to Noah. The other parents remained rooted where they stood, horror written on their faces.

Gerald carefully sidestepped Cecilia and Noah's chair and walked into the depths of the container. He drew a torch from his belt and shone a light on the coffins. Alex could hear him reporting back to his colleagues over the walkie-talkie. 'Lids are not screwed on. Martin, Cleggy, could you two please stand at the entrance and keep the parents away while I check these?'

The two officers came to stand guard, their hands folded

over their chests. Noah was pulled out onto a wheeled stretcher and taken away to an ambulance, Cecilia by his side.

'Removing the lid now,' Gerald said. There was a clang as he pulled the lid off a coffin, and it fell on the container's floor. In quick succession, he took the lids off the other three coffins.

'We'll need four more stretchers here,' Gerald said.

'Sir?' came the reply. 'Erm… bags?'

'No bags.'

The officer, Gerald, returned to the container's entrance and looked at the expectant parents. 'They're all alive. Probably heavily sedated, but alive. Please, can I ask you to stand back and let the ambulance crews do their job. We'll bring them out shortly. You can ride with them.'

Four came back in coffins, Alex thought, *just as promised, despite all the cruel misdirections.*

THIRTY-NINE

Coda

Four days had passed since the hostages were returned alive. From the field in rural Suffolk, they were initially taken to Ipswich Hospital, where they were given fluids, a clean bill of health and advice to rest. After being driven in a convoy of private ambulances to the exclusive King Edward VII's hospital in London for further tests, they were again given a clean bill of health, coffee and biscuits and advice to rest. The police agreed to hold their initial interviews in the discreet setting of the private hospital, where they were allocated an office belonging to a bariatric surgeon on leave.

When Alex asked his wife if the police interviews had yielded any useful information, Mary told him the released hostages were reticent and unhelpful. They claimed they never saw their captors' faces and could offer few details, except that they'd been held in a villa on a beach somewhere hot. 'It's almost like they were threatened not to speak to us, and it did seem like Noah and Emily were the most hostile to our questions. Even Zayn Sayal didn't have much to add, despite his training. To be honest, we didn't want to push them too hard. They're the victims here.'

Considering his assignment was now over, Alex was unsure why he had been invited to dinner with the parents. At first, he thought he'd politely decline, but then his curiosity made him reconsider. He had spent nine tense days with them in the pressure cooker that Ewald House had become. He wondered how they were doing, now their kids were back and safe. Would the released hostages also join the dinner? Was it a party? On reflection, he didn't think so. His well-honed instincts told him something else was afoot.

Alex also decided that although the five billionaires had lost large proportions of their wealth, they were still influential people, not ones he should risk upsetting. According to media reports, some of their financial moves came good too late, deals that couldn't move fast enough to meet the kidnappers' deadline. As a result, they now had liquid funds in sums unimaginable to most people. In this, Theo Salt was a well-reported exception. The fallen lawyer had become the least solvent of the lot after the hasty and unconventional disposal of his share in the law firm. The regulator called in the police. The banks froze his assets.

By the time Alex arrived at Davis Boroughs's outrageous gargoyle-fronted mansion in Hampstead, all five parents were already there. The liveried man who met him at the driveway looked down his nose at Alex's Renault Clio and shook his head as he took his keys to park the car, probably somewhere where more respectable visitors wouldn't see it. Alex didn't mind the snub from the pompous man. He'd come across this attitude before and had even given it a name: *superiority-by-proxy,* a common trait of employees who had been afflicted by arrogance from exposure to their employer's wealth. Alex had nothing to prove. Five million pounds' worth of bonuses were released from escrow into his account that morning, a million for each surviving hostage, regardless of how their release had come about. A contract was a contract, and he had done his best for them, even if, in the end, it wasn't he who had secured their safe return.

Alex was escorted to a dining room that looked like it was staged for a pantomime show with opulent gold wall curtains, huge candelabra and a crimson tablecloth embroidered with mother-of-pearl patterns. Theo Salt, whose red cheeks suggested he had already consumed his fair share of wine, was the first to greet him. 'You came!' he said with mock excitement. 'You really shouldn't have. No, really, you shouldn't have. Remind me again what you did for us, what you actually achieved?'

'Don't mind him,' Davis Boroughs said. 'Come, Alex. Sit. Join us.'

As Alex took his place next to Cecilia and Peter, Theo persisted. 'Why is he even here? He's got more cash now than I do, at least until I'm allowed to dispose of my houses.' He turned to Davis. 'Are you going to sell this place? Or maybe keep it? Yes, keep it. It would make a lovely whorehouse, something upmarket, suitable for the showbiz cocks of Hampstead.'

'Great idea,' Davis said. 'Maybe I'll call it *Jonny's Brothel*? Or is that trademark already taken? I'll need to speak to a lawyer – one who, you know, isn't suspended.'

Theo's response was a hearty belch with a hand too slow to cover it. He gave Davis a twisted, angry grin.

'We need to get some food in him,' Nadia said. 'Hello, Alex. It's nice to see you.'

Davis signalled to his waiting staff, and a convoy of waiters marched in, balancing silver platters over white-gloved hands, each coming to stand behind one of the diners. In a choreographed movement, as one, they laid the platters on the table and removed their shiny domed lids with a flourish. Alex held back a smile. Davis knew exactly what he was doing when he served his well-heeled guests hamburgers and chips.

'Once we've had some food and Theo's calmed down,' Davis said, 'I'd like to discuss where we go from here.'

Theo used his fat fingers to stuff his mouth with chips. He spoke while chewing. 'You and me, Davis,' he said, 'are going nowhere together, but thank you for the Happy Meal. It's exactly what I expected. Talk about kicking a lawyer while he's down.'

Nadia carefully removed the top bun of her burger and used a fork and knife to cut a sliver of the patty, which she chewed on slowly and then swallowed. 'It's been a terrible time, for all of us,' she said, 'but it's over now, isn't it?'

'Not quite,' Davis said. 'That's why I invited Alex. I wanted to—'

He was interrupted when a woman in a pink tracksuit, white trainers and a tanned face appeared at the dining room's door. Her hair was pulled back in a bun.

'Ah, my beautiful daughter,' Davis said.

'Hi,' Ashleigh said with a shy wave and a broad smile.

'She's thin as a rake,' Cecilia said. 'Won't you join us for dinner, Ashleigh?'

Ashleigh gave her a tiny shake of her head. 'I'm just recovering. I'm fine.'

'Zayn told me you were very courageous,' Nadia said.

'That's nice,' Ashleigh said, 'but I'm not five.' She turned to Cecilia and Peter. 'Are you two really together now, like a couple? Oh, don't worry. I'm not judging.' In a weird German accent, she added, 'One must enjoy his days on this earth, for one never knows if they are his last.'

Peter and Cecilia both looked down at their burgers. *The Sun* and *The Mirror* had carried front-page stories about their relationship. It didn't take a great leap to guess the reason they both paid Noah's ransom. The rest was pure embellishment and speculation.

Alex had called Peter after Emily was discharged from the

hospital. She had refused to go back to Ewald House with her father and vanished without saying goodbye. On the phone with Alex, Peter sounded ashamed and deflated. At Davis Boroughs's table, he and Cecilia looked like two people united by shock rather than love.

Ashleigh left them without another word. When she was gone, Davis said, 'She's recovering from kidnapping and cancer. She'll be all right.'

'Cancer?' Cecilia said. 'Is she all right?'

'She's fine,' Davis said. 'False alarm. I'd rather not get into it.'

By this point, Alex had demolished his burger and was working on the chips. The quality of the food was spectacular. Never before had he considered that a standard gastro-pub burger could be improved upon. The evening's fare was a revelation. He wondered what made the meat so tasty. Money, he guessed.

'What did you want to discuss?' Peter said to Davis.

Theo raised his empty glass and slurred his words. 'More wine, if I may.'

Davis gave Theo an impatient look while wiping his fingers one by one with a napkin. 'I'm cutting you off until you eat enough to soak the booze. Serve the man some water.'

'You're such a vulgar prick,' Theo said to Davis, 'and a spoilsport.'

'I hate drunks,' Davis said.

'Me too,' Theo slurred. He stuffed more chips into his mouth and washed them down with the water he was served. In less than a minute, he wolfed down the burger, belched again, and laid his greasy palms over his white dress shirt, imprinting trails of oily stains but looking contented.

'The kids are safe now,' Davis said, 'but I'm still furious. I barely sleep. I just… I can't let it go. What I'd really like to do is get my hands on these scum criminals, smash their heads in and drown them in buckets like rats.'

'That's a nice thought,' Theo said, sounding a smidgen more sober, 'even if it's coming from you.'

'Alex,' Davis said. 'I know you're close to these things. Could you tell us what's happening with the investigation? No one's returning my calls.'

'The latest update is…' Alex said, then hesitated. 'I'm sorry. The police operation was shut down, and the security services are no longer interested.'

'So soon?' Peter Hammerson said. 'Why?'

'The official line,' Alex said, 'is that your children are home in one piece, and resources are too stretched to spend more time on it. I'm sure you can guess the real reason. Our Prime Minister is reluctant to tackle this on the second week of her tenure. There's an election on the horizon, and public sentiment is still with the kidnappers. Even more so now, I'd say.'

'Be that as it may,' Theo said and pounded his fist on the table. 'Be. That. As. It. May.'

'Is that why Alex is here?' Cecilia said. 'To find them?'

'Him?' Theo said. 'You must be joking.'

'I won't rest,' Davis said, 'but that's not why I invited Alex.'

'I'm listening,' Alex said.

'I had a feeling we'd been deserted,' Davis said, 'and now you've confirmed it. I wanted to ask about your subcontractor, the one who ran the rescue operation. I tried to find him online, but he's a ghost. I guess that's deliberate. You said he has impressive capabilities. Do you think he could help us track down the kidnappers? I'll happily pay you a fee for the introduction.'

Alex met Davis's eyes. Clearly, the client didn't want to engage him again. It was disappointing but not entirely unexpected. 'Of course,' Alex said with as much grace as he could muster.

'If memory serves,' Theo said, 'that guy was another failure.'

'They were acting on the information they had,' Cecilia said. 'I know Bill Drake. He's worked for me in the past. Very reliable. If I'd trust someone, it's him.'

Alex forked the last chip crumb from his plate, trying to look unbothered.

'You could have just hired this Bill character yourself,' Theo said to Davis. 'Why do you need us here?'

'You don't want in?' Davis said.

'I'm in,' Peter Hammerson said. 'My daughter won't talk to me. Maybe if we catch these guys, it'll show her I care.'

'Really?' Theo said. His eyes wandered for a moment, like he was distracted by a thought. He sighed and shook his head.

'What's the matter, Theo?' Nadia said.

Theo shook his head again. 'It's not about that,' he said. 'I'm a lawyer. I should have seen it. The small print.'

'The small print?' Nadia said.

'*We'll return them in coffins*,' Theo said. 'It was staring us in the face all along. I should have picked up on it.'

'Nah,' Peter said. 'Even if you did, we couldn't know for sure. They kept saying these things… things that were meant to make us believe…'

'I'll get you Bill Drake's contact details,' Alex said to Davis. 'If anyone can find these people, he can.'

FORTY

His master's voice

Emily stopped in the hotel lobby to enjoy the coolness of the air conditioned breeze that smelled like lilac and fresh fish. She headed to the front desk, her sandals clicking on the marble floor. A dainty receptionist with a white flower in her hair welcomed her with a broad smile. 'Hello, madame. How may I assist you?'

'My name is Emily Hammerson.'

'Ah yes, of course, madame. The priest is expecting you. He is taking his breakfast by the pool. I will guide you there.'

'Thank you. I'll find him myself.'

'Visitors must be escorted. It is hotel policy, for security.'

'You don't think I'm an international terrorist, do you?'

'Please, madame, follow me.' She signalled for her colleague to take over.

The man she came to meet was sipping his coffee under a parasol, dressed in clerical black. Before him lay the remains of a half-eaten watermelon, sliced into impressively neat triangles, alongside a bread plate with a croissant's nose. Despite the scorching heat, he had not loosened his collar. He rose to greet her. They shook hands. His palm felt clammy and warm.

'Welcome, child,' he said, making a perfunctory sign of the cross in the air before returning to his seat.

Emily joined him at the table, laying her backpack against the leg of her chair. She removed the silk scarf that had protected her head from the scorching sun and scrunched it into a ball, which she laid on top of her backpack. Even in the shade, she could feel the lovely warmth. Unlike the priest, she was wearing light clothes: elephant print harem trousers and a frilly white blouse.

'I'm sorry, father,' she said. 'It's unfortunate you can't enjoy the pool. You must be boiling in that uniform.'

He took a sip of his coffee. 'I follow my orders religiously, Ms Hammerson, *religiously*. But why here? Why Laos? A greasy spoon in Highgate would have done just as well.'

'An ex-nun and a priest meeting in Luang Prabang. It has a certain air to it, a mystery. It feels…'

'Colonial?' he said.

'Maybe,' Emily said. 'Well, no. I like the heat, and I love the food – and making you work for it, Bill – or would you like me to call you Wilhelm?'

He met her gaze and did not flinch. 'Not unless I call you Robin.'

She gave him a coy smile, which he did not return.

'You may be a ruthless task mistress,' Bill said, 'but you're still the boss. Having said that…' He shook his head. 'I can't wait to take off this awful costume, hop over to Bangkok, check into a nice hotel, swim off this job, maybe find me another wife. Thai women are stunning. Why the frown? You disapprove?'

'I take it the rest of your fee arrived safely?'

'Thank you,' he said. 'You've been very generous, but the job's done now. Every time we see each other, it adds more risk, for both of us.' He sighed. 'The only reason I agreed to this meeting is because the UK government has closed its investigation. You've made Nessa Thorns Prime Minister, and congrats on that, by the way. She seems decent. Her government would like nothing more than to put the whole affair behind them. You'll be reassured to know I'm now employed by your group of parents to see if I can find, well, us.' He cleared his throat and gave her a questioning look. 'So, Ms Hammerson, now you're here, please tell me: why did you want to meet?'

A waiter approached their table. 'Would madame like anything to drink? To eat?'

'A bottle of water,' she said.

'Have some iced tea,' Bill said. 'It's very good for you in this weather.'

'Just water,' Emily said. 'Thank you.'

The waiter nodded. 'I clear dishes?'

Bill shook his head, and the waiter left them. 'How's Noah doing?' he said.

'Noah's a changed man,' Emily said. 'He's been partying with Zayn. Last I heard, he has two girlfriends on the go. Won't take my dad's calls, though.'

'Do you?'

'Dad's raised capital and started a new energy company. He'll never be poor. The guilt, though… That's something he'll have to live with.' She looked down and spoke with a bitterness she hadn't expected. 'It's not my fault he chose Noah. Even I didn't predict that particular plot twist.'

'Listen to me,' Bill said, 'and I'm telling you this as a bloke with some life experience. What happened, it's not–'

'Please don't.'

Bill sighed, forked a triangle of watermelon, and shoved it into his mouth. Still chewing, he said, 'Remember this, Ms Hammerson. You did a good thing. I don't necessarily agree with your methods, but I can't fault your reasoning. You saved millions of lives and started a movement. Even for an old cynic like me, it's refreshing. Makes a change from helping despots and corporate tough guys.'

'We're here,' Emily said, 'because I have some questions.'

'Oh, here we go,' Bill said. 'It's always like this. The client gives you absolute freedom, insists on not knowing the details, but then wants to question your methods. Am I right?'

'What would you have done if my dad hadn't paid when I was tied to the stake?'

'I'd burn you,' he said with a straight face, then shook his head. 'Except, then I wouldn't get paid, now would I? Also, the liquid we poured on you was a fire retardant. The only real kerosene was what we used for the torch and later for the real fire. Look, I'm a professional. I had a video special-effects guy ready to complete the deed in realistic high-definition, for you or one of the others.'

'Fake videos can be detected,' she said.

'They can be, but analysis takes a while. By the time they'd figured it out, your parents would have paid with extra cream on top. You told me to be ruthless but not hurt anyone. We agreed, for your own safety, that none of my soldiers could know about your involvement, so they didn't. Hence the gag when you were tied to the stake, and why I kept myself at arm's length so you wouldn't spill the beans and compromise yourself. I had the entire operation scripted to meet your *exact* requirements, *exactly*.' He wiped his mouth with a napkin, leaving traces of watermelon juice on the fabric. 'Anything else?'

'The loaded guns, Ashleigh's fake sickness, the threat to Noah's mother – were they really necessary?'

'Noah told you about that?' He patted his jacket. 'I'd kill for a cigar about now. Not sure if it'll blow my cover.'

'This is a Buddhist, communist country,' Emily said. 'No one cares.'

'Communism, eh? Is that why we ended up here?' He

pulled out a pre-cut cigar from his breast pocket, placed it in his mouth and lit it, turning away to blow smoke towards the pool. Contented, he looked at Emily. 'No one was ever in any danger, all right? None of the guns carried live bullets. The lads were told to pretend they were real, play-act. I wanted to tell you all this, but you, madam, insisted we treat you like one of the hostages and never, ever break cover, so please, please, do me a favour and don't complain now. I get that you were scared sometimes, but I was following your instructions. Cecilia Gant's pacemaker screen was a fake.'

'I guessed. That wasn't my question.'

The waiter returned with a bottle of water, which he laid on the table before her alongside a glass filled to the brim with ice cubes. Emily thanked him, and he left. She ignored the glass, uncapped the bottle and drank from it.

'You know how you trusted me to achieve your goals?' Bill said. 'I do the same with my subcontractors. "Marian",' he made quotation marks with his fingers when he mentioned her name, 'she had clear goals too, and she was free to use her best judgement to achieve them. And before you ask again, when it came to Ashleigh's cancer, we had no choice. She'd become a recluse writer, never leaving the house. We had to create a narrative that would eventually put her where she needed to be, so we could grab her at exactly the right time.'

'Maybe next time,' Emily said as Bill took another hit from his cigar, 'I'll have to be specific about hostages not being harmed psychologically.'

'Next time?' Bill said. 'Anyway, you have to admit our resident psychiatrist did a good job.'

Emily tightened her lips but said nothing.

Bill laid his cigar on the ashtray. Still pinching its end between two fingers, he met her eyes. 'How would you rate your friends' lives now, compared to before? Marian submitted her post-operation report. I'd send you a copy, but it's been shredded. We leave no evidence. Anyway, Ashleigh's new novel is out and got praise for its *raw emotional grasp of life's truths, with a maturity beyond its author's years*. Bestseller lists, readings. Her life's dream come true. Noah's finally over the death of his dad and started living a life, not hiding in his job like it's a tomb. Jonny reconciled with his wife and seems happy, and Zayn's... well, Zayn – still shagging his way through high society.'

'Zayn's grown on me,' Emily said.

'Nevertheless, Marian said you'd have to kidnap him for at least another three months of proper therapy for any breakthroughs.' He looked at her thoughtfully. 'And as for you, Mother Teresa...'

'And as for me?' Emily said.

'I'm sorry. Honour among thieves. We never manipulate the boss. Marian spent months researching your classmates to plan the best course of treatment for them. It would have been unethical to do the same to you. Still, you achieved your goal. Aren't you at least a little happy?'

'Happiness is overrated,' Emily said. She took a moment to review the man before her, to think. Then, she made her decision. 'Are you ready for your next assignment?'

'Forgive me, miss, but according to my calculations, you've spent the millions your father gave you on your promise of sobriety. Mostly they went on expenses for this project and into my pocket. Oh, and also to fix the roof of the chapel in that convent that so graciously hid you.' He tipped ash from his cigar and chuckled. 'I have a new appreciation for unscrupulous nuns.'

'This next assignment pays more,' Emily said, 'and it pays for itself.'

Bill raised the cigar to his lips. On the exhale, he blew out a cloud of smoke, which gathered in front of his face and lingered there. He looked at her curiously, then frowned. 'I hate to point out the obvious, but the hostages came back alive. That makes it difficult to do any follow-ups.'

'There will be some pre-emptive violence,' she said.

'Lethal?'

She nodded.

'You should know,' Bill said, 'taking a life, well… It hits you in ways you wouldn't expect.'

'Let me worry about that,' she said. 'And for this specific death, I feel no remorse, not even a tiny ounce of it.' She leaned forward and spoke in a quiet, serious voice, 'I want to be very clear, Bill, so there are no missteps or misunderstandings later. No matter what you're told or hear, our operation relies on one death only. This person's murder, which is well deserved, will send a clear message, a message that will put the fear of God into the hearts of our targets. Do you understand?'

He blew out more smoke and looked at her curiously. 'You're a funny one. Sometimes you seem straightforward, but then you come out with stuff like this.'

'Are you interested or not? It pays well and will help you sustain all those wives you're prospecting for.'

He waited a moment, then gave her a tentative nod. 'If the finances stack up, I'd be delighted to assist you once again, Ms Hammerson, but please, after this meeting, you will never, *ever* discuss any contract killings with me. I don't want it mentioned or even hinted at. Do you understand?'

'You refuse to do this one?'

'I didn't say that.' He reached into his pocket, took out his wallet and produced a business card that carried only a printed phone number. 'Subcontractors,' he said as he handed it to her. 'When you're ready, message this number with the words *dry cleaning*, along with a time and a location. Pick a quiet street. A biker will rendezvous with you there. You will give them an envelope with the target's name and address, a recent photo and the date and time for when it needs to happen. You have to understand: once it's been put into motion, there's no way to cancel. I have no direct contact with them. Your next bill will include a charge for laundry, plus VAT, to be paid under the usual terms. Apart from that, it's nothing to do with me.'

'Fine,' Emily said. 'You're such a drama queen.'

'I'm too old to go to prison. Being careful is my watchword.'

'All right, so, on this next project, you will be working alongside Yuxi's outfit in Asia, Obasi in the Middle East and Africa and Gustavo for the Americas. Your remit will be Europe and the rest of the world. I have a reliable group of trustees in place to deliver your instructions and then your cut. They'll be in touch.'

'You've been busy,' Bill said. 'That's an impressive crew.'

'Wait till you get your assignment.'

FORTY-ONE

Beth and taxes

CENTRAL PARK SOUTH, NEW YORK CITY, 24 DECEMBER

Media mogul Beth Grisham always made an effort to conjure up a magical Christmas for the twins, moulding traditions that her nine-year-olds, Harrison and Jack, would hopefully take with them into their adult lives, to be bequeathed to their own kids when the time comes. Christmas Eve would start with ice skating in Central Park, followed by steaming s'mores hot chocolates, the twins laughing at each other's cocoa moustaches in their cute, knitted Christmas hats. Then, home to the penthouse for family time and an early dinner of prime rib, bacon-wrapped turkey, mash and roasted vegetables, all lovingly prepared by chef Nathan. After a dessert of gingerbread men and vanilla ice cream, they'd watch a Christmas movie together, *Home Alone* or *Elf* or *The Polar Express*, with a thimble of Baileys Irish Cream for each boy.

This year was no exception. Decorations were up, and the tree was magnificent, crowned by a sparkling angel. The mound of presents was the biggest yet. A sweet cinnamon scent of mulled wine filled the penthouse. Most important of all, Beth had made sure everyone in her media empire knew that Christmas was sacred. *Don't call me unless there's a world war, and nukes have already been launched.*

The boys were finally asleep, having exhausted themselves chasing each other and playing with the one gift each was allowed to open from the pile under the tree, before the main event on Christmas Day. Harrison had been delighted for about five minutes with his robotic dinosaur before fighting Jack for the radio controller of his yellow mega-stunt car. Both toys were now back in their boxes, and Beth sat next to Mike on the sofa, watching Mariah Carey prancing in the snow and singing 'All I Want for Christmas is You'.

'Your phone keeps buzzing,' Mike said.

Beth placed a cushion on her lap. 'Let it. I'm spending time with my favourite husband.'

'Not that it's my business any more,' he said, 'but how many you got?'

'Let's see.' She counted on her fingers. 'There's grumpy Mike, usually in the mornings. There's emotionally intelligent Mike. I love him. And then there's this one: sexy Christmas Mike.'

'It's not going to work, you know,' he said, 'this routine. We've discussed it. It's done. We're done.'

'Yeah,' she said and turned to him with her eyes tightly shut. 'And here before us we have *divorce Mike*. He's so civil and polite and so… so practical. Ugh!'

'I'm here for the kids,' he said. 'Let's just enjoy the day, and maybe switch off your phone if you're not going to answer it?'

The doorbell rang, making Beth jump. Mike was obviously not going to get up, though he muted the TV and stared at the silent picture, pretending he didn't care. Mariah had been replaced by Wham. How Beth yearned to travel back in time to their good years before Mike had soured on her. She was a powerful woman by all accounts, but not powerful enough to keep his love for her alive. There were the infidelities, of course: her infidelities. Her job was stressful, and she sometimes needed relief. They meant nothing. They should not have affected her marriage. Clearly, Mike disagreed.

She got to her feet, wrapped herself in her grey Louis Vuitton shawl to feel a little more dressed, and went to answer the door. Victor, the building's reliable concierge, smiled at her, his blue uniform immaculate as usual, its buttons brushed and shiny. 'Delivery for you, Mrs Grisham.' He handed her a black box with a knotted golden ribbon. 'Merry Christmas.'

'You working Christmas Eve?' Beth said to be polite.

'Always working, Mrs Grisham. Always.'

She dropped a hundred-dollar tip into his hand, closed the door and took the present back to the sofa, where Mike was now sprawled on his back, his arms crossed over his chest. 'From one of your other husbands?' he asked.

'Maybe it's from the board? I told them not to send anything.' She pulled the ribbon open, placed the black box on the carpet and slowly removed the lid. Then, she nearly screamed.

Inside the box lay two miniature waxworks figures. They were of Harrison and Jack, looking freakishly lifelike. Next to each twin's figure, displayed in a cube of velvet foam, was a bullet with his name carved into it.

Mike sat up in a flash. 'What the hell? Beth, what have you done now? Who did you upset?'

Beth could barely comprehend his words. 'I… I don't… Look, there's a message.' With shaking hands, she tore the envelope open. Inside was a Christmas card featuring a grinning Santa Claus dressed in green and wearing a Robin Hood hat. On the card's back, in golden letters, two words were inscribed: *Lorem Ipsum*.

Beth's cell phone buzzed again, and this time she answered. It was Neil McCarthy in the newsroom. 'Neil?' she said.

'You're not answering your phone.'

'It's Christmas,' Beth said, trying to keep her voice from trembling.

'There's a video,' Neil said. 'You have to see it. It was released online ten minutes ago. I sent you a link. Watch it first, then turn on the news.'

'What's going on?' she said.

'Just watch it. I'm so sorry, Beth.'

She clicked on the link in the email Neil had sent her and instantly recognised the woman in the video, the one from the UK kidnappings, wearing a Robin Hood hat and a waistcoat and tie. Beth turned up the volume and came to sit next to Mike. 'We need to watch this,' she told him.

'Citizens of the world, the downtrodden, the exploited, the oppressed,' the woman said. 'Merry Christmas and happy holidays, if you celebrate. Robin's Brigade would like to thank you for your support so far. Today, we are pleased to announce the next phase of our plan.' A trumpet fanfare sounded, then a drum roll. 'The time has come for bigger, more ambitious actions. The rich have it all, while the poor lay broken in gutters, abused and beaten, often dead. So, I ask you this: How can it be right? An amount wasted by one billionaire on a single gala could feed a hungry village for a century, and yet, we accept it as normal, as the way of the world, good fortune for those who have it, misery for those who do not. And so, we say to you today: *No more!*'

Beth could hear her heartbeat speed up like a train on rickety tracks. She tapped the phone to pause the video and managed two breathless words, 'The boys.'

Mike leapt to his feet. Already running, he shouted back at her, 'I'll go. You check down here.' He bolted up the stairs.

With every fibre of her being, Beth wanted to follow Mike, to make sure the twins were safe, but she knew he was right. They had to ensure the entire penthouse was secure. They were seven floors up, but then, you never knew what lengths these people – these terrorists – would go to. She thought of the bullets with the twins' names on them and ran to the entrance door, double-locked it and slid the security chain into its track. From there, she sprinted around, frantically checking all the windows and the sliding balcony doors. All locked. She rushed upstairs, taking the steps three at a time, nearly twisting her ankle when she reached the landing.

Mike was in the boys' bedroom. The twins were sleeping soundly in their beds. Beth stood at the threshold, relieved, and watched them for a long time, wheezing from exertion and worry.

Back in the living room, Mike sat next to Beth as they both stared down at the phone. She took a deep breath and pressed play again.

'Our message today,' the woman on the screen continued, 'is intended for you if your net value is over a billion US dollars, no matter where you live in the world.'

Beth's hands shook so hard that Mike took the phone from her and paused the video. 'The kids are safe,' he said. 'We have nothing to worry about, okay? They're safe, and we'll protect them.'

Her head was spinning. She couldn't look at him.

'You ready?' he said.

She drew a breath and nodded.

'You have one month to fulfil our demands,' the woman said. 'Between today and the twenty-fourth of January, all of you filthy-rich individuals will send twenty per cent of your value to a crypto account, which will be provided to you by email. You'll know the email is from us because it will contain a specific code made of two words. Did you get our Christmas card? Isn't it lovely?' She smiled. 'Don't worry too much now about the details. Those will be in the email, including instructions on how to calculate your donations.'

Beth's eyes darted down to the scary box with the bullets and the figures of her twins, then back to her phone.

'What you send,' the woman continued, 'will be distributed in the same way we did last time, to those most in need: the hungry, the sick, the homeless, worldwide health programmes, good causes.' She fluttered her lashes in a way that seemed incongruous with her words. 'I'd like to be upfront with you. There is a small and necessary change from last time. A worldwide initiative has higher overheads. Therefore, a tiny percentage, 0.001 per cent of your donations, will be used to administer this ambitious, generous scheme.' She chuckled. 'After all, someone has to pay the snipers. Oh, did I mention snipers? We'll get to that in a minute, but first, please consider the bigger picture. Think of your payments as a one-off *decency tax*. You'll be helping to make the world a place that is more just, more equal, more humane. And the best part? Once you pay your dues, you won't have to worry. There's no place for fear as long as your payment reaches us on time.'

Mike wrapped his arm around Beth, but she drew no comfort from his touch – quite the opposite. For no logical reason, she felt a sudden anger towards him.

'So, you might be asking,' the woman in the video said, 'what happens if I don't comply? This is where our highly trained team of snipers comes in. They're like ghosts. There will be no warning. Your child, your partner or you will be shot in the head at a time of our choosing: on the street, at school, at your place of work or in the car park while your driver searches for her keys. Anywhere, really. If you are too selfish to share your wealth, our retribution is one hundred per cent guaranteed. You may think you can protect yourself, surround your family with an army of security guards, build walls and fences, but know this: we will lie in wait until the perfect opportunity presents itself, even if we have to wait months or even years while you worry and fret. Why put yourself through that? Is money really more important to you than peace of mind? More important than helping others less fortunate than you?' The woman gave the camera a warm smile. 'As our Christmas message comes to an end, I'd like to address the baby elephant in the room. People will say: didn't they return all the hostages alive last time despite their threats? Surely they won't do anything to us if we don't pay? Dear filthy-rich viewer, the next few hours will disabuse you of this notion. Thank you all for your time, and a reminder to our fans: please don't forget your hashtags.' The video ended.

'Turn the TV to the news,' Beth said to Mike.

'What?' Mike said, looking dazed, his eyes downcast, his face pale.

'Unmute and click the news, now. Now!'

With a shaking hand, Mike grabbed the TV's remote and did as she asked. The news channel appeared with a red *Breaking News* banner taking up the bottom section of the screen. News anchor Georgia Salem was standing against a night-time backdrop of a tree-lined street. Behind her were police cars, their blue lights flashing. Sirens could be heard in the background. 'I'll repeat what we know so far,' Georgia Salem said. 'At midnight local time, here in London, England, a person was shot to death by what police sources have told us appears to be a professional sniper hit. The self-styled Robin's Brigade group has taken responsibility for the murder in an email that was sent to news outlets a few minutes before the killing. You may remember this group kidnapped the children of five billionaires in August of this year. They have since released a video demanding payments from high-value individuals to fund charitable causes in what they call a *decency tax*, twenty per cent of their net worth.'

The picture switched to the studio, where *Evening News* presenter Sam Cartwright said, 'Thank you, Georgia. Do we have any information about the identity of the victim? Do we know who died?'

Georgia Salem appeared on screen again, holding her phone to her ear and nodding. After a short delay, she turned to the camera. 'Sam, I've just had an update from a reliable source in London's Metropolitan Police. Although this has not been officially publicised, I can now confirm that the individual who tragically lost her life here today is Emily Hammerson, daughter of Peter Hammerson. She was one of the five hostages previously held by the Robin's Brigade group. I wouldn't like to speculate at this early stage, but our viewers may remember that Peter Hammerson did not pay Emily's ransom in the second round of the game they called Heir Loss. That's heir with an "H". By targeting Emily, they seem to have just sent a message – a macabre message, one could say – to their new intended targets: *we're serious. You'd better pay up.*'

The banner on the screen changed. It now read: *Robin's Brigade shooting: Emily Hammerson dead.* The broadcast returned to the studio.

'Thank you, Georgia,' Sam Cartwright said. 'Our viewers may be wondering about the kind of sums we're talking about. We're yet to do a full analysis, so what I'm going to tell you is a back-of-an-envelope calculation. Our initial estimate is as follows: if all the billionaires pay their twenty per cent share, the total money raised would be at least 2.8 trillion, which is 2,800 billion. These sums are colossal, unbelievable. I can barely grasp them myself. I don't think I'm exaggerating when I say they will change the world. And that's not all. The rich lists are themselves only estimates, and they don't include secretive billionaires the world over. The final amount could rise to much, much more.'

Mike muted the TV and tossed the remote to the other end of the sofa.

Beth wiped her face with her hands, walked over to the

drinks cabinet and poured herself a stiff measure of Watenshi gin with a splash of tonic. She returned to sit on the sofa – across from Mike, not next to him – and stared at the TV, deep in thought.

'We should call the FBI,' Mike said.

Beth did not respond. Instead, she took slow sips of her drink.

'Did you hear me?' Mike said. 'We should talk to the Feds and get protection for the boys, at least until they catch these guys.'

Beth placed her drink on the glass table and finally looked at him. 'Maybe we should think of it like it's the IRS,' she said, 'except you can't use tricks to avoid paying taxes, and you know an incompetent federal government won't waste the money.'

'You can't be serious,' he said.

'Can't I?' Beth said.

'Beth, I mean it. You're not gonna give in to blackmail.'

'Why do you care?' She turned away from him, picked up her phone and called Neil McCarthy, the network's chief news editor. 'Neil, send a crew to my penthouse. I'll be recording a statement, and I want it out tonight, on repeat, syndicated to every corner.'

'You challenging these guys?' Neil said. 'Is that wise?'

'Not challenging.'

'Boss?' Neil said.

'They knew what they were doing when they asked for twenty per cent. It's doable, probably tax-deductible, and I'll be damned if I risk my kids' lives. No amount of money, Neil. No amount.'

'Especially not twenty per cent,' Neil said.

'Don't do that,' Beth said.

'My apologies,' Neil said. 'Message heard and received.

Media Mogul Beth Grisham wholeheartedly supports Robin's Brigade and its cause.'

'Leave out wholeheartedly,' Beth said.

'Got an initial quote for me to run with?' Neil said.

'I have always donated to good causes. I disagree with the Robin Brigade's methods, but I can see their heart's in the right place. I will therefore be making my donation without complaint.'

'I'll send a crew,' Neil said.

'And Neil,' she said, 'cynicism aside, I can live with the payment: liquidated assets, a few numbers changing columns on a spreadsheet. It will be a busy month, and it'll hurt, but we'll manage it. The thing that upsets me is what happened to Emily Hammerson. I've met her dad a few times. Peter's a decent guy. Maybe we could run a sympathetic profile of his daughter over the next couple of cycles? Something along the lines of *Her murder was senseless, but at least something good came of it*. Phrase it better, obviously. Make it about her legacy. *In her death, she saved hundreds of millions. In her death, she changed the world.*'

THE END

Author's note

As you're reading this, I'm probably at my writing desk in my garden shed, working on my next book. I left corporate life and moved to a small North Sea island, so I could spend more time writing. *The Game* is my debut novel, and I feel grateful to have it published by Bloodhound Books.

My fantastic editor asked me what happened to Prime Minister Nessa Thorns after the hostages came home safely. For *The Game*, I think she's come as far as she needed to in service of the story, but I do like her and her sidekick, Tom Smith. It's possible they'll make a return in a future book, along with some of the other characters I've grown attached to. PI Alex Czerniak is already investigating shocking events at a commune in deepest, darkest Northumberland, which I hope to publish when it's ready. For updates on when my next books are out, you can follow me on social media or join the mailing list on my website, *dagan.co.uk*.

Authors watch their debut like a newborn, with hope and trepidation as it grows and comes into its own in the world. If you'd like to support my writing journey, leaving a review for

The Game would be a kindness. Reviews make or break a book. I'm told it's a numbers game. Above all, I hope you've enjoyed reading this book as much as I enjoyed writing it.

Danny Dagan, August 2024

A note from the publisher

Thank you for reading this book. If you enjoyed it please do consider leaving a review on Amazon to help others find it too.

We hate typos. All of our books have been rigorously edited and proofread, but sometimes mistakes do slip through. If you have spotted a typo, please do let us know and we can get it amended within hours.

info@bloodhoundbooks.com

Printed in Great Britain
by Amazon

58701166R00179